STANISLAW LEM is "a major figure who just happens to be a science fiction writer....Very likely, he is also the best-selling SF writer in the world" (*Fantasy and Science Fiction*). For the past four decades he has been one of Europe's most prolific and esteemed writers, considered the single most important influence in putting science fiction into the mainstream of literature. Born in 1921 in Poland, where he lives now with his family, Lem was originally trained in medicine. He cofounded the Polish Astronautical Society and is a member of the Polish Cybernetic Association. His nearly thirty books, translated into as many languages, range from novels and thrillers to SF short stories, screenplays (SOLARIS is best known), parodies, philosophy and literary criticism. Of his SF novels translated into English, Avon has published THE CYBERIAD, THE FUTUROLOGICAL CONGRESS, THE INVESTIGATION, MEMOIRS FOUND IN A BATHTUB and THE STAR DIARIES. TALES OF PIRX THE PILOT caps his reputation as "a virtuoso storyteller" (*The New York Times Book Review*). "His imagination is so powerful and pure that no matter what world he creates, it is immediately convincing."

Other Avon and Bard Books by
Stanislaw Lem

Coming Soon

TALES OF PIRX THE PILOT

STANISLAW LEM

Translated by Louis Iribarne

 A BARD BOOK/PUBLISHED BY AVON BOOKS

A portion of this work originally appeared in *Omni* and *Penthouse* magazines.

AVON BOOKS
A division of
The Hearst Corporation
959 Eighth Avenue
New York, New York 10019

Lem, Stanislaw.
  Tales of Pirx the pilot.
  Translation of Opowiesci o pilocie Pirxie.
  CONTENTS: The test.—The conditioned reflex.—
On patrol.—The Albatross.—Terminus.
  1. Title.
PZ4.L537Tal   891.8'5'37

First Bard Printing, August, 1981

CONTENTS

TALES OF
PIRX THE PILOT

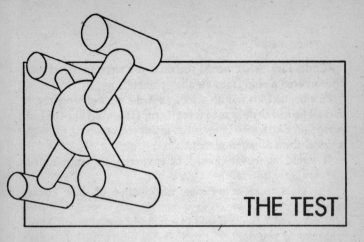

THE TEST

"Cadet Pirx!"

Bullpen's voice snapped him out of his daydreaming. He had just had visions of a two-crown piece lying tucked away in the fob pocket of his old civvies, the ones stashed at the bottom of his locker. A jingling, shiny silver coin—all but forgotten. A while ago he could have sworn nothing was there, an old mailing stub at best, but the more he thought about it, the more plausible it seemed that one might be there, so that by the time Bullpen called out his name, he was absolutely sure of it. The coin was now sufficiently real that he could feel it bulging in his pocket, so round and sleek to the touch. There was his ticket to the movies, he thought, with half a crown to spare. And if he settled for some newsreel shorts, that would leave a crown and a half, of which he'd squirrel away a crown and the rest blow on the slot machines. Oh, what if the machine suddenly went haywire and coughed up so many coins into his waiting hands that he couldn't stuff his pockets fast enough . . . ? Well, why not—it happened to Smiga, didn't it? He was already reeling under the burden of his unexpected windfall when Bullpen roused him with a bang.

Folding his hands behind his back and shifting his weight to his good leg, his instructor asked:

"Cadet Pirx, what would you do if you were on patrol and encountered a ship from an alien planet?"

Pirx opened his mouth wide, as if the answer were there and all he had to do was to force it out. He looked like the last person on Earth who knew what to do when meeting up with a vessel from an alien planet.

"I would maneuver closer," he answered, his voice muted and strangely hoarse.

The class froze in welcome anticipation of some comic relief.

"Very good," Bullpen said in a fatherly sort of way. "*Then* what would you do?"

"I would stop," Pirx blurted out, sensing that he was drifting off into realms that lay vastly beyond his competence. Furiously he racked his empty brains in search of the appropriate paragraphs from his Space Manual, but it was as if he had never laid eyes on it. Sheepishly he lowered his gaze, and as he did so, he noticed that Smiga was trying to prompt him—with his lips only. One by one he deciphered Smiga's words and repeated them out loud, before he had a chance to fully digest them.

"I'd introduce myself."

A howl went up from the class. Bullpen struggled for a moment; then he, too, exploded with laughter, only to assume a serious expression again.

"Cadet Pirx, you will report to me tomorrow with your navigation book. Cadet Boerst!"

Pirx sat down at his desk as if it were made of uncongealed glass. He wasn't even sore at Smiga—that's the kind of guy he was, always good for a gag. He didn't catch a word of what Boerst was saying; Boerst was trying to plot a graph while Bullpen was up to his old trick of turning down the electronic computer, leaving the cadet to get bogged down in his computations. School regs permitted the use of a computer, but Bullpen was of a different mind. "A computer is only human," he used to say. "It, too, can break down." Pirx wasn't sore at Bullpen, either. Fact is, he wasn't sore at anyone. Hardly ever. Five minutes later he was standing in front of a shopwindow on Dyerhoff Street, his attention caught by a display of gas pistols, good for firing blanks or live ammo, a set consisting of one pistol and a hundred cartridges priced at six crowns. Needless to say, he only imagined he was window-browsing on Dyerhoff Street.

The bell rang and the class emptied, but without all that yelling and stampeding of lowerclassmen. No sir, these weren't kids anymore! Half of the class meandered off in the direction of the cafeteria because, although no meals were being served at that time, there were other attractions to be had—a new waitress, for example (word had it she was a knockout). Pirx strolled leisurely past the glass cabinets where the stellar globes were stored, and with every step saw his hopes of finding a two-crown piece in the pocket of his civvies dwindle a little more. By the time he reached the bottom of the staircase, he realized the coin was just a figment of his imagination.

Hanging around the lobby were Boerst, Smiga, and Payartz. For a semester he and Payartz had been deskmates in cosmodesy, and he had him to thank for all the ink blots in his star atlas.

"You're up for a trial run tomorrow," Boerst let drop just as Pirx was about to overtake them.

"No sweat," came his lackadaisical reply. He was nobody's fool.

"Don't believe me? Read for yourself," said Boerst, tapping his finger on the glass pane of the bulletin board.

He had a mind to keep going, but his head involuntarily twisted around on its axis. The list showed only three names—and there it was, right at the top, as big as blazes: Cadet Pirx.

For a second, his mind was a total blank.

Then he heard a distant voice, which turned out to be his own.

"Like I said, no sweat."

Leaving them, he headed down a walkway lined with flower beds. That year the beds were planted with forget-me-nots, artfully arranged in the pattern of a descending rocket ship, with streaks of now faded buttercups suggesting the exhaust flare. But right now Pirx was oblivious of everything—the flower beds, the pathway, the forget-me-nots, and even of Bullpen, who at that very instant was hurriedly ducking out of the Institute by a side entrance, and whom he narrowly missed bumping into on his way out. Pirx saluted as they stood cheek to jowl.

"Oh, it's you, Pirx!" said Bullpen. "You're flying tomorrow, aren't you? Well, have a good takeoff! Maybe you'll be lucky enough to . . . er . . . meet up with those people from alien planets."

The dormitory was situated behind a wall of sprawling weeping willows on the far side of the park. It stood overlooking a pond, and its side wings, buttressed by stone columns, towered above the water. The columns were rumored to have been shipped back from the Moon, which was blatant nonsense, of course, but that hadn't stopped the first-year students from carving their initials and class dates on them with an air of sacrosanct emotion. Pirx's name was likewise among them, four years having gone by since the day he had diligently inscribed it.

Once inside his room—it was too cramped to serve as anything but a single—he debated whether or not to open the locker. He knew exactly where his old pants were stashed. He had held on to them, despite the fact that it was against the rules—or maybe *because* of that—and even though he had hardly any use for them now. Closing his eyes, he crouched down, stuck his hand through the crack in the door, and gave the pocket a probing pat. Sure enough—empty.

He was standing in his unpressurized suit on the metal

catwalk, just under the hangar ceiling, and, with neither hand free, was bracing himself against the cable railing with his elbow. In one hand he held his navigation book, in the other the cribsheet Smiga had lent him. The whole school was alleged to have flown with this pony, though how it managed to find its way back every time was a mystery, all the more so since, after completing the flight test, the cadets were immediately transferred from the Institute to the north, to the Base Camp, where they began cramming for their final exams. Still, the fact remained: it always came back. Some claimed that it was parachuted down. Facetiously, of course.

To kill time while he stood on the catwalk, suspended above a forty-meter drop, he wondered whether he would be frisked—sad to say, such things were still a common practice. The cadets were known for sneaking aboard the weirdest assortment of trinkets, including such strenuously forbidden things as whiskey flasks, chewing tobacco, and pictures of their girl friends. Not excluding cribsheets, of course. Pirx had already exhausted a dozen or so hiding places—in his shoes, between his stocking legs, in the inner pocket of his space suit, in the mini-atlas the cadets were allowed to take aboard. . . . An eyeglass case . . . now that would have done the trick, he thought, but, first of all, it would have had to be a fair-sized one, and secondly—he didn't wear glasses. A few seconds later it occurred to him that if he had worn glasses he never would have been admitted to the Institute.

So Pirx stood on the metal catwalk and waited for the CO to show up in the company of both instructors. What was keeping them? he wondered. Lift-off was scheduled for 1940 hours, and it was already 1927. Then it dawned on him that he might have taped the cribsheet under his arm, the way little Yerkes did. The story went that as soon as the flight instructor went to frisk him, Yerkes started squealing he was ticklish, and got away with it. But Pirx had no illusions; he didn't look like the ticklish type. And so, not having any adhesive tape with him, he went on holding the pony in his right hand, in the most casual way possible, and only when he realized that he would have to shake hands with all three did he switch, shifting the pony from his right to his left hand and the navigation book from left to right. While he was juggling things around, he managed to make the catwalk sway up and down like a diving board. Suddenly he heard footsteps approaching from the other end, but in the dark under the hangar ceiling it took him a while to make out who it was.

All three were looking very spiffy—as was customary on such occasions, they were decked out in full uniform—especially the CO. Even uninflated, however, Pirx's space suit looked as graceful as twenty football uniforms stuck together, not to mention the long intercom and radiophone terminals dangling from either side of his neck ring disconnect, the respirator hose bobbing up and down in the region of his throat, and the reserve oxygen bottle strapped tightly to his back—so tightly that it pinched. He felt hotter than blazes in his sweat-absorbent underwear, but most bothersome of all was the gadget making it unnecessary for him to get up to relieve himself—which, considering the sort of single-stage rockets used on such trial flights, would have posed something of a problem.

Suddenly the whole catwalk began to undulate as someone came up from behind. It was Boerst, suited up in the same, identical space suit, who gave him a stiff salute, mammoth glove and all, and who went on standing in this position as if just aching to knock Pirx overboard.

When the others had gone ahead, Pirx asked, somewhat bewilderedly:

"What're *you* doing here? Your name wasn't on the flight list."

"Brendan got sick. I'm taking his place."

Pirx was momentarily flustered. This was the one area—the one and only area—in which he was able to climb just a millimeter higher, to those empyreal realms that Boerst seemed to inhabit so effortlessly. Not only was he the brightest in the program, for which Pirx could fairly easily have forgiven him—he could even muster some respect for the man's mathematical genius, ever since the time he had watched Boerst take on the computer, faltering only when it came to roots of the fourth power—not only were his parents sufficiently well-heeled that he didn't have to bother dreaming about two-crown pieces lying tucked away in the pocket of his civvies, but he was also a top scorer in gymnastics, a crackerjack of a jumper, a terrific dancer, and, like it or not, he was handsome to boot—very handsome in fact, something that could not exactly be said of Pirx.

They walked the distance of the catwalk, threading their way between the girders, filing past the rockets parked next to each other in a row, before emerging in the shaft of light that fell vertically through a 200-meter sliding panel in the ceiling. Two cone-shaped giants—somehow they always reminded Pirx of giants—each measuring 48 meters in height and 11 meters in diameter, in the first-stage booster section, stood side by side on an assembly of concrete exhaust deflectors.

The hatch covers were open and the gangways already in place for boarding. At about the midway point, the gangways were blocked by a lead stand, planted with a little red pennon on a flexible staff. He knew the ritual. Question: "Pilot, are you ready to carry out your mission?" Answer: "Yes, sir, I am"—and then, for the first time in his life, he would proceed to move aside the pennon. Suddenly he had a premonition: during the boarding ceremony he saw himself tripping over the railing and taking a nose dive all the way to the bottom—accidents like that happened. And if such accidents happened to anyone, they were *bound* to happen to Pirx. In fact, there were times when he was apt to think of himself as a born loser, though his instructors were of a different opinion. To them he was just a moron and a bumbler, whose mind was never on the right thing at the right moment. Granted, he had no easy time of it when it came to words; between his thoughts and his deeds there yawned . . . well, if not an abyss, then at least an obstruction, some obstacle that was forever making life difficult for him. It never occurred to Pirx's instructors—or to anyone else, for that matter—that he was a dreamer, since he was judged to be a man without a brain or a thought in his head. Which wasn't true at all.

Out of the corner of his eye, he noticed that Boerst had stationed himself in the prescribed place, a step away from the gangway, and that he was standing at attention, his hands pressed flat against the rubber air pouches of his space suit.

On him that wacky costume looks tailor-made, thought Pirx, and on me it looks like a bunch of soccer balls. How come Boerst's looked uninflated and his own all puffy in places? Maybe *that's* why he had so much trouble moving around, why he had to keep his feet spread apart all the time. He tried bringing them together, but his heels refused to cooperate. Why were Boerst's so cooperative and not his own? But if it weren't for Boerst, it would have slipped his mind completely that he was supposed to stand at attention, with his back to the rocket, facing the three men in uniform. Boerst was the first to be approached. Maybe it was a fluke, and maybe it wasn't, or maybe it was simply because his name began with a *B*. But even if accidental, it was sure to be at Pirx's expense. He was always having to sweat out his turn, which made him nervous, because anything was better than waiting. The quicker the better—that was his motto.

He caught only snatches of what was said to Boerst, and, ramrod-stiff, Boerst fired off his answers so quickly that Pirx didn't stand a chance. Then it was his turn. No sooner had the CO started addressing him than he suddenly remembered something: there were supposed to be three of them flying. Where was the third? Luckily for him, he caught the CO's last words and managed to blurt out, just in the nick of time:

"Cadet Pirx, ready for lift-off."

"Hm . . . I see," said the CO. "And do you declare that you are fit, both physically and mentally . . . ahem . . . within the limits of your capabilities?"

The CO was fond of lacing routine questions with such flourishes, something he could allow himself as the CO.

Pirx declared that he was fit.

"Then I hereby designate you as pilot for the duration of the flight," said the CO, repeating the sacred formula, and he went on.

"Mission: vertical launch at half booster power. Ascent to ellipsis B68. Correction to stable orbital path, with orbital period of four hours and twenty-six minutes. Proceed to rendezvous with shuttlecraft vehicles of the JO-2 type. Probable zone of radar contact: sector III, satellite PAL, with possible deviation of six arc seconds. Establish radio contact for the purpose of maneuver coordination. The maneuver: escape orbit at sixty degrees twenty-four minutes north latitude, one hundred fifteen degrees three minutes eleven seconds east longitude. Initial acceleration: $2.2g$. Terminal acceleration: zero. Without losing radio contact, escort both JO-2 ships in tri-formation to Moon, commence lunar insertion for temporary equatorial orbit as per LUNA PATHFINDER, verify orbital injection of both piloted ships, then escape orbit at acceleration and course of your own discretion, and return to stationary orbit in the radius of satellite PAL. There await further instructions."

There were rumors that the conventional cribsheet was about to be replaced by an electronic pony, a microbrain the size of a cherry pit that could be inserted in the ear, or under the tongue, and be programmed to supply whatever information was needed at the moment. But Pirx was skeptical, reasoning—not without a certain logic—that such an invention would nullify the need for any cadets. For the time being, though, there weren't any, and so he had little choice but to give a word-for-word recap of the entire mission—and repeat it he did, committing only one error in the process, but that being a fairly serious one: he confused the minutes and seconds of time with the seconds and minutes of latitude and longitude. He waited for the next round, sweating buckets in his antiperspiration suit, underneath the thick coverall of his space suit. He was asked to give another recap, which he did, though so far not a single word of what he said had made the slightest impression on him. His only thought at the moment was: Wow! They're really giving me the third degree!

Clutching the pony in his left hand, he handed over his navigation book with the other. Making the cadets give an oral recitation of the mission was a deliberate hoax, since they always got it in writing, anyhow, complete with the basic diagrams and charts. The CO slipped the flight envelope into the little pocket lining the inside cover, and returned the book to him.

"Pilot Pirx, are you ready for blast-off?"

"Ready!" Pirx replied. Right now he was conscious of only one desire: to be in the control cabin. He dreamed of the moment when he could unzip his space suit, or at least the neck ring.

The CO stepped back.

"Board your rocket!" he bellowed in a magnificent voice, a voice that rose above the muffled roar of the cavernous hangar like a cathedral bell.

Pirx did an about-face, grabbed the red pennon, bumped against the railing but regained his balance in the nick of time, and marched down the narrow gangway like a zombie. He was not halfway across when Boerst—looking for all the world like a soccer ball from the back—had already boarded his rocket ship.

He stuck his legs inside, braced himself against the metal housing, and scooted down the flexible chute without so much as touching the ladder rungs—"Rungs are only for the goners," was one of Bullpen's pet sayings—and proceeded to "button up" the cabin. They had practiced it a hundred, even a thousand times, on mock-ups and on a real manhatch dismantled from a rocket and mounted in the training hangar. It was enough to make a man giddy: a half-turn of the left crank, a half-turn of the right one, gasket control, another half-turn of both cranks, clamp, airtight pressure control, inside manhole plate, meteor deflector shield, transfer from air lock to cabin, pressure valve, first one crank, then the other, and last of all the crossbar—whew!

It crossed his mind that, while he was still busy turning the manhole cover, Boerst was probably already settled in his glass cocoon. But then, he told himself, what was the rush? The lift-offs were always staggered at six-minute intervals to avoid a simultaneous launch. Even so, he was anxious to get behind the controls and hook up the radiophone—if only to eavesdrop on Boerst's commands. He was curious to know what Boerst's mission was.

The interior lights automatically went on the moment he closed the outside hatch. After sealing off the cabin, he climbed a small flight of steps padded with a rough but pliant material, before reaching the pilot's seat.

Now why in hell's name did they have to squeeze the pilot into a glass blister three meters in diameter when these one-man rockets were cramped enough as it was? wondered Pirx. The blister, though transparent, was made not of glass, of course, but of some Plexiglas material having roughly the same texture and resilience as extremely hard rubber. The pilot's encapsulated contour couch was situated in the very center of the control room proper. Thanks to the cabin's cone-shaped design, the pilot, by sitting in his "dentist's chair"—as it was called in spaceman's parlance—and rotating on its vertical axis, was able to monitor the entire instrument panel through the walls of the blister, with all its dials, meters, video screens (located fore, aft, and at the side), computer displays, astrograph, as well as that holy of holies, the trajectometer. This was an instrument whose luminous band was capable of tracking a vehicle's flight path on a low-luster convex screen, relative to the fixed stars in the Harelsberg projection. A pilot was expected to know all the components of this projection by heart, and to be able to take a readout from virtually any position—even upside down. Once seated in a semisupine position, the pilot had, to the right and left of him, two reactor and attitude control levers, three emergency controls, six manual stick controls, the ignition and idling switches, along with the power, thrust, and purge controls. Standing just above the floor was a sprawling, spoke-wheeled hub that housed the air-conditioning system, oxygen supply, fire-protection bay, catapult (in the event of an uncontrollable chain reaction), and a cord with a loop attached to a bay containing Thermoses and food. Located just under the pilot's feet were the braking pedals, softly padded and attached with loop straps, and the abort handle, which when activated (this was done by kicking in the glass shield and shoving it forward with the foot) jettisoned the encapsulated seat and pilot, together with a drogue chute of the ringsail variety.

Aside from having as its main function the bailing out of a pilot in an abort situation, the blister was designed with eight other reasons in mind, and under more favorable circumstances Pirx might have been able to enumerate them, though neither he nor his classmates found any of them that persuasive.

Once in the proper reclining position, he had trouble bending over at the waist to attach all the loose cables, hoses, and wires—the ones dangling from his suit—to the terminals sticking out of the seat. Every time he leaned forward, his suit would bunch up in the middle, pinching him, so that it was no wonder he confused the radio cable and the heating cable. Luckily, each was threaded differently, but he had to break out in a terrific sweat before discovering his mistake. As the compressed air instantly inflated his suit with a *pshhh,* he leaned back with a sigh and went to fasten his thigh and shoulder straps, using both hands.

The right strap snapped into place, but the left one was more defiant. Because of the balloon-sized neck collar, he had trouble turning around, so he had to fumble around blindly for the large snap hook. Just then he heard muffled voices coming over his earphones:

"Pilot Boerst aboard AMU-18! Lift-off on automatic countdown of zero. Attention, are you ready?"

"Pilot Boerst aboard AMU-18 and ready for lift-off on automatic countdown of zero!" the cadet fired back.

Damn that hook, anyhow! At last it clicked into place, and Pirx sank back into the soft contour couch, as bushed as if he'd just returned from a deep-space probe.

"Minus twenty-three, twenty-two, twen . . ." The count rambled on in his earphones with a steady patter.

It happened once that at the count of zero two cadets were launched simultaneously—the one scheduled to go first, and the one next in line. Both rockets shot up like a couple of Roman candles, less than 200 meters apart, escaping a midair collision by a mere fraction of an arc second. Or so the story went. Ever since then—again, if the rumors were to be believed—the ignition cable was activated at the very last moment, by a radio command signal issued by the launch-site commander stationed inside his glass-paneled booth—which, if true, would have made a mockery of the whole countdown.

"Zero!" a voice blared in his earphones. All at once Pirx heard a muffled but prolonged rumble, his contour couch shook, and flickers of light snaked across the glass canopy, under which he lay staring up at the ceiling panel, taking readings: astrograph, air-cooling gauges, main-stage thrusters, sustaining and vernier jets, neutron flux density, isotopic contamination gauge, not to speak of the eighteen other instruments designed almost exclusively to monitor the booster's performance. The vibrations then began to slacken, the sheet of racket tapered off overhead, and the thunderous roar grew fainter, more like a distant thunderstorm, before giving way to a dead silence.

Then—a hissing and a humming, but so sudden he had hardly any time to panic. The automatic sequencer had activated the previously dormant screens, which were always disconnected by remote control to protect the camera lenses from being damaged by the blinding atomic blast of a nearby launch.

These automatic controls are pretty nifty, thought Pirx. He was still miles away in his thoughts when his hair suddenly stood on end underneath his dome-shaped helmet.

My Gawd, I'm next, now it's my turn! suddenly flashed through his mind.

Instantaneously, he started getting the lift-off controls into ready position, manipulating each of them with his fingers in the proper sequence and counting to himself: "One, two three . . . Now where's the fourth? There it is . . . okay . . . now for the gauge . . . then the pedal . . . No, not the pedal—the handgrip . . . First the red one and then the green one . . . Now for the automatic sequencer . . . right . . . Or was it the other way around—first green, then red . . . ?!"

"Pilot Pirx aboard AMU-27!" The voice booming into his ear roused him from his predicament. "Lift-off on automatic countdown of zero! Attention, are you ready, pilot?"

"Not yet!" he felt like yelling, but said instead:

"Pilot Boer . . . Pilot Pirx aboard AMU-27 and ready for—uh—lift-off on automatic countdown of zero."

He had been on the verge of saying "Pilot Boerst" because he still had Boerst's words fresh in his memory. "You nut," he said to himself in the ensuing silence. Then the automatic countdown—why did these recorded voices always have to sound like an NCO?—barked:

"Minus sixteen, fifteen, fourteen . . ."

Pirx broke out in a cold sweat. There was something he was forgetting, something terribly important, a matter of life and death.

". . . six, five, four . . ."

His sweaty fingers squeezed the handgrip. Luckily it had a rough finish. Does everyone work up such a sweat? he wondered. Probably—it crossed his mind just before the earphones snarled:

"Zero!!!"

His left hand—instinctively—pulled back on the lever until it reached the halfway mark. There was a terrific blast, and his chest and skull were flattened by some resilient, rubber-like press. The booster! was his last thought before his eyesight began to dim. But only a little, and then not for long. Gradually his vision improved, though the unrelenting pressure had spread to the rest of his body. Before long he could make out all the video screens—at least the three opposite him—now inundated with a torrent of milk gushing from a million overturned cans.

I must be breaking through the clouds, he thought. His mind, though somewhat slower on the uptake, was totally relaxed. As time went by, he felt increasingly like a spectator to some strange comedy. There he was, lying flat on his back in his "dentist's chair," arms and legs paralyzed, not a cloud in sight, surrounded by a phony pastel-blue sky. . . . Hey, were those stars over there, or what?

Stars they were. Meanwhile the gauges were working steadily away—on the ceiling, on the walls—each in its own way, each with a different function to perform. And he was supposed to monitor each and every one of them—and with two eyes, no less! At the sound of a bleeping signal in his earphones, his left hand—again by instinct—fired the booster separation, immediately lowering the pressure. He was cruising at a velocity of 7.1 kilometers per second, he was at an altitude of 201 kilometers, and his acceleration was 1.9 as he pitched out of his assigned launch path. Now he could afford to relax a while, but not for long, because pretty soon he would have his hands full—and how!

He was just starting to make himself comfortable, pressing the armrest to raise the seat in back, when he suddenly went numb all over.

"The crib! Where's the cribsheet!"

This was that awfully important detail he couldn't remember at the time. He scoured the deck with his eyes, now totally oblivious of the swarm of pulsating gauges. The cribsheet had slipped down under the contour couch. He tried to bend over, was held back by his torso straps; without a moment to lose, with a sinking sensation as if perched on top of some collapsing tower, he flipped open his navigation book—which until now had been stored in his thigh pocket—and yanked the flight plan from the envelope. A mental blackout. Where the hell was orbit B68, anyway? That must be it there! He checked the trajectory and went into a roll. Much to his surprise, it worked.

Once he found himself on an elliptical path, the computer graciously presented him with the correctional data; he maneuvered accordingly, overshot his orbit, and braked so suddenly that he dropped down to -3g for a period of ten seconds, the negative gravity having little effect on him because of his exceptional physical endurance ("If your brain were half as strong as your biceps," Bullpen once told him, "you'd have been really something"); guided by the correctional data, he pitched into a stable orbit and fed the computer, but the only output was a series of oscillating standing waves. He yelled out the figures again, only to discover that he had neglected to switch over; that remedied, the CRT showed a flickering vertical line and the windows flashed a series of ones. "I'm in orbit!" he piped with glee. But the computer indicated an orbital period of four hours and twenty-nine minutes, instead of the projected four hours and twenty-six minutes. Was that a tolerable deviation? he wondered, desperately searching his memory. He was all set to unbuckle the straps—the cribsheet was still lying underneath the seat, though a damned lot of good it would do him if the answer wasn't there—when Professor Kaahl's words suddenly came to mind: "All orbits are programmed with a built-in margin of error of 0.3 percent." But just to play it safe, he fed the data into the computer, to learn that he was right on the borderline. "Well, that's that," he sighed, and for the first time he began surveying his surroundings.

Being strapped to his seat, except for a feeling of weightlessness, he hardly noticed the loss of gravitation. The forward screen was blanketed with stars, with a brilliant white border skirting the very bottom. The lateral screens showed nothing but a star-studded black void. But the deck screen—ah! Earth was now so immense that it took up the whole screen, and he feasted his eyes on it as he flew over at an altitude of 700 kilometers at perigee and 2,400 kilometers at apogee. Hey, wasn't that Greenland down there? But before he could verify that it was, he was already sailing over northern Canada. The North Pole was capped with iridescent snow, the ocean stood out round and smooth—violet-black, like cast iron—there were strangely few clouds, and what few there were looked like gobs of watery mush splattered on top of Earth's highest elevation points.

He glanced at the clock. He had been spaceborne for exactly seventeen minutes.

It was time to pick up PAL's radio signal, to start monitoring the radar screens as he passed through the satellite's contact zone. Now, what were their names again? RO? No—JO. And let's see, their numbers were . . . He glanced down at the flight plan, stuck it back into his pocket along with the navigation book, and turned up the intercom on his chest. At first there was just a lot of screeching and crackling—cosmic interference. What system was PAL using? Oh, yeah—Morse. He listened closely, his eyes glued to the video screens, and watched as Earth slowly revolved beneath him and stars scudded by—but no PAL.

Then he heard a buzzing noise.

Could that be it? he wondered, but immediately rejected the idea. You're crazy. Satellites don't buzz. But what else could it be? Nothing, that's what. Or was it something else?

A critical malfunction?

Oddly enough, he was not the least bit alarmed. How could there be a critical malfunction when he was cruising with his engine off? Maybe the old crate was falling apart, breaking up. Or could it be a short circuit? Good Lord, a short circuit! Fire Prevention Code, section 3(a): "In Case of Fire in Orbit," paragraph . . . Oh, to hell with it! The buzzing was now so loud that it was drowning out the bleeping sounds of distant signals.

It sounds like . . . a fly trapped in a jar, he thought, somewhat perplexed, and began shifting his gaze from dial to dial.

Then he spotted it.

It was a giant of a fly, one of those ugly, greenish-black brutes specially designed to make life miserable—a pestering, pesky, idiotic, and by the same token shrewd and cunning fly, which had miraculously—and how else?—stowed away in the ship's control cabin and was now zooming about in the space outside the blister, occasionally ricocheting off the illuminated instrument gauges like a buzzing pellet.

Whenever it took a pass at the computer, it came over his earphones like a four-engine prop plane. Mounted on the computer's upper frame was a backup microphone, which gave a pilot access to the computer inside the encapsulated seat in the event his on-board phone was disconnected and he found himself without a laryngophone. One of the many backup systems aboard the ship.

He started swearing a blue streak at the microphone, afraid that because of the static he might miss PAL's signal. The computer was bad enough, but soon the fly began making sorties into other areas of the cabin. As though hypnotized, Pirx let his gaze trail after it until finally he got fed up and said to heck with it.

Too bad he didn't have a spray gun of DDT handy.

"Cut it out!"

Bzzzzz . . . He winced; the fly was crawling around on the computer, in the vicinity of the mike. Then nothing, dead silence, as it stopped to preen its wings. You lousy bastard!

Then a faint but steady bleeping came over his earphones: dot-dot-dot—dash—dot-dot—dash-dash—dot-dot-dot—dash. It was PAL.

"Okay, Pirx, now keep your eyes peeled!" he told himself. He raised the couch a little, so as to take in all three video screens at once, checked the sweeping phosphorescent radar beam, and waited. Though nothing showed on the radar screen, he distinctly heard a voice calling:

"A-7 Terraluna, A-7 Terraluna, sector III, course one hundred thirteen, PAL PATHFINDER calling. Request a reading. Over."

"Oh crap, how am I ever going to hear my two JOs now?"

The buzzing in his earphones suddenly stopped. A second later a shadow fell across his face, from above, much as if a bat had landed on an overhanging lamp. It was the fly, which was crawling across the blister and exploring its interior. The blips were coming with greater frequency now, and it wasn't long before he sighted the 80-meter-long aluminum cylinder, mounted with an observation spheroid, as it flew over him at a distance of roughly 400 meters, possibly more, and gradually overtook him.

"PAL PATHFINDER to A-7 Terraluna, one-hundred-eighty-point-fourteen, one-hundred-six-point-six. Increasing linear deviation. Out."

"Albatross-4 Aresterra calling PAL Central, PAL Central. Am coming down for refueling, sector II. Am coming down for refueling, sector II. Running on reserve supply. Over."

"A-7 Terraluna, calling PAL PATHFINDER . . ."

The rest was lost in the buzzing. Then silence.

"Central to Albatross-4 Aresterra, refuel quadrant seven, Omega Central, refuel quadrant seven. Out."

They *would* pick out this spot to rendezvous, thought Pirx, who was now swimming in his sweat-absorbent underwear. This way I won't hear a thing.

The fly was describing frenetic circles on the computer's console, as if hell-bent on catching up with its own shadow.

"Albatross-4 Aresterra, Albatross-4 Aresterra to PAL Central, approaching quadrant seven. Request radio guidance. Out."

The radio static grew steadily fainter until it was drowned out by the buzzing. But not before he managed to catch the following message:

"JO-2 Terraluna, JO-2 Terraluna, calling AMU-27, AMU-27. Over."

I wonder who he's calling? Pirx mused, and he nearly jumped out of his straps.

"AMU—" he wanted to say, but not a sound could he emit from his hoarse throat. His earphones were buzzing. The fly. He closed his eyes.

"AMU-27 to JO-2 Terraluna, position quadrant four, sector PAL, am turning on navigation lights. Over."

He switched on his navigation lights—two red ones at the side, two green ones on the nose, a blue one aft—and waited. Not a sound except for the fly.

"JO-2 ditto Terraluna, JO-2 Terraluna, calling . . ." Buzz-buzz, hum-hum . . .

Does he mean me? Pirx meditated in despair.

"AMU-27 to JO-2 ditto Terraluna, position quadrant four, perimeter sector PAL, all navigation lights on. Over."

When both JO ships started transmitting at the same time,

Pirx switched on the sequence selector, but there was too much interference. The buzzing fly, of course.

"I'll hang myself!" That such a remedy was out of the question, due to the effects of weightlessness, never occurred to him.

Just then he sighted both ships on the radar screen. They were following him on parallel courses, spaced no more than nine kilometers apart, which was prohibited; as the pilot ship, it was up to him to make them adhere to the prescribed distance of fourteen kilometers. Just as he was checking the location of the blips on the radar screen, his old friend the fly landed on one of them. In a fit of anger he threw his navigation book at it, but it was deflected by the blister's glass wall, and instead of sliding down, it bumped against the ceiling, where, because of the zero gravity, it fluttered aimlessly about in space. Seemingly unruffled, the fly strolled merrily on its way across the screen.

"AMU-27 Terraluna to JO-2 ditto JO-2. I have you in range. You are hard aboard. Switch over to parallel course with a correction of zero-point-zero one. Stand by on completion of maneuver. Out."

Gradually the distance between the blips began to widen, all communication being temporarily interrupted by the fly as it embarked on a noisy little promenade around the computer's microphone. Pirx had run out of things to throw; the flight book was still hovering overhead, lithely flapping its pages.

"PAL Central to AMU-27 Terraluna. Abandon outer quadrant, abandon outer quadrant, am assuming transsolar course. Over."

He *would* try to screw things up! Pirx mentally fumed. What the hell do I care about the transsolar? Anyone knows that spaceships flying in group formation have priority. He began shouting in reply, and in this shouting of his there was vented all his impotent fury directed at the fly.

"AMU-27 Terraluna to PAL Central. Negative, am not

abandoning outer quadrant, to hell with your transsolar, am flying in tri-formation. AMU-27, JO-2 ditto JO-2, squadron leader AMU-27 Terraluna. Out."

I didn't have to say "to hell with your transsolar," he thought. That'll cost me a few points for sure. Oh, they can *all* damn well go to hell! I'll probably get docked for the fly, too.

It could only have happened to him. A fly! Wow, big deal! He could just see Smiga and Boerst busting a gut when they got wind of that crazy-assed fly. It was the first time since lift-off that he caught himself thinking of Boerst. But right now he didn't have a moment to lose, because PAL was dropping farther and farther behind. They had been flying in formation for a good five minutes.

"AMU-27 to JO-2 ditto JO-2 Terraluna. It is now 2007 hours. Insertion parabolic orbit Terraluna to commence at 2010 hours. Course one hundred eleven . . ." And he read off the course data from the flight sheet, which, by a feat of acrobatics, he was able to retrieve from overhead. The two JO ships radioed their reply. PAL dropped out of sight, but he could still hear it signaling ever so faintly. Or was that the fly he was hearing?

For a moment the fly seemed to multiply, to be in two different places at once. Pirx rubbed his eyes. Just as he suspected: there was not one, but two of them. Where did the second one come from?!

Now I'm really a goner, he reflected with absolute calm, without a sign of any emotion. He even felt relieved somehow, knowing that it no longer mattered—either way he was sunk. His thoughts were diverted by a glance at the clock: it was 2010 hours, the time he himself had scheduled for the maneuver—and he had yet to even place his hands on the controls!

The daily grind of training exercises must have taken their toll because without a moment's hesitation he grabbed both control sticks, pressed first the left and then the right one, and all the time kept his eye on the trajectometer. The engine responded with a hollow roar until it gradually tapered off to a whisper. Ouch! Something landed on his forehead, just under his visor, and remained stationary. The navigation book! It was blocking his vision, but he couldn't brush it aside without taking his hands from the controls. His earphones were alive and astir as the two flies went about pursuing their love life on the computer. If only I had a gun on me, he thought, feeling the navigation book start to flatten his nose with the increase in acceleration. In desperation he began tossing his head around like a madman; he had to be able to see the trajectometer, for crying out loud! Suddenly the book crashed to the floor with a bang—and small wonder: at 4g it must have weighed nearly 3 kilos. He immediately decelerated to the level required by the maneuver, and at 2g put the levers on hold. He threw a glance at the mating flies. They were not the least bit fazed by the deceleration; on the contrary, they looked to be in seventh heaven. Hm, another eighty-three minutes to go. He checked the radarscope: the two JO ships were now trailing him at a distance of 70 kilometers. I must have jumped out in front that time I hit 4g, he thought. Oh well, no sweat.

From now until the end of the accelerated flight he would have a little time to kill. Two g was tolerable, despite his combined weight of 142 kilos. How many times had he spent up to a half hour in the centrifuge at 4g!

But then, it wasn't exactly a picnic, either, what with your arms and legs weighing like iron, your head completely immobilized by the blinding light . . .

He verified the position of the two ships, and again thought of Boerst, picturing to himself how very much the movie star he must have looked. What a jaw that guy had! Not to mention that perfectly straight nose, those steely gray eyes . . . You can bet *he* didn't have to rely on any cribsheet! But come to think of it, so far neither had he . . . Silence reigned in his earphones. Both flies were crawling along the blister's surface such that their shadows grazed his face, and for the first time he cringed at the sight of them—at their tiny black paws, grotesquely magnified to look like suction disks, at their bodies glittering metallically in the glare of the lights . . .

"Dasher-8 Aresterra calling Triangle Terraluna, quadrant sixteen, course one-hundred-eleven-point-six. I have you on convergent course eleven minutes thirty-two seconds. Advise you to alter course. Over."

Just my luck! Pirx mentally grumbled. Always some smart-ass trying to bugger up the works . . . Can't he see I'm flying in formation?

"AMU-27 squadron leader Triangle Terraluna JO-2 ditto JO-2, calling Dasher-8 Aresterra. Negative, am flying in formation, proceed to carry out deviation maneuver. Out."

While he was transmitting, he tried to locate the unwelcome intruder on the radar. There he was—less than 1,500 meters away!

"Dasher-8 to AMU-27 Terraluna, reporting malfunction in gravimeter system, commence immediate deviation maneuver, point of intersection forty-four zero eight, quadrant Luna four, perimeter zone. Over."

"AMU-27 to Dasher-8 Aresterra, JO-2 ditto JO-2 Terraluna. Will commence deviation maneuver at 2039 hours. Yaw maneuver to commence at ditto hours behind squadron leader at optical range, northern deviation Luna sector one zero point-six. Am firing low-range thrusters. Over."

Simultaneously he fired both lower yaw jets. The two JO ships responded at once, all three veered off course, and stars glided across the video screens. Dasher thanked him as he flew off to Luna Central, and in a surge of self-confidence, Pirx wished him a happy landing—a touch of class, seeing as the other ship was in distress. He followed his navigation lights for another thousand kilometers or so, then began guiding the two JO ships back onto their original course, which was easier said than done: going off course was one thing, finding your way back onto a parabola was another. Pirx found it next to impossible, what with a different acceleration, a computer so fast he couldn't keep up with its coordinates, and the flies, which, if they weren't crawling all over the computer, were playing tag on the radar screen. Where did they get all the energy? he wondered. It was a good twenty minutes before they were back on course.

Boerst probably has smooth sailing all the way, he thought. Him? Get into trouble? Not wonderboy Boerst.

He adjusted the automatic thrust terminator to achieve a zero acceleration after eighty-three minutes, as instructed, and then saw something that turned his sweat-absorbent underwear to ice.

Above the dashboard a white panel had come unclamped. Not only that, but it was starting to work its way down, a millimeter at a time. It was probably loose to begin with, he reasoned, and all the vibrating during the recent yaw maneuvers—Pirx's handling of the ship hadn't exactly been gentle—had loosened the pressure clamps even more. With the acceleration still running at $1.7g$, the panel kept inching its way down as if being pulled by an invisible thread. Finally it sprang loose altogether, slid down the outer side of the glass wall, and settled motionlessly on the deck, exposing a set of four gleaming copper high-voltage wires and fuses at the back.

Why all the panic? he told himself. An electrical panel has come loose—so, big deal. A ship can get along without a panel, can't it?

Even so, he couldn't help feeling a trifle nervous; things like that weren't supposed to happen. If a fuse panel can come loose, what's to stop the stern from breaking off?

There were still twenty-seven minutes of accelerated flight to go when it hit him that once the engines were shut down, the panel would become weightless. Could it do any damage? he wondered. Not much. It was too light for that, too light even to break glass. Nah, not a chance . . .

What were the flies up to? He followed them with his gaze as they zoomed and buzzed and circled and chased each other around the outside of the blister before landing on the back of the fuse panel. That's when he lost track of them.

He took a reading of the two JO ships on the radarscope: both were on course. The face of the Moon now loomed so large on the front screen that it took up half of it. He recalled how during a series of selenographic exercises in the Tycho Crater, Boerst, with the help of a portable theodolite . . . Dammit, what a pro that guy was! Pirx kept an eye out for Luna Base on the outer slope of Archimedes. It was camouflaged so well among the rocks that it was almost invisible from high altitude, all except for the smooth surface of the landing strip with its approach lights—when in the night zone, that is, and not, as presently, when it was illuminated by the Sun. At the moment the Base was straddling the crater's shadow line, the contrast with the blinding lunar surface being so intense that it overpowered the weaker approach lights.

The Moon looked as if untrodden by human foot. Long shadows stretched all the way from the Lunar Alps to the Sea of Rains. He recalled, too, how on his first trip there—they were just passengers then—Bullpen had called on him to verify whether stars of the seventh magnitude were visible from the Moon, and how, dumb as he was, he had tackled the problem with the greatest of enthusiasm. He had clean forgotten, the dope, that no stars were visible from the Moon by day because of the solar glare reflected by the lunar surface. It was a long time before Bullpen stopped ribbing him on account of those stars.

The Moon's disk continued to swell, gradually crowding out the remaining darkened portion of the screen.

"That's funny—I don't hear any more buzzing." He glanced sideways and flinched.

One of the flies was sitting and cleaning its wings on the exposed side of the panel, while the other fly was busy courting it. A few millimeters away, its copper terminal gleaming below the spot where the insulation ended, was the nearest cable. All four cables were exposed, about as thick in diameter as a pencil, and all in the 1,000-volt range, with a contact clearance of 7 millimeters. It was just by accident that he knew it was 7. Once, as an exercise, they had torn down the entire circuitry system, and when he, Pirx, couldn't come up with the exact clearance, his instructor had read him off the riot act.

In the meantime, the one fly took time off from its wooing and started venturing out along the live terminal. A harmless enough thing to do—unless, of course, it suddenly got an urge to hop over to the next one, and, judging by the way it sat there, humming, at the very end of the terminal, that's precisely what it intended to do. As if it didn't have room enough in the cabin! Now, thought Pirx, what would happen if it put its front paws on the one wire and kept its hind feet on the other . . . ? Well, so what if it did. In the worst case it might cause a short circuit. But then—a fly?! Would a fly be big enough to do that? But even if it were, nothing much could happen; there would be a momentary blowout, the circuit breaker would switch off the current, the fly would be electrocuted, and the power would be restored—and good-bye fly! As if in a trance, he kept his eyes fixed on the high-tension box, secretly cherishing the hope that the fly would think better of it. A short circuit was nothing serious, a glitch, but who knows what else might happen. . . .

Only eight more minutes of gradual deceleration until touchdown. He was still staring at the dial when there was a flash—and the lights went out. It was a momentary blackout, lasting no more than a fraction of a second. The fly! he thought, and waited with bated breath for the circuit breaker to flip the power back on. It did.

The lights stayed on for a while—dimmer and more orangish-brown than white—before the fuse blew a second time. A total blackout. Then the power came on again. Off again. On again. And so it went, back and forth, with the lights burning at only half their normal amperage. What was wrong? During the brief but regular intervals of light, he managed, with considerable squinting and straining of the eyes, to pinpoint the trouble: the insect was trapped between two of the wires, a charred sliver of a corpse that continued to act as a conductor.

Pirx was far from being in a state of panic. True, his nerves were a trifle frayed, but then, when had he ever been completely relaxed since the launch count? The clock was barely legible. Fortunately, the instrument panel operated on its own lighting system, as did the radarscope. And there was just enough juice being supplied to keep the backup circuits from being tripped, but not quite enough to light the cabin.

Only four minutes left until engine cutoff. Well, that was one load off his mind—the thrust terminator was programmed to shut down the engine automatically. Suddenly an icy chill ran down his spine. How could the kill-switch work if the circuit was shorted?

For a second he couldn't recollect whether they operated on the same circuit, whether these were the main fuses for the rocket's entire power supply. Of course—they had to be. But what about the reactor? Surely the reactor must have had its own power network. . . .

The reactor, yes, but not the automatic switch. He knew because he had set it himself. Okay, so now all he had to do was to shut off the power. Or maybe he should just sit back and give it a chance to work on its own.

The engineers had thought of everything—everything except what to do when a fly gets into your cabin, a fuse panel comes unclamped, and you wind up with such a screwy short circuit!

Meanwhile the lights kept shorting out. Something had to be done about it. But what?

Simple. All he had to do was to flip the master switch located in the floor behind his seat. That would shut off all the main power circuits and trip the emergency system. Then all his worries would be over. Hm, he thought, not bad the way these buckets are rigged.

He wondered if Boerst would have been as quick on his feet. Probably, if not quicker . . . Yikes, only two minutes left! Not enough time for the maneuver! He sat up: he had clean forgotten about the others.

He closed his eyes in a moment of concentration.

"AMU-27 squadron leader Terraluna, calling JO-2 ditto JO-2. Reporting short circuit in control room. Will be necessary for me to postpone lunar insertion maneuver for temporary equatorial orbit—uh—indefinitely. Proceed to execute maneuver at previously designated time. Over."

"JO-2 ditto to squadron leader Terraluna. Will commence joint lunar insertion maneuver for temporary equatorial orbit. You are nineteen minutes away from lunar landing. Good luck. Good luck. Out."

Pirx hardly heard a word because in the meantime he had disconnected the radiophone cable, the air hose, and another small cable—his straps were already undone. No sooner had he made it to his feet than the kill-switch flashed a ruby-red. The cabin sprang briefly out of the dark, only to be plunged back into an orangish-brown blur. The engine cutoff had failed. The red signal light kept staring at him from out of the dark, imploringly. A buzzer sounded: the warning signal. The automatic terminator was inoperative. Fighting to keep his balance, Pirx jumped behind the contour couch.

The master switch was housed in a cassette inserted in the floor. The cassette turned out to be locked. Natch! He tried yanking on the lid; it wouldn't give. The key. Where was the key?

There *was* no key. He tried forcing the lid again. No luck.

He sprang to his feet and stared blindly into the forward screens, where, its surface no longer silver but an alpine-snow white, there now loomed a gigantic Moon. Craters came into view, their long, serrated shadows creeping stealthily along the surface. The radar altimeter could be heard clicking steadily away. How long had it been operating? he wondered. Little green digits flashed in the dark, and he read off his present altitude: 21,000 kilometers.

The lights never stopped blinking as the circuit breaker continued to kick on and off. But now it was no longer pitch-dark when they went out; now the cabin's interior was flooded with moonlight, an eerie, luminous glare that paled only imperceptibly beside the dim, soporific lighting inside the cabin.

The ship was now flying a perfectly straight course, gaining velocity as the residual acceleration reached $0.2g$ and the Moon's gravitational pull increased. What to do? What to do?! He rushed back to the cassette and kicked it with his foot. The metal casing refused to budge.

Hold everything! My Gawd, how could he have been so stupid! All he had to do was to find a way to reach the other side of the blister. And there *was* a way! By the exit, at the point where the blister narrowed tunnellike to form a funnel ending with the air lock, there was a special lever painted a bright enamel red, beneath a plate that read FOR CONTROL SYSTEMS EMERGENCY ONLY. One switch of the lever was all that was needed to raise the glass cocoon a meter off the ground, leaving just enough clearance underneath. Once on the other side, all he had to do was to clear the lines, and with a piece of insulation . . .

He was at the handle in less than no time.

You moron! he thought, and he grabbed the metal handle and yanked until his shoulder joint cracked. The lever, its metal rod glistening with oil, was fully extended, but the blister hadn't wiggled an inch. He stood staring at the glass bubble in stunned bewilderment, at the video screens ablaze with moonlight, at the blinking light overhead . . . He jerked on the lever again, even though it was out as far as it would go. Nothing.

The key! The key to the cassette! He fell flat on the floor

and searched under the seat. There was nothing to be seen
except the cribsheet.

The lights blinked; the circuit breaker switched. Now
when the lights dimmed, the moonlight cast everything in a
stark, skeleton-bone white.

It's all over, he thought. Should he fire the ejection rocket
and bail out in the encapsulated seat? No, it wouldn't work;
without any atmospheric drag, the parachute wouldn't brake.
"Help!"—he wanted to yell, but there was no one to whom he
could call in distress: he was all alone. What to do?! There
just *had* to be a way out!

He scrambled back to the emergency lever and almost tore
his arm out of his socket, now so frantic he wanted to cry. It
was all so dumb. . . . Where was the key? And why the
malfunction in the emergency lever? The altimeter. At one
sweeping glance, he read off the displays: 9,500 kilometers.
The saw-toothed ridge of Timocharis now stood out against
the luminous background in sharp relief. He even had visions
of where his ship was about to drill a hole in the pumice-
covered rock. A loud crash, a blinding explosion, and . . .

During a brief interval of light, his frantically shifting gaze
fell on the set of four copper wires. The little black speck
spanning the cables—all that was left of the incinerated
fly—was clearly discernible, even from a distance. Sticking
out his neck and shoulder like a soccer goalie about to make a
flying save, Pirx lunged forward with all his weight, and was
almost knocked unconscious by the force of the collision. He
bounced off the blister's glass wall like an inflated inner tube
and crumpled to the floor. The outer shell did not so much as
jiggle. Struggling to his feet, panting, with a bleeding mouth,
he got ready to make another flying lunge at the glass wall.

That's when he happened to glance down.

The manual override. Designed to give rapid, full-thrust
acceleration in the 10g range. Operated by direct mechanical
control and capable of providing an emergency thrust lasting
less than a second in duration.

But the greater the rate of acceleration, he suddenly realized, the faster his descent to the lunar surface. Or would it be? No, it would do just the opposite—it would have a braking effect! But wouldn't the reaction be too short to act as a brake? The braking had to be continuous. So much for the override. Or was it?

He made a dive for the control stick, grabbing it on his way down, and pulled for all he was worth. Without the contour couch to cushion his impact, he could have sworn all his bones had been fractured when he hit the deck. Another pull on the stick, another powerful lurch. This time he landed on his head, and if it hadn't been for his helmet's foam-rubber liner, his skull would have been shattered.

The fuse panel started sizzling, the blinking suddenly stopped, and a soft and steady electric light lit up the cabin interior.

The two bursts of acceleration, fired in quick succession by manual control, had been enough to dislodge the minute sliver of carbon from between the wires, thus eliminating the short circuit once and for all. With the salty taste of blood in his mouth, Pirx made a diving leap for the couch, but instead of landing in it, sailed high up over the back and rammed his head into the ceiling, the blow softened only somewhat by his helmet.

Just as he was getting set to leap into the air, the now activated kill-switch cut off the rocket, and the last trace of gravitation disappeared. Propelled by its own momentum, the spacecraft was falling straight toward the rocky ruins of Timocharis.

He bounced off the ceiling, spit, and the bloody saliva floated next to him in a galaxy of silver-red bubbles. Frantically he twisted and turned and stretched out his arm toward the couch. For added momentum he emptied his pockets and threw their contents to the back of him, the force of which propelled him downward, gradually and gently. His fingers, now so taut that his tendons threatened to snap, at first barely scraped the nickel-plated tubing before getting a firm grip on the frame. He didn't let go. Like an acrobat doing a handstand on parallel bars, he tucked in his head and pulled himself into an upright position, grabbed hold of the seat belt, and lowered himself down on it, at the same time wrapping the belt around his trunk. Not stopping to buckle the belt, he stuck the loose end between his teeth; it held. Now for the control levers and the braking pedals!

The altimeter showed 1,800 kilometers to lunar surface. Would he be able to brake in time? Impossible—not at a velocity of 45 kilometers per second. He would have to pull out of the nose dive by describing a steep turn. There was no other way.

Firing his pitch rockets, he accelerated to 2g, 3g, 4g. Not enough! Not nearly enough!

As he applied full thrust for the pullout recovery, the lunar surface, shimmering quicksilverlike on the video screen, and so like a permanent fixture until now, began to quiver and slowly subside, his contour couch squeaking under the increasing pressure of his body. The ship was going into a steep arc directly over the lunar surface, an arc with a radius large enough to compensate for the tremendous velocity. The control stick was pushed to the limit. Pressed against the spongy backrest, with his space suit not connected to the air compressor, he could feel the air being squeezed out of his lungs and his ribs being bent inward. He began seeing gray spots and waited for the blackout, his eyes riveted to the radar altimeter, which kept grinding out one set of digits after another: 990 . . . 900 . . . 840 . . . 760 . . .

He knew he was at maximum thrust, but he kept exerting pressure on the handgrip nonetheless. He was performing the tightest possible loop, yet kept on losing altitude as the digital values continued to drop—albeit at a slower rate—and he continued to find himself on the descending arm of the steep arc. Despite a paralysis of the head and eyeballs, he kept his eyes trained on the trajectometer.

As always when a space vehicle approached the danger zone of a celestial body, the trajectometer displayed not only the ship's flight curve—along with its projected course, faintly indicated by a pulsating line—but also the convex profile of the Moon, over which the maneuver was being executed.

At one point the flight curve and lunar curve seemed to converge. But did they intersect? That was the question.

Intersect—no, though the peak of the curve definitely formed a tangent. So there was no way of predicting whether he would simply skim over the lunar surface—or slam right into it. The trajectometer operated with a margin of error of 7 to 8 kilometers, and Pirx could only guess whether his flight curve ran 3 kilometers above the boulders—or below.

His eyesight began to dim—the 5 g's were beginning to take their toll—but he remained conscious. He lay there, partially blind, his fingers tightly gripping the controls, and felt the seat's foam-rubber cushion give way under the g-force. Somehow he couldn't quite bring himself to believe that he was done for. Unable to move his lips, he started counting mentally in the dark, slowly and deliberately: Twenty-one . . . twenty-two . . . twenty-three . . . twenty-four . . .

At the count of fifty, it crossed his mind that if there was to be an impact, it would have to be now. Even so, he kept his hands on the controls. It was starting to get to him now—the suffocating sensation in the chest, the ringing in the ears, a throat all clogged with blood, the reddish-black in the eyes. . . .

His fingers relaxed their grip, and the control stick slid back on its own. He saw nothing, heard nothing. By degrees the darkness began to lift, turned grayer, and breathing became easier. He tried opening his eyes, only to discover that they had been open the whole time—his eyelids were completely dried out.

He sat up.

The gravimeter showed $2g$; the forward screen—nothing

but a star-infested void. Not a sign of the Moon. What had happened to it?

It was there, all right—below him. He had pulled out of his lethal nose dive and was now cruising up and away with a diminishing escape velocity. How close had he shaved it? he wondered. The altimeter must have recorded the exact amount of clearance, but somehow he was not in the mood for taking a readout. Suddenly the alarm signal stopped. My Gawd, it had been on the whole time! A big help *that* was! Why not hang a church bell from the ceiling?! If you're headed for the cemetery, then at least let a guy go out in style! There was another buzzing noise, this time very faint. The other fly! It was alive, the bastard! Alive and buzzing the blister's ceiling. Suddenly he had an awful taste in his mouth, a taste similar to that of coarse canvas. . . . The safety belt. He had been munching on it absentmindedly the whole time.

He fastened the safety belt and grabbed hold of the controls; he still had to steer the ship back onto the assigned orbit. The two JO ships were nowhere in sight, which came as no surprise. Even so, he had to complete the mission and report to Luna Navigation. Or should he report first to Luna Base—because of the malfunction? Damned if he knew! Or maybe he should just keep quiet. No way! The moment he touched down they would spot the blood—which, as he now noticed for the first time, was splattered all over the ceiling. Besides, the on-board flight recorder would have the whole story on tape—the way the circuit breaker went berserk, the malfunction in the emergency lever . . . Boy, a swell piece of machinery these sports give us! They might as well send us up in a coffin!

Okay, so he'd report it. But where? Then he had a brainstorm. He leaned forward, loosened his shoulder strap, and groped under the seat for the cribsheet. Why the hell not? Now's when it could really come in handy.

At that instant he heard something creak behind him—as if a door were being opened.

A door? Behind him? He knew perfectly well there was no door behind him. But even if he'd wanted to, he couldn't have turned around because of the straps. A streak of light fell across the screens, wiping out the stars still visible on them, and the next thing he heard was the CO's soft and subdued voice:

"Cadet Pirx."

He made an attempt to get up, was restrained by the straps, and fell back against the seat, convinced that he was hallucinating. Out of nowhere, the CO suddenly appeared in the passage separating the glass shell from the rest of the cabin. He stood before him in his gray uniform, fixed him with his gentle gray eyes, and smiled. Pirx was altogether confused.

The moment the glass bubble went up, Pirx automatically started undoing his straps, then rose to his feet. The video screens in back of the CO went blank.

"A good performance, Pirx," said the CO. "*Quite* good."

Pirx was still dumbfounded. Then, as he was standing at attention in front of the CO, he did something that was strictly against the rules: he turned his head around, twisting it as far as his partially inflated neck collar would let him.

To his amazement, the entire access tunnel had been dismantled, hatchway and all, making it look as if the rocket ship had split in half. In the evening light he made out the catwalk, where a group of people was now standing—the cable railings, the ceiling girders . . . Pirx stared at the CO with a gaping mouth.

"Come along, son," said the CO, who reached out and shook Pirx's hand firmly. "On behalf of Flight Command, I commend you—and . . . offer you my personal apology. Yes, it's . . . only right. Now, come along. You can clean up at my place."

He started for the exit, with Pirx trailing in his footsteps, still a little stiff and wobbly on his feet. It was chilly outside, a breeze was blowing through the sliding panel in the ceiling.

Both ships were parked in the exact same place as before. Attached to the nose of each were several long and thick cables, droopingly suspended in space. They had not been there before.

His instructor, who was among those waiting on the catwalk, made a remark, which Pirx had trouble hearing through his helmet.

"What?" he instinctively blurted out.

"The air! Let the air out of your suit!"

"Oh, the air . . ."

He pressed the valve, and the air made a hissing sound as it was released. From where he stood on the catwalk, he could make out the two men in white smocks waiting behind the railing. His rocket ship looked as if it had a fractured beak. At first he felt only a strange apathy, which turned to amazement, then disillusionment, and finally anger—pure and unmitigated anger.

They were opening the hatch of the other ship. The CO was standing on the catwalk, listening to something the men in white smocks were telling him.

A faint banging noise could be heard coming from inside.

Then, from out of the cabin staggered a writhing hulk of a man in a brown uniform, his helmetless head bobbing around like a blurry blotch, his face contorted in a mute shriek. . . .

Pirx's knees buckled.

It was . . . Boerst.

He had crashed into the Moon.

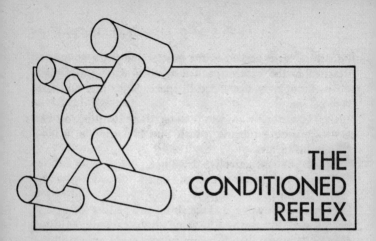

THE CONDITIONED REFLEX

It happened in his fourth year, shortly before the summer break. Pirx, fresh out of basic training, had passed his qualifying tests on the mock-ups, logged two unsimulated flights, and soloed once to the Moon. By now he fancied himself something of a rocket jockey, a space ace, whose real home was among the planets and who had only one set of clothes—his g-suit, much the worse for wear, of course—the first to sound the time-honored meteorite alert and with a brilliantly executed maneuver save his ship, himself, and his less keen-eyed buddies from certain disaster. That was how he liked to think of himself, anyway; and it always pained him, while shaving, to observe how unscathed his manifold experiences had left him: not a single telltale nick! Not even the nastiest of these experiences—the time the Harelsberg machine went off in his hands as he was setting his ship down in the Sinus Medii—had rewarded him with a single gray hair. Oh, well, maybe it was wishful thinking—but gee, how nice to have just a sprinkling of gray around the temples, a few crow's-feet at least, the kind bearing witness to prolonged concentration on the reference stars. Unfortunately, it was not meant to be; he was what he was—a smooth-faced, chubby-cheeked cadet. And so, while running his razor over his face, swallowing his shame, he would go on inventing all sorts of adventures, one more spine-tingling than the next, designed to show him off to his full heroic stature. Matters, who either knew of his frustration or merely intuited it, advised him to grow a mustache. Whether or not his advice was sincerely meant, the next day Pirx, in the privacy of his morning shave, stood before the mirror balancing a black shoelace on his lip—and nearly cracked up. From that day on, he had reason to doubt Matters's sincerity, though not that of Matters's sister—Matters's very *cute* sister—who once confided that he had the look of a "decent, regular sort of fella." That was the last straw.

Nothing really bad happened that night at the discothèque; at least, none of his worst fears was realized. True, he danced the wrong dance once—something he discovered only after it was too late—but she was tactful enough not to rub it in. The rest of the evening went off without a hitch. He managed to stay off her feet and even to keep a straight face (his was the sort of grin that could stop traffic), and wasn't refused when he offered to take her home. They got off at the last stop and traveled the rest of the way afoot, giving him time to brood. What could he do to prove to her that he was far from being the "decent, regular sort of fella" she took him to be? Ooo, how those words rankled! But by the time they got to her place, he'd fallen into a blue funk. For all his mental exertions, he'd drawn a blank; worse, they had left him altogether tongue-tied, his head like a void, differing from the cosmic version only in that it was consumed by a grim determination. Then he was struck by a meteorlike brainstorm: why not kiss her, ask her for a date, and squeeze her hand—suggestively, passionately, perversely . . . or something like that (echoes of something he had read somewhere)? A false alarm. There was no kiss, no asking for a date, and no hand squeezing. But when she said good night in that titillatingly throaty voice of hers, turned, and reached for the door handle, the demon in him was aroused. Was it that he detected a note of irony in her voice, real or imagined? Who knows. The fact was that, quite spontaneously, the moment she turned her back on him, so breezy in her bearing, so confident in her feminine charm, so very much the belle . . .

Anyway, the moment she turned around, he gave her a formidable whack on the fanny. Oh, was she surprised! All he caught as he spun on his heel and took off lickety-split, hell-bent for safety, was a muffled "Ouch!" Matters, whom he approached the next day as though he were a time bomb, made no mention of the incident.

Nevertheless, his rash behavior continued to nag at him. He had acted impetuously, without any forethought—something for which he seemed to have a special talent. A slap on the rump. Now was that something worthy of a "decent, regular sort of fella"?

He was inclined to think it was. Regardless, the effect of this episode with Matters's sister—whom he had avoided like the plague ever since—was to cure him of his early morning habit of posing before the mirror. Before that, he had sunk so low on several occasions that, not content with one mirror, he had enlisted an additional hand mirror, to find a profile that, however insignificantly, might satisfy his Great Expectations. Fortunately, he was not so consummate an idiot as not to see the absurdity of these asinine poses. Besides, it was not for signs of any masculine sexiness that he was looking—heavens, no!—but *grit*. For he had read Conrad, and whenever he would ponder, with cheeks aglow, the great galactic silence, the lonely valor of men, he always had trouble picturing a hero of eternal night, a loner, having such a—dimplepuss. He soon gave up his morning posing once and for all, thereby demonstrating what superior willpower he had.

These concerns, though festering, paled beside his upcoming oral with Professor Merinus, popularly nicknamed "the Merino." To tell the truth, Pirx wasn't all that anxious about the exam; only a few times had he been tempted to hang around the Department of Navigational Astrodesy and Astrognosis, at whose entrance students used to waylay those coming out of the Merino's office—not to congratulate the lucky few who passed, but to hear what new and tricky questions had been devised by "the Ornery Ram," as that pitiless interrogator was called. The old man, though he had yet to set foot inside a spaceship, to say nothing of stepping on the Moon, was possessed of such theoretical omniscience that he knew every stone of every crater in the Sea of Rains, could recite every butte and bluff of every planetoid, and was equally at home among the far-flung regions of Jupiter's moons. It was said that he was an expert on meteors and comets yet to be discovered (in the next millennium), this ability mathematically to project future trajectories owing to his favorite pastime: the perturbational analysis of celestial bodies. And precisely this prodigious knowledge of his made him cantankerous among those whose own knowledge was microscopic by comparison. But Pirx was not the least bit intimidated by him, for he had discovered his Achilles' heel. The professor had his own terminology, one uniquely his in the world of scientific scholarship. Guided by his own innate cunning, Pirx went to the library and got out all of Merinus's major works. Not to read them, of course. Oh, no. He only thumbed through them, jotting down some two hundred of the Merino's favorite verbal eccentricities. Once he had committed them to memory, he felt sure of passing. He was not disappointed. The old professor, attending closely to the style of his delivery, fidgeted and squirmed, twitched his scraggly brows, and hung on every word as if harking to the trills of a nightingale. The clouds that normally darkened his face scattered. He looked almost young again. Pirx, spurred on by this sudden transformation, and by his own pluck, really poured it on. And even though he completely flubbed the last question—it presumed a knowledge of a four-part formula, unobtainable even with the help of Merinosian rhetoric—the professor, somewhat apologetically, awarded him with a big fat B.

But the taming of Professor Merinus was nothing compared to the anxiety aroused by what was known as the "loony dip," the last and final phase of his qualifying exam.

There was no bluffing one's way through the "loony dip." The candidate first reported to Albert, officially employed as janitor in the Department of Behavioral Astropsychology, but in reality the chairman's right-hand man, whose word carried more weight than the combined wisdom of the tenured faculty. Albert, formerly the factotum of Professor Balloe, who had retired the year before—to the delight of the students, but to the distress of Albert ("No one ever appreciated me half as much as Professor Balloe emeritus")—then took the candidate down to a small room in the basement. There he had his face cast in paraffin. Into the nostrils of this facial mask, once it was removed, were inserted two metal tubes. After that, the candidate was sent back upstairs to the "pool." It was not really a pool at all—students never like to call anything by its proper name—but a large room containing a tank filled with water. The candidate, or, in cadet slang, the "patient," was made to strip and climb into the water, which was gradually heated until it matched his body temperature. For some the cutoff point came at twenty-eight, for others at thirty degrees Celsius. Once the test subject's body temperature was reached—signaled by an upraised arm of the freely floating "patient"—one of the assistants attached the paraffin mask. Salt was then added to the water—not potassium cyanide, as was attested by those who had already been through the "loony dip," but ordinary table salt, in amounts large enough to allow the "patient" (also referred to as the "drowning victim") to float just below the surface without sinking. Breathing was made possible by the metal tubes protruding above the water. That, in essence, was all there was to the test, the scientific name for which was the Sensory Deprivation Experiment. Blind and deaf, without any sense of smell, taste, or touch (after a very short while the water ceased to exert any sensation), lying with arms folded on his chest like an Egyptian mummy, the "victim" was soon submerged in a simulated weightless condition. For how long depended on the subject's endurance.

It looked harmless enough. Yet when a man was subjected to this condition for any length of time, he became susceptible to the strangest sensations. The experiences of past test subjects were amply documented in textbooks on experimental psychology; yet while nothing prevented one from reading up on them, the experiences themselves were too varied to be of much help. One-third of the candidates were lucky to last three hours; five or six hours was considered exceptional. Perseverance had its rewards, too, as the summer training assignments were awarded on the basis of the class grade list: the one with the highest grade was assigned a "special" mission, rather than a routine assignment at one of the many circum-Terra stations. But there was no way of predicting who would "tough it out" and who wouldn't; the "dip" was designed to test severely the subject's psychological stability.

Pirx got off to an auspicious start, disregarding the fact that he unnecessarily kept his head underwater before the mask was installed. In the process he consumed a quarter of a liter of water that, as he now had occasion to verify, was treated with ordinary salt.

Once the mask was in place, his first sensation was of a slight buzzing in the ears and of being immersed in total darkness—his eyes were kept forcibly shut by the mask's tight fit. He relaxed his muscles and was gently buoyed by the water. Then something unexpected: an itching sensation in his nose and right eye. Now what? He couldn't very well scratch through the mask. Hm. Nobody ever reported having an *itch* before. Maybe this was to be his own special contribution to experimental psychology. He rested, perfectly poised, the water neither warming nor cooling his naked body. Before long it was completely lacking in any sensations. One wiggle of his toes would have told him they were wet, but he also knew that hidden in the ceiling was a video recorder and that every twitch of his body meant a minus point. By monitoring himself internally, he was able to distinguish his own faint heartbeat. Soon the discomfort passed; even the itching abated. Albert had installed the metal tubes so adeptly that he could hardly feel their presence. For that matter, he was slowly being divested of any feeling: a vacuum, the more alarming for being so painless. He was losing all sense of spatial relationship, of the position of his arms and legs; only his memory told him where they were. He tried to calculate how long he had been underwater with his face imprisoned in white paraffin. To his surprise, he discovered he hadn't the faintest idea of how much time had elapsed since his submersion in the "loony dip"—and he'd always been able to guess the time to within a few minutes' accuracy.

He hadn't got over his surprise when he discovered that his body, his face—everything—was gone. Not what one would call a pleasant feeling; on the contrary, it was terrifying. Slowly but surely, he was dissolving into this water, whose presence was as unreal to him as his own body. Even his heartbeat had faded. He listened intently. Nothing. Silence engulfed him, was transformed into a low murmur, a monotonous white drone, against which he was defenseless—he couldn't plug his ears. After a while, when he was sure enough time had elapsed so that he could risk a few minus points, he decided to move his arms.

There was nothing to move, which was more a cause for amazement than alarm. Okay, the textbooks *had* said something about "total sensory deprivation"—but who would have believed it could be *this* total?

A normal reaction, he assured himself. The thing is not to move. Whoever toughs it out the longest will get the highest grade. For a while he sustained himself on this maxim, though for how long he didn't know.

The situation went from bad to worse.

The darkness in which he was submerged—which he embodied—began teeming, flickering with dimly incandescent circles swirling about on the periphery. He swiveled his eyeballs and was consoled, though it wasn't long before this feeling eluded him as well.

The sum of all these sensations—the flickering lights, the monotonous drone—was a harmless prelude, a trifle, compared to what came next.

Anyone who has ever had his hand or arm fall asleep when the blood supply has been temporarily cut off knows how wooden it seems to the touch. Uncomfortable as it is, the condition is usually short-lived. The deadening numbness affects only a few fingers, or a hand, momentarily turning it into a lifeless appendage on an otherwise normal, sensate body. But Pirx was deprived of all sensation—save that of terror.

He was disintegrating not into different personalities but into a manifold terror. Of what he didn't know. He was residing neither in reality (how could he without a body to perceive it?) nor in a dream (he was too conscious of where he was, of his own responses, to be dreaming). No, it was something else, not comparable to anything he'd ever experienced, not even to an alcoholic or narcotic stupor.

He remembered reading about it. He was experiencing what was known as "disorganization of the cortex caused by sensory deprivation of the brain."

It sounded innocent enough. The real thing was something else again.

He felt scattered, diffused. Up, down, right, and left no longer meant anything to him. Where was the ceiling? He couldn't remember. How could he? Without a body, without eyes, he had lost all sense of direction.

Wait a sec, he thought. Let's get this straight. Space has three dimensions. . . .

Words without meaning. He tried to summon up some sense of time, kept repeating the word "time." . . . It was like munching on a wad of paper. Time was a senseless glob. It was not he who was repeating the word, but someone else, some intruder who had wormed his way inside him. Or he inside him. And that someone was enlarging, swelling, transcending all boundaries. He was traveling through unfathomable interiors, a ballooning, preposterous, elephantine finger—not his own, not a real finger, but a fictitious one, coming out of nowhere . . . sovereign, overwhelming, rigid, full of reproach and silly innuendo. . . . And Pirx—not he but his thought processes—reeled back and forth inside this preposterous, fetid, torpid, nullifying mass. . . .

Poof! The finger disappeared. Pirx spun, spiraled, plummeted like a rock. Tried to scream but couldn't.

Scintillating shapes—faceless, spherical, gaping, dispersing every time he tried to confront them—advanced, bore down on him, swelled his insides. . . . He was a thin-walled, membranous receptacle, strained to the bursting point.

He exploded—splattered into random and disjointed fragments of night, which fluttered aimlessly in space like flakes of charred paper. Throughout this flurry of oscillating movements there was the awareness of some terrific exertion of will, some last-ditch effort to traverse the realm of murky oblivion that had once been his own body but was now reduced to an insensate, chilling nothingness—to reach out and touch someone, to catch one final glimpse of him. . . .

"Hold it," something said in an astonishingly clear and matter-of-fact voice, one decidedly not his own. Some sympathetic onlooker? Where? He could have sworn he'd heard a voice. No, it was only his imagination playing tricks on him.

"Hold it. If others have lived to tell about it, then it can't be fatal. So just hang in there."

The words spun around until they were emptied of their meaning. Then it started up again: the slow dismemberment, the breaking up, the crumbling apart of everything like gray, water-soaked tissue, melting like a snowcapped peak warmed by the sun. Swept up by it, he was freighted passively away.

I'm a goner, he thought in earnest, convinced that this was death, that it was not a dream. It swamped him—no, not him, but *them,* his manifold selves, too prolific to be counted.

What am I doing here? Where am I? In the ocean? On the Moon? Taking part in some experiment . . . ?

He refused to believe it was an experiment. What—vanish because of a little paraffin and a tankful of salt water? Hey! Enough of this crap. And he began to fight back against whatever it was; he exerted every muscle; it was like trying to heft a boulder. But there was nothing left of him, not enough to make his muscles flinch. During his last glimmer of consciousness he mustered the strength to groan—feeble and distant, the sound was like a radio signal from another planet.

For a second or so he almost revived, only to surrender to an even blacker, more nullifying ordeal.

He was not in any physical discomfort. If only it *had* hurt! If only he could have experienced a twinge of real pain, the kind that bestows limits, presence, confirmation of self. . . . But it was painless, a numbing surge of nothingness. He felt the air rush into him—spasmodically, in snatches, not into his lungs but into that wilderness of shuddering, stunted thought-scraps. Whine, groan—anything to hear your own voice. . . .

"You can moan without thinking of the stars," said some intimate yet strangely anonymous voice.

Whine? Moan? How could he? He was dead. Extinct. Defunct. Look: he was a hole, a sieve, a labyrinth of tortuous caves and passages, transparent, porous. . . . Oh, why hadn't they told him it would be like this? Cold and clammy streams . . . they were running through him . . . freely . . . without obstruction. . . . The bastards! Why hadn't they told him?!

Soon the sensation of airy transparency gave way to raw fear, and it persisted—even after the darkness, convulsed by shimmering spasms, had vanished.

The worst was yet to come, but it defied description, even clear recollection; there was no vocabulary for it. Yes, the "victims" were the richer for the experience, the hellish nature of which escaped their professors—but it was scarcely an experience to be envied.

Pirx had to undergo still more punishment. He would vanish for a while, then return to life, not singly but in multiple versions; have his brain eaten completely away, then recover long enough to be plunged into a series of abnormal states too intricate to articulate, whose leitmotif was a conscious and ineradicable terror transcending time and space.

Pirx had had a bellyful.

Later Dr. Grotius said:

"Your first groan came at the one-hundred-thirty mark, your second at the two hundred twenty-ninth. All told, a loss of three points—but not a single jerk! Fold one leg over the other, please. I'm going to test your reflexes. . . . Tell me, how did you manage to stick it out so long, especially toward the end?"

Pirx was sitting on a neatly folded towel, the more pleasant for being coarse. He felt like Lazarus himself. Not that it showed on the outside, but inwardly he felt resurrected. He had tested a full seven hours. The highest grade in the class! Never mind that he had died umpteen thousand times during the final three hours; he'd done it without a peep. After they fished him out of the tank, after they dried him off, gave him a body massage, an injection, and a generous swig of cognac, they hustled him off to the examination room, where Dr. Grotius was waiting for him. Along the way he caught a glimpse of himself in the mirror: the stunned, comatose, bleary-eyed look of someone just recovered from a bout with malignant fever. He stared into the mirror—not because he expected to see his hair streaked with gray, but on a whim—took one look at his broad-boned pie face, wheeled around, and marched off, trailing wet footprints on the parquet flooring.

Dr. Grotius labored long and hard to get him to recount his experience. Seven hours was no small feat. He regarded Pirx differently now, less with sympathy than with the fervor of an entomologist on discovering some rare species of moth or insect. Possibly he saw in him the makings of a scholarly article.

Pirx, it must be said, was not the most obliging of research subjects. He sat the whole time in stunned silence, batting his eyes like a halfwit. Everything seemed flat and two-dimensional, receding or moving closer the moment he tried to grasp it. A typical reaction. But his response to the doctor's questioning aimed at prying further details out of him was anything but typical.

"Ever been in there yourself?" He answered a question with a question.

"No." Grotius backed off in some astonishment. "Why do you ask?"

"You should try it sometime," suggested Pirx. "That way you'd see firsthand what it's like."

By the second day he felt fit enough to joke about the "loony dip." From then on, it was back and forth to the Main Building, where the summer training missions were posted daily on a glassed-in bulletin board. But when the weekend rolled around, his name was still not on the list.

On Monday he was told to report to the commandant's office.

Pirx, though not immediately fazed, examined his conscience beforehand. Was it for sneaking that mouse aboard Osten's ship? Nah, that was ancient history by now. Anyway, what was one measly mouse? Big deal. How about the time he hooked up the AC/DC to Maebius's mattress springs, using an alarm clock for a timer? But that was just a lowerclass-man's prank, a twenty-two-year-old's idea of a practical joke. The commandant was a bighearted guy; he'd understand. Up to a point. Or was it for Operation Zombie?

Operation Zombie was Pirx's own brainstorm. He of course had help from friends—what were friends for, anyway? It was his smoothest, slickest job ever: a little gunpowder in a paper cone, a trail three times around the room, payload under the desk—there he might have overdone it a bit—then back out into the corridor through the slit under the door. And the way Barn had been "primed": for one whole week Pirx made sure the nightly bull sessions were devoted exclusively to "extraterrestrial beings." Pirx—nobody's fool—was shrewd enough to cast people in different roles—some telling horror stories, others acting as skeptics—so Barn wouldn't be the wiser. Except for occasionally sneering at the partisans of the "beyond," Barn kept aloof from these metaphysical debates. But, man, what a sight he made, barrel-assing out of his room at midnight, bellowing like a water buffalo with a tiger on its tail! The flame, as planned, had sneaked under the door, snaked three times around the room, and—whamo!—exploded under the table, toppling books and starting a small fire. A couple of buckets of tap water took care of it, but it left a nice hole in the floor, not to mention the lingering stench of cordite. The operation, though technically flawless, proved a flop: Barn still refused to believe in spirits. Yep, Operation Zombie it was. Pirx got up early, slipped on a fresh shirt, took one last peek into his *Flight Book* and *Basic Navigation*—just to be on the safe side—and went to face the music.

The commandant's office was a dream come true. For Pirx it was, at any rate. Walls totally obscured by celestial maps, constellations like golden-brown drops of honey against a navy-blue field. A small blank Moon globe on the desk; books and degrees galore on the walls; another globe against the wall—only this one bigger, more elaborate. The second one was a real marvel of technological splendor: press the right button and bingo! the orbital path of any artificial satellite was immediately simulated, from the latest to the oldest—those pioneering satellites dating from the fifties.

Practically any other day Pirx would have been enthralled by such a globe, but not today. The commandant was busy writing when he came in. "Please be seated; I'll be right with you," he heard him say. At last, taking off his glasses—until about a year ago he had got along without them—the commandant gave him a good long gander, as if laying eyes on him for the first time. That was his way—not only with Pirx but with everyone. It was a gaze designed to rattle even the saintliest of men. And Pirx was hardly a saint. He couldn't keep still. Either he found himself sprawled out in the grossly casual manner of a millionaire aboard his own private yacht, or precariously balanced on the edge of his seat. Finally—mercifully—the commandant broke the silence.

"Well, Pirx, how are things?"

He'd addressed him informally—a good omen. Pirx said he couldn't kick.

"Took a dip, did you?"

Pirx nodded. Hey, what gives? Pirx kept his guard up. Maybe it was for sassing Dr. Grotius. . . .

"There's a trainee's berth up on Mendeleev. Know where that is?"

"That's an astrophysics station on the Far Side," replied Pirx. He felt a slight letdown. He had been nurturing a quiet hope—so quiet he had been reluctant to admit it to himself, for fear of blowing it—that it would be something else. Like a flight mission. With all the ships and planets in the cosmos, he *would* have to land a routine station assignment, and on the Far Side, no less. Once the "in" term for the lunar hemisphere not facing Earth, it was now in common parlance.

"Right. Do you know what it looks like?" asked the commandant, wearing a facial expression that said he had something up his sleeve. Pirx briefly toyed with the idea of bluffing.

"No," he answered.

"If you sign on, I'll supply you with all the specs." The commandant patted a stack of papers.

"You mean it's voluntary?" Pirx shot back with undisguised alacrity.

"Correct. The mission I have in mind is . . . could turn out to be . . . very—"

He deliberately broke off in mid-sentence to measure what effect his words would have on the wide-eyed, incredulous Pirx. Slowly the cadet drew a solemn breath, held it, and sat there as if oblivious of the need to exhale. Blushing like a maiden at the sight of her Prince, he waited for another dose of sweet-sounding phrases. The commandant cleared his throat.

"Well, well," he said soberingly, "I may have been exaggerating. Anyway, you're mistaken."

"Beg your pardon?" stammered Pirx.

"I mean you're not the world's only salvation. Not yet, at least."

Pirx, red as a beet, squirmed in his seat and fidgeted with his hands. The commandant, a man notorious for his methods, had just finished painting a paradisiacal vision of Pirx the Hero (Pirx already had dreams of returning from his Heroic Exploit and, while being paraded through a packed cosmodrome, hearing awed whispers of "That's the one! That's the one!"), and now, unknowingly it seemed, he was beginning to play down the Mission, to trim it down to the size of a routine training assignment.

"The station is manned by astronomers—they're sent out there, do their month's service, and that's that. The work is routine, requiring no specialized skills. Candidates used to be screened on the basis of the standard first- and second-degree tests. But that was before the accident. Now we need people who have undergone more rigorous testing. Pilots would be ideal, but you can't very well farm a pilot out to a routine observatory. You can understand that."

Pirx could understand. The whole solar system was begging for pilots, astrogators, navigators—always in short supply, even in the best of times. But what "accident" was the commandant referring to? Pirx observed a prudent silence.

"It's a small station, situated in the most cockeyed place imaginable—not on the crater floor, as you'd expect, but just below the northern summit. There was a big to-do about the choice of location, international prestige rather than sound selenophysics being the deciding factor—as you'll see in a moment. Anyhow, last year a section of the wall collapsed and wiped out the only road, making access difficult, and possible only by day. Plans were under way for a cable railway, but work was halted when it was decided to transfer the station down below in a year's time. At night the station is cut off from the outside world. All radio communication is suspended. Why is that?"

"Sir?"

"Why does all radio communication cease?"

That was the commandant for you. What had begun as a harmless briefing on his Mission had suddenly been turned into an exam! Pirx broke out into a sweat.

"Since the Moon has no atmosphere or ionosphere, radio communication is maintained by ultrashortwave frequency. . . . A network of relay stations, similar to TV transmitters, was constructed to—"

The commandant, his elbows propped on the desktop, twiddled his ball-point in a display of forbearance as Pirx went on expounding on things any schoolchild would have known. He was venturing into territories where his limited knowledge left much to be desired.

"These transmission lines"—he hurtled on, coming upon more familiar waters—"have been installed on both the Far

Side and the Near Side. Eight are located on the Far Side, linking up Luna Base with Sinus Medii, Palus Somnii, Mare Imbrium—"

"You can skip that," the commandant suddenly interrupted in a fit of magnanimity. "Nor is it necessary to hypothesize on the origin of the Moon. Proceed."

Pirx blinked.

"Radio interference occurs when the relay network enters the terminator . . . when one half of the network lies in darkness and the other half in light—"

"I know what a terminator is. There's no need to explain it," the commandant said benignly.

Pirx coughed and blew his nose. Still, he couldn't go on coughing or blowing his nose forever.

"In the absence of any lunar atmosphere, the Sun's corpuscular radiation bombards the Moon's crust, causing— uh—interference of the radio waves. This interference is what causes inter—"

He was floundering.

"The interference interferes—absolutely right!" said the commandant, coming to his aid. "But what *causes* the interference?"

"A secondary radiation, known as the No—the No—"

"Nov—" The commandant prodded gently.

"The . . . Novinsky effect!" Pirx finally blurted out. But the interrogation didn't end there.

"And what produces the Novinsky effect?"

This last question had him altogether stumped. There was a time when he'd known the answer, but he had since forgotten. He had gone into the exam with the facts down cold, like a juggler balancing a pyramid of wildly improbable things in his head. But the exam was over now. He was desperately going on about electrons, forced radiation, and resonances when he was cut short by a sympathetic head-shake from the commandant.

"Uh-uh," said the stern and uncompromising man. "And

Professor Merinus gave you a B for the course. . . . Hm. Do you suppose he might have made a mistake?"

Pirx's armchair was slowly being transformed into a live volcano.

"I wouldn't wish to cause my colleague any embarrassment, so I think the less said about this the better. . . ."

Pirx sighed.

"But during your comprehensive examination I shall see to it that Professor Laab . . ."

He left the rest to Pirx's imagination. Pirx gulped, but not from the concealed threat; the commandant's hand was slowly scooping up the papers that were to have accompanied his Mission.

"Why isn't a cable communications system practicable?"

"Too costly. At the moment only one concentric cable is in operation—the one connecting Luna Base with Archimedes. There are plans to install a cable network within the next five years," Pirx fired away.

Not mollified, the commandant picked up the thread.

"To resume, then. The Mendeleev station is cut off at night. But communication or no communication, the work went on as usual—until recently, that is. One day last month, when the station failed to respond to any calls following the usual nighttime intermission, the Tsiolkovsky team set out and found the main hatch open, and inside the chamber—a body. The station was being manned by a team of Canadians, Challiers and Savage. The body in the chamber was Savage's. His helmet was punctured. Death due to asphyxiation. Challiers's body was found the next day at the foot of the Sun Gap—the victim of a fall. Otherwise the station was in perfect order: the monitoring systems checked out, stores untouched, not a sign of any damage or mechanical malfunction. You probably read about it."

"Yes, I did," said Pirx. "But it was reported in the papers as a double suicide. A case of temporary insanity brought on by a . . . psychosis of some kind . . ."

"Bull!" the commandant suddenly blurted out. "I knew Savage. From our days in the Alps. A guy like that would never have snapped. No, sir. The papers were full of it. You can read the report yourself, the one released by the joint inquiry commission. Listen here, Pirx, you fellas are given the same screening as pilots; the only difference is that you can't fly until you're breveted. And like it or not, you've got to put in your summer duty. If you sign on, you'll fly tomorrow."

"And my partner?"

"I don't know his name. Some astrophysicist. The station can't function without them. I'm afraid he won't be exactly thrilled by your company, but, well, you might just pick up a little astrography in the process. Now you're sure you understand the nature of your assignment? The commission ruled it was an accident, but certain aspects still remain under a cloud of . . . let's call it ambiguity. Something unexplainable happened up there—exactly what, we don't know. That's why it was decided the next team should include someone with the psychological qualifications of a pilot. I saw no reason to turn down their request. Chances are, nothing sensational is going to happen. Of course you'll have to keep your eyes and ears open. But remember, you're not up there to play detective; no one is expecting any startling new discoveries or breakthroughs in the case. No, that's not your mission. What's the matter? Aren't you feeling well?"

"Huh? No, no—I feel fine," answered Pirx.

"I thought so. Well, think you can behave sensibly? Unless I'm mistaken, it's already going to your head. Maybe we should call off—"

"I will behave sensibly," said Pirx in the most emphatic voice he could muster.

"I doubt it," said the commandant. "I'm sending you up there with some reluctance. If it weren't for the grade—"

"The dip!" Pirx let it slip.

The commandant pretended not to have heard this last remark. He gave him the papers first, then his hand.

"Takeoff tomorrow at zero eight hundred hours. Travel light. You've been up there before, so you know what it's like. Here's your plane ticket and your reservation on the *Transgalactic*. You'll fly straight to Luna Base; from there you'll be transferred."

He added a few more words. To wish him luck? By way of farewell? Pirx couldn't tell. He was too far away in his thoughts to comprehend. His ears were already full of the roar of boosting rockets, his eyes blinded by the desiccating white glare of rocky lunar terrain, his face wrought with stunned bewilderment—the same look that must have accompanied the two Canadians to their mysterious deaths. He did an about-face and bumped into the large globe by the window; took the front steps in four lunarlike bounds; and was nearly run over by a car, whose screeching brakes brought everyone—excluding Pirx—to a standstill. Luckily the commandant had gone back to his papers and thus was spared this opening display of "sensible behavior."

In the course of the next twenty-four hours, there was such a bustle of activity around, for the sake of, on behalf of, and with a view to Pirx, that at times he almost pined after the salty, lukewarm bath where nothing happened.

A person can be adversely affected as much by a lack of as by a surfeit of impressions. But Pirx was in no frame of mind to formulate such insights. All the commandant's efforts to soft-pedal, reduce, and even dismiss the Mendeleev mission had been, to put it mildly, in vain. Pirx boarded the plane with a facial expression that made the comely stewardess recoil instinctively—though she was guilty of a gross injustice, for as far as Pirx was concerned she might just as well not have existed. Marching up the aisle like the commander of an armed legion, he took his seat; he, this William the Conqueror of the Space Age, this Cosmic Crusader, this Lunar Benefactor, this Explorer of Awesome Mysteries, this Monster Tamer of the Far Side (speaking potentially, of course, and hypothetically, which made his present bliss no less delectable; on the contrary, it made him profoundly benevolent toward his fellow passengers, who never suspected who was traveling with them in the belly of the big jetliner). He looked on them with the same amused detachment as Einstein, in the waning years of his life, must have felt watching children at play in a sandbox.

The *Selene,* a new vessel from the *Transgalactic* fleet, lifted from a Nubian cosmodrome deep in the heart of Africa. Pirx felt deeply satisfied. He didn't exactly have visions of a plaque being installed here in his honor—that much of a dreamer he was not; but he was not very far from it. All the more bitter, then, were the drops of gall that began to creep into his cup of self-contentment as he boarded the *Selene.* That nobody aboard the jet had recognized him—well, that was bad enough. But aboard the spaceship? He took his seat on the lower deck—in tourist class, no less—and found himself surrounded by a bunch of wildly garrulous, camera-toting, jibber-jabbering Frenchmen. Pirx—sandwiched among a lot of loudmouthed tourists!

No one doted or fussed over him. No one offered to help him into his suit or to inflate it; no one asked how he was feeling or strapped on his oxygen bottles. For a while he consoled himself with the thought that it was to avoid recognition. Tourist class was like the seating compartment of any jet, except that the seats were bigger, roomier, and the NO SMOKING—NO STANDING sign stared one right in the face. Pirx tried to dissociate himself from this crowd of astronautical neophytes by adopting a more professional pose, folding one leg over the other, deliberately neglecting to fasten his safety belt—but to no avail. The only time he was noticed by the crew was when he was told to buckle up—this coming not from the pretty stewardess but from one of the copilots. Finally one of the Frenchmen—quite unintentionally, it seemed—offered him a jelly bean, which he took and chewed on until the gooey filling gummed up his teeth, then sank back resignedly into his cushioned seat and surrendered himself to his reveries. Gradually he renewed his faith in the perilousness of the Mission, savoring the impending danger in peace, without haste, looking forward to his upcoming trial like a confirmed wino being handed a moss-covered bottle of wine dating from the Napoleonic Wars.

Pirx was seated next to a port. No matter how strenuously he tried to ignore the familiar sight below, he couldn't resist. From the moment the *Selene* settled into its circum-Terra orbit, before escaping onto a translunar course, his eyes were glued to the viewport. The most thrilling moment came when Earth's surface, crisscrossed by roads and canals, speckled with cities, was gradually cleansed of any human presence; when nothing was visible below save the planet's soft, round bulge, blotchy and cloud-flecked; when the eye, moving from the violet-black of oceans to the familiar shapes of continents, failed to locate a single trace of man's technological genius. At an altitude of several hundred meters, Earth looked empty— eerily empty—and newborn, the warmer regions being denoted by a faint coating of green.

As often as he had been a spectator to this abrupt transition, it never ceased to jolt him into an awareness of something—something to which he found it hard to reconcile himself. Was it the lurid manifestation of man's microscopic stature in relation to the cosmos? The transposition to another—planetary—scale? The visualization of mankind's feeble and ephemeral efforts expended over the millennia? Or was it the overcoming of that frailty, the transcending of the blind and indifferent force of gravitation exerted by that formidable mass? The leaving behind of rugged mountain massifs, of polar shields, to brave the shores of other celestial bodies? These reflections, these unarticulated sensations, soon gave way to others as the ship changed course and, threading the gap in the radiation zone hugging the North Pole, shot up to the stars.

The stargazing stopped the second the lights went on.

Luncheon was served, during which the engines labored to create a semblance of gravity. The meal over and the lights once again extinguished, the passengers sat back in their seats and got their first glimpse of the Moon.

They were approaching from the side of the Moon's southern hemisphere. A few hundred kilometers below the pole was the crater Tycho, a yawning white Sun-drenched pockmark with luminous bands radiating in all directions, whose stunning regularity had enthralled generations of Earthly astronauts, only to become, once the mystery of its symmetry was solved, the subject of student jokes. First-year students, for example, were made to believe that the circular white depression constituted the "Moon's axle hole" and that the luminous rays were in fact thickly drawn meridians.

The closer they came to the bright sphere suspended in a black void, the more evident it was that the Moon was indeed a congealed, lava-caked version of the world as it must have existed billions of years ago, when the hot Earth wandered with its satellite through meteorite clouds and masses of planetisimals; when a continuous hailstorm of rock and iron pelted and pierced the Moon's thin outer crust, tossing up huge amounts of magma onto the lunar surface; and when, the universe cleansed and purified at last, the era of tectonic cataclysms over, the airless planet died on the battlefield, to become a stony mask ravaged by bombardments—the inspiration of poets, the lyrical lamp of lovers.

The *Selene,* with is four-hundred-ton payload of freight and flesh, turned its tail to the expanding disk and commenced braking, slowly and in stages, until its gently throbbing hull roosted on one of the cosmodrome's huge steel cone assemblies.

This was Pirx's third lunar landing; on one of them, his solo, he had soft-landed in a practice field located a kilometer and a half from the passenger terminal.

He saw nothing of the field this trip; the *Selene*'s generous ceramite-plated frame was immediately hoisted onto a hydraulic winch and lowered into a hermetically sealed hangar. Customs inspection. Any narcotics? Alcohol? Material of an explosive, corrosive, or toxic nature? Uh, Pirx suddenly remembered that he had some toxic liquid in his possession— namely, a small flask of cognac, a present from Matters. He stashed it in his back pocket. Then came the health inspection—vaccination certificate, baggage sterilization (to guard against contamination)—which he whipped through in nothing flat.

He paused outside the gate to check whether anyone was on hand to greet him.

Later he stood on the mezzanine overlooking the hangar, an enormous concrete chamber hewn in the rock, with a hemispherical ceiling, level floor, and fluorescent light panels that flooded the interior with artificial sunlight. The place was aswarm with battery-powered dollies wheeling out baggage, cylinders of compressed gases, vats, crates, tubing, cable coils. . . . Looming darkly, stolidly in the background was the cause of all this commotion—the *Selene,* its midships a gaping wound, its stern anchored far below the concrete in a cavernous shaft, its bow jutting up through an opening to the next level.

Pirx stood idly around, then remembered he still had to get squared away. An agent at the Port Authority office handed him an overnight pass, told him his ship wasn't scheduled to leave for another eleven hours, then ducked out of sight, leaving him completely in the lurch. Pirx strode back out into the hallway, a little dazed by this display of bumbling inefficiency. Not a boo about whether they were to fly directly to the Tsiolkovsky station or over Mare Smythii. Come to think of it, where was his lunar sidekick? And the commission? And their work agenda?

The more he thought, the more disgruntled he became, his irritation gradually coalescing into a gnawing sensation in the pit of his stomach. He was hungry. Chow time. The directory was in six languages; he studied it carefully, hopped on the right elevator, and rode down to the pilots' cafeteria, where he was directed to the public cafeteria: this one was for pilots only.

That took the cake. He was about to make his way over to the damned restaurant when he remembered something: he had forgotten to claim his knapsack. Back upstairs to the hangar. To learn that his baggage had been sent to his hotel room. In disgust he stomped off to lunch without his pack. On the way he was caught up by two waves of tourists: some Frenchmen—the same ones—and a crowd of Swiss, Dutch, and Germans, just returned from a selenobus tour of the crater Eratosthenes. The French, doing what people normally did when getting their first taste of lunar gravitation, bunnyhopped instead of walked, bounced off the ceiling—to the squeals and cheers of the women—relished the slow descent from a height of three meters. The Germans, being more reserved by nature, filed into the spacious dining room, draped the backs of their chairs with camera gear, binoculars, tripods—with everything but high-powered telescopes—and over soup swapped samples of Moon rock fobbed off on them by the selenobus crews. Pirx sat hunched over his soup, drowning in a German-French-Greek-Dutch potpourri. Amid the general euphoria he was the only glum-faced customer. A Dutchman, taking pity on him, convinced that he was suffering from space sickness ("Your first trip to the Moon, no?"), offered him a pill. That was the drop that made his cup run over. Pirx skipped the second course, bought four packages of fruitcake at the snack bar, and took the elevator up to the hotel, venting his scorn on the porter. The man had offered to sell him a piece of the Moon—that is, a chunk of vitrified basalt.

"Get lost, you two-bit peddler! I was here before you were—" he barked and, trembling with rage, left the stupefied man standing there with jaw agape.

His room, a double, was already occupied by a short-to-medium-size man in a faded windjacket, sitting under the overhead lamp. Ginger-haired with a sprinkling of gray, a few wisps dangling over the forehead, a sunburned face, bespectacled. He took off his glasses the moment Pirx entered the room. His name was Langner—Dr. Langner—the astrophysicist who was to accompany him to Mendeleev. Pirx, already prepared for the worst, pronounced his name, mumbled something, and sat down. Langner looked to be a man in his forties—an old man in Pirx's book—but still fairly fit for his age. He didn't smoke, probably didn't drink, and didn't look like the talkative type. He was reading three books at once: a logarithm table, another brimming with formulas, a third with spectrograms. He kept a miniature calculator in his trouser pocket, using it sparingly but with effortless ease. From time to time, without taking his eyes off his formulas, he threw a question at Pirx—to which the cadet responded with a mouth full of fruitcake. Their cubicle was furnished with a set of bunkbeds and a shower stall barely big enough to accommodate someone on the beefy side, and was plastered with multilingual sings bearing entreaties to conserve water and electricity. Fortunately, breathing was permitted: a short while later, oxygen was delivered to their room. Pirx washed down his snack with tap water, so cold it set his teeth on edge—reservoirs just below the basalt crust, he thought. That's funny. It was eleven by his watch, seven by the room's electric clock, and ten past midnight by Langner's.

They switched their watches to Lunar Time, knowing they would have to change again soon. The Mendeleev station was in a different time zone. The whole Far Side was in another time zone.

Lift-off was still nine hours away when, without a word, Langner got up and left the room. Pirx sat and did nothing for a while, later moved his chair into the light, browsed through some ragged-looking magazines lying on the table, and finally, in a fit of restlessness, went out. The corridor wound around before opening onto a small lounge where several armchairs stood facing a recessed TV set. A track and field meet was being telecast by special relay from Australia. Though not much of a track fan, Pirx flopped down into one of the chairs and watched until his eyelids drooped. As he stood up, he shot a half meter into the air: he had forgotten about the reduced gravity. Nothing to do but loaf around. When could he change out of his civvies and into his g-suit? Where were his instructions? Why all the stalling?

He would have nosed around, even raised hell, if what's-his-name, Doctor Langner, hadn't treated the whole thing so casually. Better to keep his mouth shut.

The track meet was over. Pirx switched off the set and shuffled back to his room. Gosh, if he had known it was going to be like this . . . While he was taking a shower he heard voices through the dividing wall: the tourists, still rhapsodizing over lunar splendors. Ho-hum. For lack of anything better to do, he changed his shirt. He was just stretching out on his bunk when Langner reappeared with a fresh supply of books. Four of them this time.

Pirx started to get the creeps. He began to suspect Langner of being one of those scientific fanatics, a younger version of Professor Merinus.

Spreading out some new spectrograms on the table and studying them more intently than Pirx had ever scrutinized his favorite pinup, Langner suddenly asked:

"How old are you?"

"A hundred and eleven," Pirx said, and added, when the other looked up, "in binary."

Langner broke out in a smile—his first—a smile that lent him an almost human look. He had strong, immaculately white teeth.

"The Russians are picking us up in one of their ships," he said. "We'll stop off at their station on the way."

"The Tsiolkovsky station?"

"Yes."

The Tsiolkovsky station was on the Far Side. That meant

another stopover. Pirx wondered how they would cover the remaining thousand kilometers. Not by land, surely. By ship? He refrained from asking, not wishing to betray his ignorance. Langner was about to say something, but it was too late. Pirx was sound asleep—in his clothes.

He woke up with a start. Langner was bent over his bunk, touching his arm.

"It's time," he said, not wasting any words.

Pirx sat up. Langner, judging by the stack of computations on the table, had been up the whole time, reading and writing. At first Pirx understood him to mean that it was time for dinner, but soon found out he was referring to takeoff. As he slung on his knapsack, he noticed that Langner's was even bulkier and heavier. Rocks, he guessed. Later he discovered that aside from a few personal items—a couple of shirts, some toilet soap, a toothbrush—it held only books.

They moved directly to the upper level, this time without having to pass any inspections, customs or otherwise, and found a lunar shuttle waiting for them—a squat, dome-shaped vehicle, supported by three elbowlike legs measuring twenty meters in height. The ship's original silver finish was now a dingy gray. Pirx had never been aboard such a ship. An astrochemist who was to have joined them failed to show in time. They took off without him, right on schedule.

The Moon's lack of atmosphere meant that no aerodynamic vehicles such as helicopters or airplanes could be used for transportation—only rocket-propelled ships. Not even hydroplanes, the vehicles most suited for rugged terrain, were practical, requiring as they did a large supply of air. Rocket ships were fast, but fickle about where they were landed: they had a special aversion to mountains and cliffs.

Their shell-shaped, three-legged insect rumbled, roared, and went up candlestick-straight. The passenger cabin was twice as large as a hotel single. Portholes in the walls, a large round port in the ceiling, cockpit under the belly, snugly situated between the exhaust ducts for maximum ground visibility. Pirx felt a little like a parcel being shipped to an unknown destination. Not a clue as to the whys and wherefores.

It was the same old story.

They pitched into a parabola, the cabin tilting sharply, the ship trailing its long "legs," the Moon scudding by underneath—a huge convex swelling of rock and dust, seemingly untrodden by human foot. In space there is a point somewhere between Earth and the Moon where both spheres appear equal in size. Pirx distinctly recalled the illusory impression from his first lunar flight: Earth, icy blue, wrapped in mist, its continental contours blurred beyond recognition, had seemed less real than the Moon—suspended like a stone pendant, its stationary mass looming almost palpably.

They were flying over the Sea of Clouds, the crater Bullialdus already behind them, Tycho now situated to the southeast, a halo flinging its luminous rays clear across the south pole to the Far Side, the supreme symmetry of its rocky skull made even more awesome, more overwhelming from high altitude. Refulgent with sunlight, Tycho became the center of a dazzling design, its luminous white arms embracing and traversing Mare Humorum and Mare Nubium; its northernmost spur, the most prominent of all, vanishing over the horizon in the direction of Mare Serenitatis. But once past Circus Clavius to the east, once they began losing altitude over the equator and were flying over the Sea of Dreams on the Far Side, the illusion of symmetry was lost and the deceptively dark, smooth surface of the "sea" revealed its flaws and cracks. To the northeast the sawtoothed ridge of Verne stood out in brilliant relief. The closer they came to the lunar surface, the more authentic the view, the truer the image: plateaus, plains, crater basins, and ringed mountains riddled by cosmic bombardments; wreaths of debris and lava, overlapping and interlacing, as if the will unleashing this titanic shower had not been content with the ravages already inflicted. Before Pirx could locate the Tsiolkovsky massif, the shuttle, nudged by a brief burst of power, righted itself; his last glance was of the ocean of darkness swallowing the Moon's whole western hemisphere, leaving only the blazing tip of Lobachevski Peak protruding above the terminator. The stars in the upper port came to a standstill. The shuttle went down like an elevator; as they plunged through the engine flare converging around the stern, gases rocked the ship's skirt with all the booming force of an atmospheric entry. Their seats automatically reclined; the stars remained fixed in the port above; the downward plunge was gradually slowed by the timid but stubborn resistance of the rumbling retro-rockets. Suddenly the braking jets resounded full blast.

All right! We're standing on the column! Pirx thought, just to remind himself that he was a full-fledged—if not yet licensed—astronaut.

There was a jolt, a clank, then a hard thud, similar to a sledgehammer hitting a slab of rock; the cabin seesawed gently up and down; the hydraulics hissed and gurgled until the ship's wobbly, twenty-meter-long legs finally wedged into the rubble.

The pilot applied a little pressure to the oil lines to quell the rocking; there was a long *pshhh*, and the cabin stabilized.

Crawling out through the deck hatch, the pilot opened a wall locker, and lo! their space suits.

Pirx's sudden elation was quickly aborted. There were, it turned out, four suits: the pilot's, a small, a medium, and a large. The pilot was suited up in nothing flat, but waited for the others before putting on his helmet. Langner was equally quick getting into his. But Pirx—flushed, sweaty, and inwardly fuming—was having a tough time of it. The medium-size suit turned out to be too small; the large, too large. When he tried on the medium, his head rammed into the impact liner of his helmet. In the large he floated around

like a seed in a hollowed-out gourd. He was not without
friendly advice, though. The pilot was quick to point out that
better a baggy suit than one too tight, and suggested stuffing
the gaps with underwear from his pack. If that didn't do the
trick, he would gladly lend him a blanket. For Pirx the very
idea of stuffing his suit was somehow blasphemous, and he
rebelled against it with all his astronautical soul.

He settled on the smaller one. The pilot and Langner held
their peace. The pilot, leading the way, then opened the air
lock; when all were inside, he unscrewed the manhole cover
and pushed open the outer hatch.

If not for Langner, Pirx would have hopped right out onto
the scree, which, in view of the twenty-meter drop, would
have meant a sprained ankle or worse. Despite the lesser
gravity, the weight of his space suit would have made the
impact equivalent to jumping down into a pile of extremely
loose rock from one story up.

The pilot lowered a collapsible ladder, and one by one they
egressed onto the Moon.

There were no welcoming parties, no one with flowers, no
trumpet blasts. In fact, there was not a living soul in sight.
About a kilometer away, its armor-plated dome grazed by
oblique rays of awesome lunar sunlight, the Tsiolkovsky
station rose prominently above the plain. A little higher up,
hewn in the rock, was a small landing pad, now occupied by a
double row of rockets—transports, judging by their size.

Their ship, listing slightly to one side, hunkered down on
its triadic, steel-footed assembly, blackening with exhaust the
rocks directly beneath its thrust chambers. The terrain to the
east was relatively flat, if an endless boulder-cluttered
plain—some stones were the size of apartment houses—could
be called flat. Rearing gently eastward, it fringed off into a
wall of vertical faults to become the central massif of the
Tsiolkovsky mountain. A blazing Sun, poised ten degrees
above the ridge, blinded them every time they turned their

gaze in its direction. Pirx, like the others, lowered his sun visor, but it failed to cut down the glare altogether, at most enabling him to look without squinting. Cautiously picking their way in and out of the shifting boulders, they shoved off for the station, eventually losing sight of the shuttle when they had to cross the flat-bottomed basin. The station commanded a view of the basin and the surrounding landscape, three-fourths of the structure being recessed in a wall of highland mass strangely evocative of a stone fortress from the Mesozoic era. Its lopped-off cornices bore a striking similarity to ancient turrets, but only from a distance; the closer one got to them, the more these "turrets" abandoned their symmetrical shape, the more clearly one saw their deep cracks, too easily mistaken for black stripes from far off. The terrain was fairly navigable by lunar standards. Each bootstep raised a cloud of dust—the celebrated lunar dust— that would climb waist-high, gird them in immaculate white, and refuse to settle, forcing them to walk three abreast. When they reached the station, Pirx cast a backward glance and saw three tubular, serpentine trails, brighter than any dust or powder he had ever known on Earth.

On the subject of lunar dust Pirx was somewhat knowledgeable. He recalled how amazed the first explorers had been by its behavior. Although they had anticipated it, according to all laws known to them even the finest-particle dust should have settled in an airless vacuum; not lunar dust—but oddly enough, only during the daytime, under conditions of sunlight. Later it was discovered that electrical phenomena behave differently on the Moon. Lightning, thunder, St. Elmo's fire, and other atmospheric discharges common to Earth are unknown on the Moon. Lunar rocks, because they are subjected to a constant bombardment of particle radiation, have the same charge as the dust mantling them. And since electrical charges of the same polarity are mutually repellent, the dust, if disturbed, remained in suspension, frequently for hours, thanks to this electrostatic repulsion. The more sunspots there were, the "dustier" the Moon. But the dust cloud phenomenon ceased at night—a night so biting cold that a man's only protection was his specially designed double-ply Thermoslike space suit, which even in the Moon's thinner atmosphere weighed like holy hell.

These scientific musings were soon interrupted by their arrival at the station's main entrance. They were given a warm welcome. The station's scientific supervisor, Professor Ganshin, was an exceptionally tall man—tall even by Pirx's standards, whose own height had always been seen as a compensation for his chubbiness. But Ganshin looked down on him—not figuratively, but literally. His colleague, Dr. Pnin, a physicist, turned out to be even taller—a towering two meters.

There were four other Russians present, not counting those who may have been on duty. The station's upper level housed an astronomical observatory and a radio station. A sloping concrete passage, tunneled through solid rock, led up to a small radome—huge gyrating dishes of the grid type. Through the side ports the eye made out, at the station's edge, a shimmering, perfectly symmetrical spiderweb: the radio-telescope, the most powerful on the Moon.

The station was deceptive, being much larger than it looked. There were, besides the station proper, several underground storage tanks containing water, air, and food; and transformers for converting solar energy into electricity, housed in a wing sequestered deep inside a rocky crevasse, so that it was not visible from below. And something else, the most sumptuous thing of all: a gigantic hydroponic solarium under a dome of steel-reinforced quartz, in the center of which, surrounded by myriad flowers and large vats of algae, the main source of vitamins and protein, there stood, of all things, a banana tree. Pirx and Langner were treated to their first Moon-grown banana. With a congenial smile, Dr. Pnin explained that bananas were excluded from the crew's daily menu, being reserved strictly for guests.

Langner, no amateur when it came to lunar engineering, began probing his host for details concerning the quartz dome's construction, whose ingenious conception had aroused his admiration even more than the bananas. And it was, without doubt, ingenious. Because of its exposure to vacuum conditions, the dome had to withstand a constant pressure of nine tons per square meter, which, taking into account its surface area, yielded an impressive 2,800 tons. Under such atmospheric pressure, the confined air mass could easily burst the quartz bubble to smithereens. Having to dispense with ferroconcrete, the engineers had reinforced the quartz with welded ribs, transferring the main pressure load, roughly three million kilograms' worth, onto the iridium plate at the apex. Powerful branching steel cables were strung outside, radially, where they were anchored deep within the surrounding basalt crust, transforming the dome into a bizarre "tethered quartz balloon."

It being lunchtime at the Tsiolkovsky station, they went directly from the solarium to the dining room. It was Pirx's third meal of the day—the first was aboard the *Selene,* the second at Luna Base. From the looks of things, that's all people did on the Moon: eat lunch. The dining room, which also functioned as a lounge, was rather cozy in size, paneled—not wainscoted—in natural pine, still redolent of resin. This uncanny touch of "worldliness," after exposure to the blinding lunar landscape, was a welcome relief. But Professor Ganshin informed them that the wood paneling was only veneer, installed to ease the crew's homesickness.

Neither during nor after lunch was any mention made of anything even remotely connected with the Mendeleev station. Not a word about the accident, the fate of the two Canadians, or even about their upcoming departure. The prevailing mood was that of a leisurely social visit.

The Russians fairly doted on them. Eager for news—any kind of news—they continuously plied their guests with questions. What news from Earth? From Luna Base? In a rush of sincerity, Pirx owned to having a basic dislike for tourists; by the responses, he had a sympathetic audience. Time passed. The Russians later took turns slipping in and out. They soon discovered why: a solar prominence had been sighted from the observatory—and was it ever a beaut! At the mere mention of the words "solar prominence," Langner became a man totally obsessed. The whole table, in fact, was seized by that sort of self-obliterating passion common to the profession. Upstairs they examined the lab photos, then the film recorded by the coronograph, both of which revealed the prominence to be one of exceptional magnitude—750,000 kilometers in length. To Pirx it had the look and shape of some antediluvian monster with flaming jaws. But no one besides Pirx was at all interested in zoological comparisons. As soon as the lights came back on, Ganshin, Pnin, Langner, and a third astronomer launched into a heated discussion, with eyes aglitter and ears deaf to anything else. When someone alluded to lunch, the group shifted back into the lounge, there to begin, as soon as the table was cleared, a fury of computations on paper napkins.

Dr. Pnin, noticing how baffled and bewildered Pirx was by all the shop talk, invited him to his room, which was minuscule in size but equipped with a large window that afforded a wonderful view of the massif's eastern summit. A low-lying Sun, gaping like the Gates of Hell, was superimposing on the riot of rock below an anarchy of shadow, an eerie excrescence of black, conjuring behind every boulder a hellish shaft that seemed to lead straight to the Moon's interior. A dissolution of nothingness into mountain peaks, leaning towers, spires, and obelisks, all sprung from an inky realm; a fire turned to stone, petrified, arrested in midflight; a wild configuration in which the eye quickly lost itself in a tangle of irreconcilable forms, finding dubious relief only in those circular pits of black, those gouged-out sockets brimming with shadow, that were, in fact, the pools of miniature craters.

It was a spectacle like no other. Pirx had been on the Moon several times—which he made a point of reiterating six times throughout the conversation—but never at this time of day, nine hours before sunset. He and Pnin kept each other company for quite a while. Pnin insisted on calling him his "colleague" and "friend," leaving Pirx to fumble with the grammar to avoid using any direct forms of address. The Russian had a fantastic collection of photos from his mountaineering days, when he, Ganshin, and three other comrades had gone alpine climbing during a brief furlough Earthside.

Attempts had been made to coin the phrase "Moon climbing," but it failed to catch on, the term "Lunar Alps" only confusing the issue.

Pirx, an ardent climber himself, even before his matriculation into the Institute, had found in Pnin a soulmate. He asked him how lunar mountain climbing differed from mountaineering on Earth.

"As a rule of thumb," Pnin said, "use the same techniques you would use back home. There is no ice up here—except, and then only rarely, in very deep cracks. And no snow, either, of course. That makes the climbing look deceptively easy. What makes it even more deceiving is that you can take a thirty-meter fall without seriously injuring yourself. But never let that enter your head."

Pirx looked puzzled. "Why is that?"

"The lack of atmosphere," Pnin explained. "No matter how long you work the terrain, you'll never get the knack of judging distances. Not even with a telemeter—besides, who wants to lug around a telemeter? It's like this. You'll scale a peak, look over the side of a cliff, and swear it's fifty meters down. Maybe it really is fifty, but it could just as well be five or ten times that. I remember once. . . . Well, anyway, you know the old saying. Once you tell yourself you're going to fall, sooner or later you will. Fracture your skull on Earth and it will heal. Here, one solid jolt on the helmet, a punctured visor—and it's all over. So don't forget. When you climb, do the same things you would normally do in mountainous terrain; take the same chances you would take Earthside. With one exception: ravines. Even if it looks like only ten meters across—that's a meter and a half by Earthly standards—toss a rock over to the other side and observe its flight. But my advice—my sincere advice—is: avoid any jumps. Because once you've cleared twenty meters, no cliff will seem too steep, no mountain too high. And remember, there's no mountain rescue service up here. . . ."

Pirx inquired about the Mendeleev station. Why was it built high up under the ridge and not down below? And was it a rough climb?

"No, not really. Only a few outcrops left by the slides, up around the gap—the road, you see, was wiped out by the avalanche. It would be tactless of me to comment on the choice of location, especially after what happened. . . . But surely you must have read about it."

Pirx flushed with embarrassment and stammered something about having had exams at the time. Pnin smiled, then turned grimly serious.

"Well, to begin with. . . . The Moon has become internationalized; each country has its own sphere of scientific research—this hemisphere, for example, belongs to us. When it turned out that the Van Allen Belt was interfering with the process of cosmic radiation on the side facing Earth, the English asked our permission to build a station in our hemisphere. We agreed to it. Since we were at work on a station of our own on Mendeleev, we proposed they take it over from us, provided they reimburse us for materials already accumulated. They accepted but then turned the project over to the Canadians. Well, English or Canadians, it made no difference to us. Since we had already conducted a preliminary land survey of the area, one of our group, Professor Animtsev, was invited to join the Canadian planning team as a consultant on local conditions. Then we learned that the English wanted back in. They sent out their man Shanner, who advised that secondary radiation pencils at the bottom of the crater could adversely affect future research. Our experts disagreed, but by this time the English had decided to make the station their own and to locate it just under the ridge. Costs skyrocketed, with the Canadians agreeing to foot the bill. But that was none of our business. We don't go around peeking into other people's pockets.

"Anyway, once the site was selected, a road survey was done. Animtsev tipped us off that the British were planning to lay concrete bridges across the ravines along the projected route but that the Canadians had rejected the idea as being too costly—double the original estimate. They decided to blast two ribs into the face of Mendeleev, using directional charges. I warned them that they ran the risk of disturbing the equilibrium of the basalt's crystal core. But they wouldn't listen. Well, what could we do? They weren't kids, you know. We had all the selenological experience on our side—but then we thought if they won't listen, we can't force them to take our advice. Animtsev cast his dissenting vote, and that was that. They started blasting. One silly mistake compounded by another. The English built three slide barriers, got the station up, and brought in their crawler transports. So far, so good. But the station wasn't three months in operation when, at the foot of the overhang, just under the Gap—the ridge's western pass—cracks started to appear. . . ."

Pnin got up, opened a desk drawer, and produced several large photographs.

"There," he said, pointing to the cracks, "you're looking at what is—or was—a kilometer-and-a-half-long wall. The road ran roughly a third of the way up the side—there, where you see that red line. The Canadians were the first to sound the alarm. Animtsev—who had hung around, still trying to convince them of their errors—told them, 'Look, there's a three-hundred-degree difference in temperature between day and night. The cracks are sure to expand. It's no use. You can't shore up a kilometer-and-a-half-long wall! Close the road, and since the station is already up, build a cable railway up there.' Well, they began calling in the experts—from England, Canada. . . . It was a farce: those who corroborated Animtsev's opinion headed back as fast as they had come. The only ones left were those who advocated—cement. Yes, that's right. They began pouring cement into those cracks. They injected, they put up abutments, they injected more cement, then more abutments, because whatever they cemented during the day would crack overnight. By this time the couloirs were beginning to spill over, but the walls held. To divert any worse slides they put up a system of wedges. That's when Animtsev told them: 'You're worried about a few landslides when the whole wall is about to cave in!'

"Poor Animtsev. I couldn't bear to look at him when he came to see us. The man was frantic. He could see it coming but was helpless to do anything about it. Granted, the English have their share of top-notch specialists. But, you see, this wasn't a problem for a specialist, it wasn't a selenological problem. Their prestige was at stake! They had built that road and were damned if they were going to back out. Animtsev protested for the umpteenth time and finally resigned. We later heard that the English and Canadians had quarreled about what to do with the wall—the shoulder of what's known as the Eagle's Wing. The Canadians were all for blowing it up—let's destroy the road, they said, and build a safer one later on. The English didn't like the idea. Anyway, it was wishful thinking; Animtsev estimated it would have taken a six-megaton hydrogen blast, and the UN charter expressly prohibits the use of radioactive materials as explosives. . . . Well, they kept bickering back and forth until, finally, the wall really did collapse. . . . The English wrote that it was all the fault of the Canadians for having rejected their original proposal—those concrete via-ducts. . . ."

Pnin pondered a blowup of the Gap; black dots marked the place where the landslide had obliterated the road and its abutments.

"The station is reasonably accessible by day—just a few traverses along the outcrop I mentioned earlier—but almost impossible at night. We're not back on Earth, you know. . . ."

Pirx understood; the Russian was alluding to the fact that the side of long lunar nights was not illuminated by Earth's generous lamp.

"Infrared doesn't help?"

Pnin grinned.

"Infrared goggles, you mean? But how, my friend, when the surface temperature drops to minus 160 degrees within an hour after sunset? Theoretically, I suppose, radar might work, but have you ever tried climbing with a radarscope?"

Pirx admitted he hadn't.

"And I wouldn't advise you to, either. It's an exceedingly complicated way of committing suicide. Radar is fine on level terrain, but not when you're scaling—"

Langner and the professor came in: time to shove off. A half-hour flight and a two-hour hike still lay ahead of them, and sunset was only seven hours away. Only? thought Pirx, for whom seven hours seemed like an ample amount of time.

Dr. Pnin insisted on accompanying them to Mendeleev. The visitors politely protested, saying that it was not really necessary, but their hosts merely shrugged off their protests. Ganshin asked, as they were getting ready to leave, if there were any messages they wanted relayed to Earth. It would be their last chance: once they were inside the terminator, all radio communication would be suspended.

Pirx was tempted to send Matters's sister "Greetings from the Far Side" but lost his nerve. They thanked their hosts and went below, where, again, the Russians insisted on escorting them to their ship. Pirx broke down at this point and complained about his g-suit. The Russians offered him one of theirs, which he gladly exchanged, leaving the old one to hang in the Tsiolkovsky pressure chamber.

The Russian suit was unconventional in a number of ways. For one thing it had three, instead of two, visors: one for high Sun, one for low, and one—shaded dark orange—for dust. The air-valve arrangement was different, and it was rigged with inflatable boots that cushioned the impact of rocks and gripped even the slipperiest surface; they called it the "high-mountain model." Even the coloring was different: half in black and half in silver. When you stood with the black side facing the Sun, you broke out in a sweat; with the silver you were braced by a delicious coolness.

Pirx found the idea had one basic flaw in it: a man couldn't always be pointed in the direction of the Sun. So what was he supposed to do? Walk backward?

The others chuckled and called his attention to a color alternator located on his chest. If he adjusted the knob, the colors could be reversed: black in front, silver in back, and vice versa. The mechanics of it were interesting. The suit's outer ply was made of a clear, tear-resistant nylon fabric; between it and his body was a thin air barrier filled with two different kinds of dye, or rather semiliquid substances—one aluminized, the other carbonized. Pressure came from the air respirator.

It was time to leave for the launchpad. Earlier he had been too blinded, having just emerged from the Sun, to notice anything inside the pressure chamber. Now he had occasion to observe that one of the walls operated on the same principle as a piston. "The advantage being," said Pnin, in reply to his question, "that you can let in or out any number of people at one time, with no appreciable air loss." Pirx, on hearing this, felt a slight twinge of envy; the Institute's chambers were antiquated boxes by comparison, at least five years behind the time, a five-year lag in technology being tantamount to a whole epoch.

The Sun's course seemed to have been arrested. Walking in inflated boots for the first time was a strange sensation, a little like floating on air, but the feeling was gone by the time they reached the ship.

Professor Ganshin bumped helmets with him and shouted a few parting words, there was a flurry of handshakes in heavy gloves, and the threesome followed the pilot into the belly of the ship, which had shifted slightly from the added weight.

The pilot waited until the others were a safe distance away before igniting the engines. The inside of Pirx's suit resonated with the sullen rumble of gathering thrust. Gravitation increased, but they felt nothing on takeoff. Stars swung in the ports; a rocky wilderness dipped below the rim and vanished from view.

They were flying low. The only one with any ground visibility was the pilot, whose eye was fixed on the fleeting landscape below. The ship hung vertically, like a helicopter, the blast of pulling engines and a vibrating hull being the only signs of surging speed.

"Stand by for landing!" Pirx couldn't tell if the voice in his headset had been the pilot's, coming over the on-board radio, or Pnin's. Their seats tilted back. Pirx took a deep breath, felt light enough to float up to the ceiling, and gripped the armrests. The pilot braked sharply; rockets blazed and squealed; fiery implosions licked the outside walls; the gravitation climbed and fell. . . . Pirx heard a couple of hollow thuds in quick succession. They had landed. Then something unexpected. The ship, which had already gone into its rocking motion, seesawing up and down on its insectlike legs, suddenly listed to one side and, accompanied by a clattering cascade of rock, started to slide downhill. . . .

We've crashed! Pirx thought. Instinctively, without panicking, he braced himself. The other two lay perfectly still. Engine shutoff. He grasped the pilot's dilemma at once: the craft was lamely, fitfully sliding along with the debris; a burst of thrust, instead of lifting them, could, with a sudden lurching of one of the legs, capsize or hurtle them onto the rocky fragments below.

Gradually, the clattering and grating of heaving rock beneath the ship's steel feet let up. A trickle of shingle clanking against metal, a final shifting of bedrock under the weight of the ship's telescoped legs, and the cabin stabilized at a ten-degree angle.

The pilot crawled up out of the deck hatch, somewhat jittery in his gestures, and started making apologies. Ground profile had changed, he said, another landslide down the northern gully. . . . He had put her down on the scree, close to the wall, to save them a long hike.

Pnin to that: A fine way to take shortcuts. A lava bed was not a cosmodrome. And: One should avoid taking any unnecessary risks.

This brief exchange ended, the pilot let the others get by him. They filed through the air lock, climbed down the footladder, and stepped onto the scree.

The pilot remained aboard ship to await Pnin's return, while the others set out for the station, the towering and lanky Russian in the lead.

Pirx had always felt at home on the Moon. Until now, that is. The terrain around the Tsiolkovsky station was a boardwalk promenade in comparison with his present surroundings. Their ship, listing on its maximally stressed legs, mired in a mass of ejecta, was parked some three hundred steps beyond the shadow cast by Mendeleev's main wall. The Sun, a blazing chasm against the black sky, grazed the ridge, creating a mirage of melting rock. But the expanse of vertical walls rising up out of the darkness to heights of one, and, in the distance, two kilometers—that was no illusion. Stark-white alluvial cones ran down out of the gullies and spilled out onto the flat, deeply crevassed crater bed below; the blurry outline of boulders—blurred by dust clouds that took hours to settle—marked the latest cave-ins. The floor of the crater, a bed of fissured lava, was likewise mantled with luminous dust; the whole Moon, in fact, was powdered with the microscopic debris of meteors—that desiccating rain that had been pelting the surface for millions of years. The trail—a trail in name only, being rather a heaping up of block and slab, every bit as rugged as the rest of the terrain—was marked with aluminum stakes, anchored in cement and capped with ruby-red balls; on both sides of this trail cutting up through the talus, one half bathed in light, the other half black as galactic night, loomed a wall surpassing in grandeur the giants of the Alps or the Himalaya.

The diminshed lunar gravity had allowed the rocky matter to assume nightmarish shapes, able to withstand the test of ages; forms so bizarre that the eye, no matter how accustomed to the sight of it, sooner or later went astray as it meandered up to the summit, the unreality, the implausibility of the landscape being heightened by the spectacle of powdery white pumice rising up like soap bubbles, of heavy chunks of basalt being hurtled through space in eerie slow motion, noiselessly subsiding in the talus below, more dreamlike than real.

A few hundred paces up the trail the rocks changed color. Riverbeds of rosy-hued porphyry framed the ravine ahead of them. Stone mesas, piled several stories high in places, their razor-thin edges delicately intertwining, stood there tenuously, begging to be nudged, to be toppled down in a wild and uncontainable rockslide.

Pnin guided them through this forest of petrified eruptions

leisurely but infallibly. Now and then he would put his space boot on a slab; if it wobbled, he would stop and brood, then either proceed on a straight course or maneuver around it, intuiting by means of signs recognizable only to him whether or not it could sustain a man's weight—sound, the warning signal of mountain climbers, being wholly absent here. Suddenly, for no apparent reason, one of the stone witches they had passed earlier broke loose and started down the slope, slowly and somnolently at first, then bouncing and ricocheting to touch off a stampede of stone, a furious rush of rock and rubble that was gradually enveloped by milky-white swirls of dust. It was a spectacle bordering on a hallucinatory vision—collisions without noise, a mute avalanche without tremors or vibrations, thanks to the inflated boots. When they veered sharply around the next hairpin bend farther up, Pirx beheld the trail left by the avalanche—a cloud of serenely undulating waves. Instinctively, with unease, his eyes scanned the horizon in search of the ship; it was safely parked in the same place as before, a kilometer or two away, its shiny hull and three hyphenlike legs clearly visible. A weird lunar spider resting on the site of an old avalanche, on what only a short while ago had seemed so precipitous but now lay flat as a tabletop.

As they neared the shadow zone, Pnin quickened his step. Until now the terror, the extremity of the landscape had so engaged Pirx that he had neglected to notice Langner. He was struck now by the surefooted agility with which the little astrophysicist moved.

They came to a four-meter-wide rift. Leaping broadjump-style, Pirx managed to get too much into it, went sailing high up and over the ravine, and, pedaling his legs wildly, overjumped the opposite ledge by some eight meters. This kind of lunar hopping was a new experience, one that made a mockery of the tourists and their clowning acrobatics back at Luna Base.

They slipped into the shadow. Occasionally a Sun-glazed

wall would break up the darkness with its reflection, casting them and their surroundings in a bright radiance. The transition from sharp light to thick shadow made them lose sight of one another. Soon they were braced by a nocturnal cold. Pirx felt it penetrate the layers of his antithermal suit—not a biting, bone-clamping cold, more like a mute and icy presence. The twenty-degree drop in temperature made the aluminized layers of his suit vibrate. When his eyes had grown more accustomed to the dark, he observed that the balls atop the aluminum poles emitted a strong red light— beads in a ruby necklace that snaked its way up the slope before dissolving in the light. The serrated, rock-ribbed skyline flung its three precipices down to the plain, each traversed by a narrow, shelflike ledge of displaced rock. He could have sworn the serpentine chain of stakes led up to one of these shelves, but he also knew that it was an illusion. Higher up, the sundered wall of Mendeleev was grazed by an almost horizontal column of sunlight—a mute explosion, splashing buttes and crevasses with a blinding incandescence.

"Over there's the station," he heard Pnin's voice say in his headset. The Russian, straddling night and day, cold and heat, was pointing up the mountain; but beyond a series of rocks, black even in the Sun, Pirx could see nothing.

"You see the Eagle? There's the head; there you see the beak; and over there the wing."

At first Pirx saw only a mass of light and shadow, then a hooked crag bulging over the eastern sunlit ridge, deceptively close because it was so clear in outline, unobscured by fog. Suddenly he saw the Eagle. The wall they were scaling was the wing; higher up was the head, a prominence framed by stars; the crag was its beak.

He glanced at his watch. They had been at it for forty minutes, with another hour of climbing ahead of them.

Before entering the next shadow zone, Pnin stopped to switch on his A/C unit. Pirx took advantage of the pause to ask which way the road had run.

"That way." Pnin pointed down below.

Pirx saw only a huge gash, emptying out onto a cone-shaped talus littered with boulders.

"That's where the wall gave way," said Pnin. He pointed to a deep notch in the skyline. "There you see the Sun Gap. Our seismographs back at Tsiolkovsky registered the tremors. By our estimates, a half ton of basalt spilled down—"

"Hold it," interrupted Pirx, a trifle bewildered. "How did they get the supplies up there?"

"You'll see when we get there," said the Russian, hitting the trail again.

Pirx fell in behind him, puzzling over the riddle. Did they backpack in every liter of water, every oxygen cylinder? No, impossible. They were moving along at a faster clip now. The last of the aluminum markers was buried at the top of the cliff. Darkness. They switched on their headlamps, the beams flitting aimlessly from one rocky hump to another, and started out along the ledge, which narrowed in places to two handwidths, in others to a trail wide enough for a man to stand up on with legs apart. They edged along the shelf, which was faintly undulating but otherwise level, its rugged surface making it good for footholds. Still, one false step, one dizzy spell . . .

Why haven't we roped up? wondered Pirx. The light ahead of him suddenly came to a standstill. Pnin had stopped.

"The rope," he said.

He handed one end to Pirx, who looped it through his belt buckle and tossed it back to Langner. Pirx, leaning against a boulder, surveyed the area.

The inside of the crater lay below him in all its pristine clarity: the black lava gorges, now shriveled to a net of cracks; the submerged cone in the center, throwing a long shadow. . . .

Where was the ship? No sign of it. What about the trail? The hairpin turns? All that met the eye was an expanse of rocky basin, caught partially in a blinding glare, partially in a black configuration of shadows stretching from one rock pile to another. The luminous rocky powder accentuated the sculpture of the terrain—that grotesque proliferation of constantly diminishing craters, numbering in the hundreds in the vicinity of Mendeleev alone, ranging from a half kilometer in diameter to those barely visible to the naked eye; each crater perfectly round, with a gentle, tapered outer slope and an even steeper one converging toward a hill, a cone, or a navellike hollow in the center; the smallest being a replica of the larger ones, and all of them circumscribed by a rock-walled colossus measuring thirty kilometers in diameter.

This proximity of chaos and precision somehow jarred the mind: the proximity of waste and creation, both governed by a uniform design, implying simultaneously a mathematical perfection and the anarchy of death. He turned his gaze upward. The Sun Gap was still spewing a torrent of white fire.

The wall began to recede a few hundred paces past the ravine. They hiked, as before, in shadow, its thickness modulated by the light refracted by the vertical cudgel rising some 200,000 meters up out of the murk, and traversed a tongue of scree that frayed off at the top into a moderately steep slope. Pirx was gradually overcome by a strange torpor, not so much physical as mental, the effect, presumably, of his intense concentration, of this surge of impressions: the Moon, the rugged highland, glacial night alternating with blazing heat, and this ubiquitous, all-encompassing silence that reduced the sound of a human voice inside a space helmet to something as unlikely, as incompatible with its surroundings, as a goldfish on the Matterhorn.

Pnin rounded an aiguille—and was engulfed by fire. Pirx was blinded by the same burst of light before he understood: the Sun. They had reached the upper stretch of road, the only part salvaged in the avalanche.

They walked three abreast now, with both sun visors lowered.

"We're almost there," said Pnin.

The road was indeed passable. Hewn—or rather blasted—in the rock, it ran under the Eagle's Wing clear up to the top of the ridge, where a low-slung saddle overlooked a natural rock basin. Thanks to the basin, the station was kept supplied even after the slide. A cargo ship, rigged with a special rocket launcher, flew in the supplies and fired the canisters into the basin. Though a few were lost in every shipment, most of the canisters were able to withstand the shock of impact, thanks to their extremely durable armor casings. In the old days, before there were any stations in operation, the only way of supplying expeditionary teams in the Sinus Medii had been by "spacelift." Since parachutes were not deployable in an airless atmosphere, special shock-resistant canisters made of duralumin and steel had been designed. These were dropped like bombs and later collected by members of the teams, who sometimes found them scattered over areas a kilometer square. Now, many years later, the containers were again being put to good use.

A trail led from the pass, out along the ridge, to the northern peak of the Eagle's head; three hundred meters below the peak, its dome shimmering bright, was the station. With a semicircle of boulders on the downslope and boulders pressing it on all sides, the bubblelike structure was wedged right into the cliff. A few of these boulders crowded the concrete platform by the entrance.

"Couldn't they have found a better place?" exclaimed Pirx.

Pnin, one leg already on the platform, paused.

"For a moment I thought I heard Animtsev talking," he said. Pirx detected a trace of laughter in his voice.

Pnin headed back—alone—four hours before sundown. But, in fact, he walked out into a lunar night, the way back being already blanketed by impenetrable darkness. Langner, a veteran of many lunar expeditions, told Pirx that the cold they had met on the way up was nothing compared to the cold that came within an hour after nightfall, when the rocks had had time to cool.

Pnin was supposed to report back the moment he reached the shuttle. An hour and twenty minutes later, a voice came over the station's radio—Pnin's voice. They exchanged only a few words. They were in a hurry . . . bad lift-off conditions . . . ship listing . . . feet anchored in the scree. . . . Pirx and Langner slid back a metal shutter and watched the lift-off— not the very beginning, because a ridge blocked their view of the landing site, but in time to see a fiery line stitch the dense and shapeless black, trailed by a reddish-brown glow—dust swirls reflecting the exhaust flare. The smoldering javelin climbed higher and higher, the ship invisible except as a glowing piece of string that became more and more attenuated, vibrant, frazzled—the normal pulsation of an engine working at full blast. Then, their heads craning toward the sky, where a fiery trajectory was inscribing itself on a starry backdrop, they watched as the straight line tilted gently and described a beautiful arc over the horizon.

Now there were just the two of them, in the dark—they had doused the lights for a better view of the blast-off. They slid back the shutter and exchanged glances. Langner mustered a faint smile, then, with a slight stoop, dressed in his checkered flannel shirt, marched over to the table, to his pack, and began removing his books. Pirx, leaning against a concave wall, stood with his legs apart as if on a deep-space probe. His mind was aswarm with images: Luna Base, with its chilly basements, narrow hotel corridors, elevators, and bouncing, basalt-swapping tourists; the flight to Tsiolkovsky station, their visit with the Russians, the silver grid of the radartelescope strung between ridge and black sky; Pnin's lecture; the second flight; and finally that eerie trek through a landscape of extremes, of icy cold and blinding heat, and those abysslike gorges staring into his visor. . . . Golly, so much in the space of just a few hours. Time, grown gigantic, had swallowed and devoured these images, and now they were reasserting themselves, fighting for supremacy. He closed his hot, parched eyelids for a moment, then opened them again.

Langner was arranging his books on a shelf in meticulous order, and Pirx got his first real insight into the man. The calm, leisurely way he went about shelving his books, one next to the other, by subject, came not from insensitivity or dullness of intellect. Langner was not oppressed by his surroundings, by this desiccating world; he made it serve him. He had volunteered for station duty and felt not the slightest twinge of homesickness. His home was precisely here, among these spectrograms and computations and the phenomena giving rise to them; he was at home wherever he could quench his thirst for knowledge; he had a purpose in life. He was, in short, the last man in whom Pirx would have confided his romantic dreams of greatness. Pirx envied him his self-assurance, his self-confidence, but only for a split second, because he also sensed some deep incompatibility between them. Here they were, two men who had little to say to one another, forced to spend this first night together. Then tomorrow, and the next night . . .

Pirx let his eyes roam about the cabin. Curving, foam-padded walls. Recessed light panels in the ceiling. Several color reproductions sprinkled among shelves of reference works, and a small plaque inscribed with two columns of names: their predecessors. Corners were crowded with empty oxygen cylinders, tin cans filled with colorful mineral samples, and lightweight metal chairs with nylon webbing. A small table, a swivel desk lamp. Through a crack in the door he caught a glimpse of the radio station.

While Langner began sorting out a shelf stacked with photographic plates, Pirx maneuvered around him and went to explore the rest of the station. To the left, branching off a tiny vestibule, stood the door to the kitchen; straight ahead was the hatch to the pressure chamber, with two other doors to the right, both leading to tiny cubicles. He opened the door to his room: bare except for a bed, a folding chair, a collapsible writing desk, and a few bookshelves. The ceiling dropped down over the bed at an angle, as in an attic, but it was curved instead of sloping, matching the station's exterior design.

He made his way back to the vestibule. The chamber hatch, rounded at the corners and hermetically sealed by a thick rubberized silicone gasket, was mounted with a spoked wheel and a small lamp, which, when lit, meant that the outer hatch was open and there was a vacuum inside. The lamp was off at the moment. He opened the door, tripping two lights, which revealed a narrow compartment with sheer metal walls and a vertical iron-rung ladder in the center, the ladder leading up to a hatch in the ceiling. Under the first rung was a chalk outline, partially obliterated by footsteps: the place where Savage's body had been discovered. The body had been lying with its legs tucked up and on its side, frozen to the rough concrete slab where the blood had escaped from his eyes and mouth.

Pirx studied the blurry outline for a while, then withdrew. As he was sealing the airtight door, his head suddenly snapped back: footfalls overhead. It was Langner, who had climbed the ladder mounted opposite the vestibule and was prowling about the observatory. Pirx poked his head up through a round opening in the floor and took stock of the hardware: a slip-covered telescope the size of a small cannon, astrographs, cameras, plus two other fair-size pieces of equipment—one a Wilson cloud chamber, the other a high-voltage spark-gap chamber, rigged with an attachment for photographing ionization trails.

The station was designed for monitoring cosmic radiation, and the photographic plates were everywhere. The orange packets containing them were sandwiched between books, stacked under shelves, stuffed into drawers, plopped on the floor beside beds, and even strewn about the kitchen.

That was all there was to the station, not counting the huge water and oxygen tanks stored underground, deep beneath the station's floor in the Mendeleev massif.

Above each compartment was a CO_2 gauge and a perforated air vent. The air-conditioning system silently took in air, purified it of carbon dioxide, added the right amount of oxygen, and forced the mixture back out into the cabins. Pirx welcomed every footstep, every thud coming from the observatory; the moment the noises stopped, the silence swelled to the point that he could hear the whispering murmur of his own blood, as clearly as he had that time in the "loony dip," though the latter had one distinct advantage: you could quit at any time.

Langner came down from the observatory and started making supper, but so quietly and competently that everything was on the table by the time Pirx came in. "Pass the salt, please." "Any bread left in the can?" "Tomorrow we'll have to open a new one." "Tea or coffee?" That was the extent of their table talk—which, at the present moment, suited Pirx just fine. What meal was this? Their third of the day? Fourth? Breakfast of the following day? Langner said he had some developing to do and scooted along upstairs. But Pirx was left with nothing to do.

Suddenly he understood. He had been sent up here for one reason only: to keep Langner company. Astrophysics? Cosmic radiation? That wasn't his line. And Langner wasn't about to break him in, either, by teaching him how to handle an astrograph. No, he was here because he had earned the highest grade in the class, because the psychologists said he wouldn't go batty. So, fourteen nights and fourteen days in this sardine can, waiting for no one knew what, investigating no one knew what.

Suddenly the Mission, which only a while ago had seemed such a blessing, was showing him its true face: a blank. Protect Langner and himself? Okay, but from what? Hunt for clues? *What* clues? No one seriously believed that he, dumb clod that he was, would stumble onto something overlooked by a commission of lunar experts.

He went on sitting at the table. He knew there were dishes to be washed. That he would have to be stingy with the tap water—water, that precious commodity flown in in ice blocks and fired into the basin at the foot of the station on a two-and-a-half-kilometer parabola. They couldn't afford to waste a drop of the wet stuff.

He knew all that and still didn't budge. He couldn't even muster the energy to lift his arm when it fell limply onto the edge of the table. His head was still reeling from the heat and the waste and the darkness and the silence that pressed on this steel shell from all sides. He rubbed his burning eyes that felt sand-whipped, stood up, and, feeling twice his normal weight, cleared the table and dumped the dirty dishes into the sink and started rinsing them with a trickle of warm water. And as he stood there scrubbing the dishes, turning them over in his hands, scraping off the little globs of fat, he smiled at his own dreams, which had been left behind somewhere on the trail leading up to the Mendeleev ridge, dreams that now seemed so distant in time and place, so absurdly inappropriate, that he did not even need to feel ashamed of them.

Langner never changed; whether you shared his company for a year or a day, he never altered his routine. He worked diligently, but always according to schedule, never hurrying. He was a man without any vices, eccentricities, or tics. Now, when you live with someone in such close quarters, the smallest trifle can begin to grate. Someone hogs the shower, or won't open a can of spinach because he doesn't like spinach, or grumps a lot, or starts sporting a prickly stubble, or shaves but pampers himself in front of the mirror. . . . But Langner was not that sort. He ate everything, but without gusto. He never bellyached or sulked. When it was his turn to wash, he washed. When he was asked something, he replied.

He was neither unsociable nor overbearing. And it was precisely this neutral, neither-here-nor-there behavior of his that began to get on Pirx's nerves, because the first evening's impression—when the image of the physicist fastidiously arranging his books on the shelf had seemed the embodiment of a quiet and unassuming heroism, of a truly enviable and noble-minded dedication—well, that impression had become tarnished, to say the least, to the point that his partner—his compulsory partner—now struck him as lackluster, even boring. Not that he actually was bored or irritated by Langner's company. Because meanwhile he had found something else to occupy him—at least temporarily. Now that he was more at home in his surroundings, he began reviewing all the known facts in the case.

The avalanche had occurred when the station had been only four months in operation. Contrary to what one would have expected, it transpired not at dawn or dusk but in the middle of a lunar afternoon. Suddenly, with no advance warning, three-fourths of the overhanging wall known as the Eagle's Wing had collapsed. By coincidence, that same day the station's four-man crew had been mustered to receive a convoy of transports. They were all eyewitnesses to the tragedy.

Subsequent studies showed that the deep incisions on the Eagle's main rib had indeed disturbed the crystal core and upset its tectonic equilibrium. The English shifted the burden of blame onto the Canadians, and the Canadians onto the English, their mutual loyalty being manifested only by their consistent failure to heed Professor Animtsev's advice. The four crew members standing in front of the station, less than a mile from the scene of the accident, later described how the blinding wall had split in two, collapsing the system of wedges and barriers, how the avalanche swept away the road and spilled into the valley below, and how, for the next thirty hours, the basin had been a sea of undulating white. In the space of just a few minutes the flood of swirling debris had been carried by the slide's momentum clear across to the other side of the crater.

Two transports had been within range of the avalanche. The one bringing up the rear of the column had been buried instantly by a ten-meter-thick layer of rubble. The other had already reached the upper road, was just out of range of the main flow, when an enormous mass of debris jumped the last of the barriers and swept the vehicle over the side of the three-hundred-meter cliff. At the last minute its driver managed to open the hatch and drop down onto the shifting scree. He became the disaster's lone survivor, outliving his companions by only a few hours. For the witnesses those few hours became a living hell. The driver, a French-Canadian named Roget, who either remained conscious or regained consciousness later on, started radioing for help from somewhere inside the white cloud—his receiver had been damaged, but not his transmitter. There was no locating the injured man. The multiple refractions caused by the waves bouncing off the boulders—so mammoth the people moved in and out of the dusty labyrinth as through a city in ruins—made it impossible to get an accurate fix. Radar was out because of the iron sulfide content of the rock. An hour later, another avalanche, originating from up around the Gap, forced the men to call off their search. This second slide, though smaller than the first, portended still others. There was nothing to do but wait. And wait they did, all the while hearing Roget's voice loud and clear at the station, the basin in which he was stranded acting as a dish reflector. Three hours later the Tsiolkovsky team arrived and drove out into the dust cloud with their ground crawlers, but the shifting talus kept tipping their vehicles on end—the reduced gravity made the angle of inclination commensurately greater on the lunar scree than Earthside. Rescue teams, dispatched into those areas not accessible to the crawlers, combed the rubble three times. One of the searchers fell into a crevasse; only his immediate transfer to Tsiolkovsky and prompt medical treatment saved his life. Despite this near-fatality, the search went on, prodded by the sound of Roget's ever weaker but still audible voice.

Five hours later the voice fell silent, though they knew he was still alive. Every space suit had, in addition to a voice transmitter, a miniature automatic sensor hooked up to the respirator. The sensor relayed, electromagnetically, every breath to the station, where a special tracking device, similar to a "magic eye," projected it as a luminous green butterfly-shaped blip, dilating and contracting in rhythm to the man's respiration. The phosphorescent "butterfly" indicated that the unconscious Roget was still breathing. The pulsations grew steadily weaker, slower, but no one left the radio station. The people crowded inside waited, in helpless despair, for the inevitable.

Roget continued breathing for another two hours. Finally the green light on the magic eye flickered and shrank for good. The mutilated body was located some thirty hours later, stone-hard, so badly mangled that he was buried together with his aluminized space suit, as in a coffin.

Later a new road was staked out—the same rocky trail used by Pirx on his ascent to the station. The Canadians were all set to abandon the project, but their persistent English colleagues solved the logistical problem in a manner originally conceived during the assault on Mount Everest. It was rejected at the time as unworkable.

News of the accident circulated in numerous, often conflicting versions until the clamor finally subsided, to become a tragic chapter in the chronicle of man's struggle with the lunar wilds. Meanwhile, astrophysicists on field assignment continued to take turns manning the station. Six lunar days and nights passed. Just when it seemed the sorely tested station had given rise to its last sensation, Mendeleev's radio station failed to acknowledge Tsiolkovsky's transmission at dawn. Again the Tsiolkovsky team set out on a rescue—or rather reconnaissance—mission. They arrived by ship, landing at the foot of the slide.

They reached the station when the crater floor was still untouched by the Sun's rays. Except for the metal shell under the peak, glinting in the horizontal shaft of light, the entire basin was under a mantle of darkness. They found the outer hatch open, and down below, at the foot of the ladder, Savage's body, slumped to the floor in a way that suggested he had slipped and fallen from the rungs. Death was attributed to asphyxiation, caused by a punctured faceplate. Faint traces of dust, later found lining the inside of his gloves, suggested that he had been returning to, not leaving, the station, though the traces could easily have remained from a previous climb. The body of the second Canadian, Challiers, was discovered only after a meticulous combing of the neighboring ravines and gullies. Rescuers lowered on three-hundred-meter ropes brought up the body from the base of the cliff, no more than fifty steps away from the place where Roget had expired.

No matter how they tried to reconstruct the sequence of events, not a single plausible hypothesis could be advanced. That's when a combined English-Canadian commission decided to conduct an on-the-spot inquiry.

The inquiry disclosed that the hands of Challiers's watch had stopped at exactly twelve o'clock—whether noon or midnight, it was impossible to say—and Savage's at two. In the case of Savage, an expert's examination of the watch's works revealed that the mainspring had been fully wound; hence the time shown on the watch's face did not necessarily coincide with the time of death.

Everything inside the station was found to be in perfect order. The log, recording only events of scientific relevance, contained nothing that could shed the faintest light on the

unexplained fatalities. Pirx went through it carefully, entry
by entry. They were written in the usual laconic style.
Astrographic survey taken at such-and-such a time, so-and-so
many plates exposed under such-and-such conditions. . . .
Not a single reference, however oblique, to whatever had
transpired that night, Savage's and Challiers's last. Not only
was the station found to be in perfect order, but all the
evidence indicated that death had taken its inhabitants by
surprise. An open book, with Challiers's notes in the margin,
was found lying face up, with another book on top to keep the
pages from turning, under a burning lamp. A pipe, which had
tipped over on its side and spilled a few cinders onto the table,
lightly scorching the Bakelite top, lay beside it. Savage, from
the looks of things, had been making supper. In the kitchen
they found freshly opened cans, a mixing bowl full of omelet
batter, and on the little white eating table, place settings for
two and slices of stale bread.

The commission concluded that one of them had interrupted his reading, laying down his pipe in the manner of
someone intending to be out of the room for only a few
minutes. The other had walked off in the middle of preparing
supper, leaving behind a greased frying pan and not even
bothering to shut the refrigerator door. Two men had suited
up and stepped out into a lunar night. Together? Separately?
And, above all, why?

The two Canadians had been stationed at Mendeleev long
enough—two weeks, to be exact—to know their way around.
With sunrise only twelve or so hours away, the question
naturally arose: Why hadn't they waited until dawn, assuming their intent was to climb down to the crater floor? And in
Challiers's case, that was fairly safe to assume, going by the
location of his body. But Challiers must have realized, as
Savage must have, that it was an act of lunacy to go down the
face of the mountain. The wall made a gradual and easy
descent before falling off abruptly in the place where the

avalanche had left a gaping hole. The new road bypassed the canyon, traveling a straight line along the route staked out by the aluminum markers. Everyone, even one-time visitors to the station, was aware of the danger. And yet here was one of its permanent staff members, a man who should have known better, attempting to navigate a sheer precipice. Why? A deliberate suicide? But would someone bent on committing suicide simply interrupt his reading, put aside his book and pipe, and go out to meet certain death?

And Savage. How to explain Savage's punctured visor? Was he on his way into or out of the station? Had he gone out to look for Challiers when he failed to show up? Or had they left together? If that were so, how could he have let him go down the cliff?

There was no end to the unanswered questions.

The only item not in its proper place was a packet of photographic plates, the type used to record cosmic radiation. It was found lying on the kitchen table alongside two empty, spotlessly clean plates.

The commission postulated the following sequence of events. That day—the day of the accident—it was Challiers's watch. Distracted by his reading, he suddenly noticed the time—eleven o'clock. Eleven was the time he was scheduled to restock the plates. The plates were exposed outside the station, a hundred paces up the slope, in a shaft tunneled in the rock—small and not too deep, with lead-lined walls to permit only the zenith rays to hit the plates. A routine exercise, one of the many performed at the station. Challiers, then, putting down his book and pipe, got up, grabbed a new packet of plates, suited up, and left the station through the pressure chamber. He went up to the shaft, climbed down the recessed ladder, switched the plates, and started back with the exposed ones.

On his way back, he made a detour. Subsequent examination of his space suit, severely damaged in the fall, disclosed no malfunction in his respirator unit, ruling out the possibility of a sudden loss of memory due to anoxia.

The members of the commission hypothesized that Challiers must have suffered a momentary blackout, reasoning that he knew the terrain too well to have made a wrong turn. He could have had a fainting spell, an attack of dizziness, lost his sense of direction—whatever the reason, he went along in the mistaken belief that he was returning to the station. In reality, he was bound straight for the cliff, lying only a hundred meters or so ahead of him.

Savage, alarmed by his partner's absence, interrupted his kitchen duty and tried to make radio contact—the transmitter was later found switched on, the frequency setting on ultrashortwave for local transmission. Admittedly, it might have been switched on earlier—if, say, someone in spite of the radio blackout had tried to make contact with the Tsiolkovsky station. But this was deemed highly improbable—first, because the Tsiolkovsky radio had received no calls, distorted or otherwise, and second, because both Savage and Challiers knew better than to attempt any communication just before the dawn, the time when interference was at its peak. Failing to make contact—Challiers by this time was dead—Savage, after suiting up, rushed out into the dark in search of his partner.

In his anxiety over Challiers's silence, over his sudden and inexplicable disappearance, Savage must momentarily have lost his bearings. Or, as seemed more likely, since he was the more experienced climber of the two, he must have exposed himself unnecessarily to danger while combing the area, taken a fall, and shattered his visor in the process. Sealing the breach with his hand, he struggled back to the station and scrambled up the dome, but before he could seal the outer hatch and lower himself into the pressure chamber, his oxygen supply ran out and he collapsed in a fatal coma on the last rung of the ladder.

Not satisfied with the commission's version of the dual tragedy, Pirx checked the personality profiles. He paid special attention to Challiers's, since, according to the commission, he was the inadvertent cause of the two deaths—his own and that of his partner. Challiers, at thirty-five, was an established astrophysicist and an accomplished mountain climber. A man in excellent health, with no known history of any illness, dizzy spells or otherwise. Previously he had done service on the Moon's Near Side, where he was one of the founding members of the Club of Acrobatic Gymnastics, a typically lunar kind of sport whose adepts were capable of turning double-quadruple flips and of shouldering twenty-five-man pyramids. And this was the same Challiers who suddenly, for no apparent reason, was supposed to have suffered an attack of vertigo a hundred feet away from the station? A man who, even assuming he had been overcome by dizziness, was too weak to take the easiest way back, down the slope, but not too weak to make a detour by way of the cliff, knowing that to reach the salvaged portion of the road he would have to scale the wall of boulders at the rear of the station—and at night, no less?

There was one other detail that to Pirx's way of thinking (and not only his) directly contradicted the version set forth in the official record. Everything at the station was in its proper place, with one exception: the packets of plates found lying on the kitchen table. Supposing Challiers had really gone up to the shaft, made the switch, but instead of making a detour by way of the cliff, come straight back by the usual route, bringing the exposed plates with him. Now, then, why had he left them on the table? And where was Savage at the time? The commission theorized that the plates in the kitchen were from a previous batch, that one of the scientists must have accidentally left them lying on the table. Yet no plates were ever found on Challiers's body, a circumstance the commission attributed to his fatal fall—that is, they could have slipped out of the pocket of his space suit and vanished in one of the thousand or more crevices lining the talus.

To Pirx this smacked of stretching the facts to suit the hypothesis.

He shoved the records back into their files, the files into the drawer. He no longer needed them; he already knew them by heart. He told himself—intuited with absolute certitude—that the missing clue was not to be traced to psychology, that the fatalities were caused by something other than a fainting spell, vertigo, or momentary blackout. The answer, he knew, lay somewhere inside or outside the station. With that in mind, he set out to inspect it, compartment by compartment, not in search of clues but simply to familiarize himself with its operational systems. He would do it leisurely; he had time. The pressure chamber seemed like a logical place to begin. First the inner door. Chambers of this type were usually equipped with a mechanism for releasing both the inner and outer hatches, and this one was no exception. The system was designed so that when the outer hatch was open, the inner door could not be opened, this to safeguard against accidents caused by a simultaneous opening of both hatches. As an added precaution, the inner hatch was designed to open toward the inside, so that in an emergency the pressure inside the station would slam it shut with a force of nearly eighteen tons, though the system was far from foolproof: a hand or an object—a tool, for example—could always get caught between the door and the frame, triggering an explosive decompression.

To further complicate matters, the hatch was continuously monitored by a control located in the radio station. An open hatch was registered by a red light on the console, automatically tripping a green monitoring signal. This was a nickel-ringed eye, centered on a tracking screen. A pulsating "butterfly" in the eye meant that the subject outside the station was breathing normally; a calibrated line monitored his position, relative to the output source. The oscilloscope, rotating in unison with the dome-mounted radar antenna, displayed the station's environment in phosphorescent outline. Each sweep of the oscilloscope flooded the tube with that familiar fluorescent glow, a space-suited body showing up as a blip of considerable luminosity. By monitoring this elongated emerald-green speck, one could plot its movements against the dimly illuminated background. The upper half of the screen corresponded to the terrain below the northern summit, the bottom half to the southern zone, which included the cliff area, strictly off limits at night.

The remote respiration monitor and the radar tracking system functioned independently of one another. The "eye" was activated by a transmitter connected to the space suit's oxygen-inlet valve; it operated on a near-infrared frequency, the radar beam on half-centimeter radio waves.

The system was equipped with one tracker and one eye, since station regulations prohibited more than one egress at a time. The one remaining inside the station was required to keep the other under constant surveillance, hastening to the rescue in event of an emergency.

In practice, the plate change was so routine and consumed so little time that the one staying behind could, simply by keeping the door to the radio station open, monitor the instruments without interrupting his kitchen duty. Radio contact could also be maintained, except during the predawn hours when the terminator, that boundary between night and day, whose arrival was always announced by a torrent of static, rendered voice communication next to impossible.

Pirx experimented with the play of signals. He opened the hatch; the red light flashed, the willow-green "eye" went on but remained dormant, its winglike appendages collapsed into listless threads in the absence of any input. The oscilloscope sweep rotated on the face of the tube, conjuring up rigid silhouettes of rock: stone spirits inhabiting a petrified landscape. Not a single light pulse marred its orbital sweep, confirming the lack of input on the breathing monitor.

The next time Langner went out to change the plates, Pirx was able to observe the monitoring system in action.

The red signal flashed, then faded as Langner opened and closed the outer hatch behind him. The butterfly began to palpitate within a few minutes, the pulsations growing more accelerated as the astrophysicist started up the slope at a brisk pace. The light pulse transmitted by his space suit lingered on the screen after each sweep of the tracing beam. Suddenly the butterfly contracted, the screen went blank, the pulse vanished, as Langner descended into the shaft. The lead-lined walls were intercepting the wave transmissions, thought Pirx. Simultaneously the main console flashed a crimson ALARM and the profile on the screen changed.

Then Pirx understood why. The radar antenna, its grid constantly gyrating, had reduced the angle of inclination to sweep increasingly distant sectors. The system was responding to the "unknown": the subject had momentarily slipped out of the range of its electromagnetic vision. Three or four minutes later the butterfly resumed its fluttering motion and the radarscope picked up the missing target. Both components were again registering it, as Langner, now up out of the shaft, began heading back to the station. The alarm signal stayed on; unless switched off manually, it would stay on for another two hours before being shut off automatically. The shutoff was to prevent the system, if inadvertently left on, from consuming too much battery-stored electricity.

The more expert he became at the station's operational systems, the less complicated he found them to be. Langner never once got in the way of his experiments. To him the commission's report seemed plausible enough. "Accidents do happen," he said.

"The plates?" he said in reply to Pirx's objection. "The plates mean nothing. People do funny things when they're in a panic. Logic is the first thing to desert them, quicker than life. When that happens, anyone will act irrationally. . . ."

Pirx decided to drop the matter.

The long lunar night was nearing the end of its second week. Pirx, for all his sleuthing, was no wiser now than at the beginning. Maybe he was up against one of those unsolvable, one-in-a-million-type cases. . . . Bit by bit, he began lending Langner a hand with his experiments. He had to pass the time somehow. He even learned how to operate an astrograph (It's turning out to be a routine training mission after all, he thought) and took turns trekking back and forth to the shaft.

At last it came, the thing he had been waiting for: dawn. Eager for news of Earth, he fiddled with the radio dials, but for all his tinkering could pull in only a hailstorm of cosmic crackle announcing the sunrise. Soon it was time for breakfast. After breakfast there were plates to be developed. Langner sat poring over one in particular, having stumbled across a handsome specimen of mesonic decay. He called Pirx over to the microscope, but Pirx reacted indifferently to the wonders of nuclear transformation. Then it was time for lunch, an hour at the astrographs, some stargazing. . . . By then it was suppertime. Langner was already about in the kitchen when Pirx—it being his turn today—stuck his head through the door and said he was on his way out. Langner, who was trying to decipher a complicated recipe printed on a box of dehydrated eggs, told him, in a mumbling voice, to hurry—the omelets would be ready in ten minutes.

Suited up, with a fresh packet of plates in hand, tie-down straps secured to his neck ring, Pirx opened the doors to the kitchen and radio station, squeezed into the chamber, slammed the hermetic door shut, flipped the hatch, and crawled outside, leaving the hatch cover slightly ajar for a speedy return.

He was circumscribed by cosmic darkness, incomparably

thicker than any on Earth, where the atmosphere always emits a faint radiation of light. He took his bearings by the stars; where the patterns of known constellations were truncated by a starless black, a rocky presence made itself felt. He switched on his headlamp and, with a pale concentration of light bobbing rhythmically before him, made his way up to the shaft. He swung his heavy boots gracefully over the rim—lunar lightness was easy to master, far easier than readjusting to Earth's gravity—groped for the top rung, and lowered himself into the well.

As he squatted down and bent over the plate racks, his headlamp flickered and went out. He gave his helmet a pat; the light came back on. A loose contact, he thought. He had just started to collect the plates when the headlamp blinked—and went out again. Pirx deliberated in the dark. He wasn't worried about the return trip—he knew the trail by heart. Besides, there were always the station's dome lights—one green, the other blue—to guide him. But one false step in the dark and he ran the risk of damaging the plates. Another blow to the helmet: it worked; the light came back on.

Losing no time, he jotted down the temperature, fitted the plates into their holders, but just as he was transferring the cassettes to the carrying case, the damned headlamp gave out again. This time he set aside the plates and gave his helmet several raps in a row. By now he had observed a certain pattern: when he stood up straight, the lamp worked fine; the moment he bent over, it went out. From then on he tried to hold his back straight while crouching down—an awkward position.

Finally the light went completely dead. There was no going back to the station now, not with the plates scattered helter-skelter. Leaning his back against the lowest rung, he unscrewed the lamp's outer cap and pushed the mercury-vapor lamp deeper into its socket, then screwed the cap back on. The light was working again, but fitfully; as happens sometimes, the thread refused to grab. He tried every which way to get it back on; finally, running out of patience, he shoved the glass cover into his pocket, quickly picked up the old plates, replenished the racks, and started back up the ladder.

He was a half meter from the top when another light, wavering and fugitive, mingled with his own. He glanced up but saw only a star-pierced sky trapped in the well opening.

Your eyes are playing tricks on you, he thought.

He surfaced and, suddenly gripped by a vague unease, broke into a run, taking the downslope in enormous bounds—those long lunar hops that gave the illusion of speed, being, in fact, six times slower than the Earthly kind.

He was already standing by the dome, one hand clutching the rail, when a second burst of light cleaved the darkness. A flare! To the south! The metal bubble blotted any view he might have had of the rocket flare itself, but not the eerie luminescence reflected by the overhanging rocks, which lunged out of the dark and just as quickly retreated. He scampered monkey-fashion up to the peak of the dome. Impenetrable darkness. He regretted not having a flare gun with him. He switched on his radio. Static—the same goddamned lousy static! His eye fell on the hatch; it was open, a sign Langner was still inside.

"You dummy! Flare, my foot! It was a meteor! What you saw was a meteor colliding with the rocks at cosmic velocity!"

He dropped down into the chamber, sealed the hatch behind him, waited for the air pressure to reach a level of 0.8 kilogram per square centimeter, then opened the inner hatch. Undoing his helmet on the run, he stormed into the vestibule.

"Langner!"

Silence. Still in his g-suit, he barged into the kitchen. One sweeping glance told him it was empty. Dinner plates on the table, bowl of omelet batter on the counter, frying pan next to the red-hot burner . . .

"Langner!" he bellowed at the top of his lungs. He flung down the exposed plates still in his hand and ducked into the radio station. Deserted. Something told him it was a waste of time to look in the observatory. So those *were* flares he had seen! Was it—yes, it had to be! Langner! But why had he left the station?

Then he saw it. The green eye was pulsating: Langner was out there—breathing, alive. He checked the scope. The tracing beam was picking up a small, tapered light pulse at the very bottom of the screen. Langner was heading for the cliff!

Without taking his eye from the screen, Pirx started screaming into the microphone:

"Langner! Stop! Stop! Hey, come back! Langner, stop!"

The receiver crackled with interference. The willow-green wings pulsated—not in rhythm to normal breathing, but sluggishly, tenuously, at times becoming alarmingly inert, signaling a possible respirator breakdown. The blip on the radar had reached the outer periphery; it was at the bottom of the coordinate grid, or roughly a kilometer and a half from the station, far enough to put Langner among the towering outcrops under the Gap. Then it ceased moving, flaring up with every sweep of the tracing beam, always in the same place.

Maybe he had fallen. Maybe he was lying unconscious. . . .

Pirx dashed out into the corridor. Quick—outside! Get your ass into the pressure chamber! He got as far as the airtight door; as he was racing past the kitchen, something black against white had caught his eye. The photographic plates! They were lying right where he had dropped them in all the panic over his partner's sudden disappearance. . . .

He stood before the chamber door, too dumbfounded to move.

The whole thing was like a replay, a repeat performance. Langner cuts out in the middle of making supper, I take off after him, and—neither of us comes back. The hatch will be open. . . . In a few hours the Tsiolkovsky team will start radioing the station. . . . No one will answer. . . .

A voice yelled, "Get going, you fool! What are you waiting for? He's out there! Caught in an avalanche, for all you know. You can't hear anything up here, remember? He's still alive, pinned down somewhere, hurt, but alive, breathing! Come on, what are you waiting for?!"

He didn't move. All of a sudden he spun around, stormed into the radio station, and checked the displays. Situation unchanged. The butterfly's quivering, tenuous pulsations came at regular four- to five-minute intervals now; the blip on the radar was still hovering on the edge of the cliff. . . .

He checked the position of the antenna. It was at the lowest possible angle, automatically positioned for maximum detection range.

He brought his face up close—very close—to the breathing monitor and remarked something peculiar. The green butterfly was not only furling and unfurling its tiny wings at regular intervals; it was also vibrating—like the breathing pulsations, but more accelerated and somehow overlapping them. Langner's death throes? Convulsions? My God, the man was dying out there and all he, Pirx, could do was stand there, mouth agape, and monitor the movements of the cathode-ray tube, now aflutter with a double pulsation! Unexpectedly, acting purely on impulse, he grabbed the antenna cable and tore it out of the wall plug. At that point, something amazing happened: the butterfly, its antenna disconnected, cut off from any input, kept right on pulsating. . . .

Guided by the same blind impulse, he lunged toward the console and enlarged the antenna angle. The blip under the Gap began drifting toward the edge of the screen. The radar kept sweeping the area at closer and closer range, then—suddenly—it picked up a second blip, this one larger and stronger than the first. Another space suit!

A man. It was moving like a man. Slowly, deliberately, it

was proceeding downhill, skirting the obstacles in its path, now to the right, now to the left, heading straight for the Gap, toward that other, more distant dot—that other man?

Pirx's eyes bulged. There were two dots—one close and mobile, the other far off and stationary. The Mendeleev station was manned by a team of two: Langner and himself. But the display said three. Impossible. The instrument had to be lying.

In less time than it took to think, Pirx was back in the chamber, armed with flare gun and cartridges. A minute later he was standing on top of the dome, firing as fast as he could load, straight down, in the direction of the Sun Gap. He had trouble ejecting the hot cartridges; the gun's heavy butt kicked in his hand. There was no report, no loud bang, only a slight recoil followed by fiery efflorescence, a burst of brilliant green, then a purple glare; a shower of red drops, of sapphire stars. . . . He fired indiscriminately, not being choosy about the colors. Finally, out of the impenetrable dark came a reply—an orange star that exploded over his head and showered him with iridescent ostrich feathers. Then another, this one in saffron-gold . . .

Pirx kept firing away, with Langner returning his fire. The gun flashes began to converge. Before long he discerned the figure of a man, eerily silhouetted against the brilliance. Pirx suddenly went limp, felt woozy. He was drenched from head to foot. Dripping as if he'd just stepped out of the bathtub, still clutching the flare gun, knees buckling, he sat down and dangled his legs through the open hatch, and waited—short of breath—for his partner to join him.

What had happened was this. After Pirx left, Langner had been so preoccupied with his powdered-egg recipe that it was a while—exactly how many minutes he couldn't recall—before he remembered to check the monitors. It was clear that he did so around the time Pirx was tinkering with the headlamp. The moment Pirx disappeared from the radar's scanning range, a servomechanism gradually reduced the antenna angle until the polarized pencil beam reached all the way to the foot of the Sun Gap. When a blip appeared on the screen, Langner automatically assumed it to be a space suit, the "magic eye," now dormant because of Pirx's momentary absence, confirming his suspicion. Whoever was out there— and he knew it had to be Pirx—was either unconscious or suffocating. Langner lost no time in suiting up and going out.

Actually, the radar had picked up one of the aluminum stakes, the one at the top of the cliff, nearest the station. Langner might have discovered his mistake if not for the "eye," which seemed to corroborate the radar input.

The papers later reported that the "eye" and the radar tracking system were both controlled by an electronic brain; that at the time of Roget's death, this brain had recorded the Canadian's breathing pattern, storing it in its memory; and that given the same input data, it was "programmed" to reproduce the same pattern again. In effect, the phenomenon had been the result of a "conditioned reflex."

There was a much simpler explanation. The station's monitoring system was controlled not by an "electronic brain" but by an automatic sequencer. The convulsive breathing pattern was the result of a simple mechanical failure—in this case, a burned-out condenser. When the outer hatch was inadvertently left open, the voltage jumped circuits, and that in turn was transmitted on the magic-eye grid as a "vibration." Only at first glance did it resemble a dying man's breathing pattern; closer inspection revealed it to be what it in fact was: a glitch.

Langner had been lured to the cliff in the mistaken (as it turned out) belief that Pirx was stranded. He had used his headlamp to navigate in the dark and, when circumstances required it, the flares. That accounted for the two bright flashes seen by Pirx on his way back from the shaft. Within four or five minutes Pirx was up on the station dome, trying to capture Langner's attention with the flares. And that's how the drama ended.

In the case of Challiers and Savage, the sequence of events was somewhat different. Savage, too, might have urged the departing Challiers to hurry back, just as Langner had done with Pirx. Then again, Challiers might have lost track of the time while reading, and fallen behind schedule. Whatever the reason, he neglected to close the hatch. But by itself the mechanical malfunction would not have been enough to cause the fatalities. Something else was needed, some purely fortuitous, coincidental factors. Because something must have distracted Challiers in the shaft long enough for the radio antenna, its inclination enlarging with every sweep, to reflect the aluminum marker on the cliff.

What could have distracted him? A mystery. A headlamp malfunction? The odds spoke against it. Yet something definitely had delayed him, and in the interim there had appeared that fatal blip that Savage, and later Langner, had mistaken for a space suit. Subsequent tests established that the delay must have been at least thirteen minutes long.

Savage had gone down to the cliff to look for Challiers. Challiers, returning from the shaft to find the station deserted, then saw the same image later observed by Pirx, which made him go out in search of Savage. Savage probably got as far as the Sun Gap, realized the blip was a reflection of the aluminum marker, but took a fall on his way back and punctured his faceplate. Or he may not have suspected a mechanical malfunction but, driven by his failure to locate Challiers, might have been lured into treacherous terrain and fallen. The exact circumstances of his death were never ascertained. Certain it was, however, that both Canadians were dead.

Logically the accident must have struck around dawn. For if not for the radio blackout, the man on duty at the station could have communicated, without having left the kitchen, with the one outside. Haste must also have been a factor, since only when the outer hatch was left unsealed did the mechanical failure manifest itself. Too, the person bent on saving time was more apt to *lose* time through his haste—by dropping a packet of plates, by upsetting the plate rack. . . . Too, a radar blip is indistinct enough for a metal marker located 2,000 meters away to be mistaken for a man's space suit. The convergence of all these factors made such a tragedy not only possible but probable. Finally, the man on duty must have been in the kitchen, or somewhere else, but in any case not in the radio station, where he would have seen that his partner was correctly oriented, and would not have taken the blip in the southern perimeter for a space suit.

It was no coincidence that Challiers's body was found within a close radius of the spot where Roget had perished. He fell and landed directly below the site posted with the aluminum marker, deliberately placed there as a warning. Challiers was obviously steered in that direction by the radar input.

The technical cause was simple and straightforward—to the point of being trivial. All it required was a series of coincidences and the presence of such factors as radio interference and an open pressure-chamber hatch.

More noteworthy were the psychological factors. When the monitoring device, in the absence of any input, displayed the internal voltage oscillation as a "breathing," pulsating butterfly, and when the radar screen projected a space-suit-like image, both men, first Savage and then Challiers, had been quick to accept these as reliable visual presentations, each believing the other to be in mortal danger. The same held true for Pirx and Langner.

Such responses were only natural for men intimately acquainted with the details of Roget's death, of that long and agonizing ordeal luridly and dramatically transmitted on the "magic eye."

If, then, as was purported, it was simply a case of a "conditioned reflex," then it was manifested not by the hardware but by humans. Half-unconsciously, each of them, Pirx and Langner, had been aware of a possible repetition of Roget's fate, this time with one of themselves as the victim.

"Now that we know all the circumstances," said Professor Taurov, a cyberneticist from the Tsiolkovsky team, "tell us, Pirx—what tipped you off? You said yourself you didn't understand the cause-and-effect mechanism. . . ."

"I don't know," said Pirx. The blinding white of the Sun-glazed peaks throbbed through the window. Their needle tips—like baked bones—pierced the thick black firmament. "The plates, I guess. As soon as I saw them, I realized I had done exactly what Challiers had done with them—dumped them on the table. The plates—well, okay, that could have been a coincidence. But we were having omelets for supper—the same thing they were having that night. That was one too many; it had to be more than just a fluke, I figured. Yep, the omelets are what saved us. . . ."

"Yes," said Professor Taurov. "The open hatch was indeed a function of the omelets—or, more accurately, of your haste to make it back in time for supper. There your perceptions were quite apt. But," he added, "they would *not* have saved you if you had trusted blindly in the monitors." He paused. "On the one hand, we have no choice but to trust in our technology. Without it we would never have set foot on the Moon. But . . . sometimes we have to pay a high price for that trust."

"That's true," said Langner, rising up from his chair. "But, gentlemen, I must tell you what impressed me most about my cosmic colleague. As for me, that little stroll down the cliff . . . well, it fairly ruined my appetite. But this one"—he placed his hand on Pirx's shoulder—"after all that happened, he polished off I don't know how many omelets. Amazing! I mean, I always thought of him as a decent, regular sort of fellow. . . ."

"Huh?!" said Pirx.

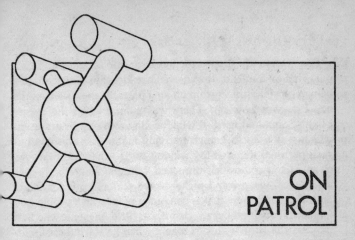

A red-shingled cottage, as yummy-looking as a raspberry gumdrop, stood on the floor of the little see-through box. One jiggle of the box and three little pigs came tumbling out of the bushes, so like three rosy-pink pearls. Simultaneously, a black wolf, its serrated, red-lined jaw chomping up and down at the slightest nudge, popped out of its hole by the forest—a make-believe forest painted on the rear wall, but amazingly lifelike—and made a beeline for the pigs. (The wolf was probably magnetized.) Now, it took a pretty steady hand to head off a massacre. The trick was to maneuver the pigs through the cottage door—not the most obliging of doors, by the way—by tapping the bottom of the box with the nail of your little finger. The box was no bigger than a ladies' compact, but challenging enough to consume half a lifetime. But at the moment it was as good as useless, due to the zero gravity. Pirx gazed down at the accelerator controls, wistfully. A flick of the finger, the barest amount of thrust, and he would have just enough gravity to tinker with the pigs' destiny—which beat staring idly into space any day.

Regrettably, saving three rosy-pink piglets from an attacking wolf was not reason enough to justify activating the reactor, not according to the flying regs, anyway, which strenuously forbade any aimless maneuvers in space. Aimless, my foot!

Pirx reluctantly slipped the box back into his pocket. Other pilots before him had stowed even wackier things aboard, this being especially the custom on long patrol flights, such as the one Pirx was now on. There was a time when the Base's Flight Command used to wink at this splurging of uranium, which was used to launch not only manned spaceships but such personal items as toy windup birds—the kind that feed on bread crumbs—self-propelled hornets that chase after mechanical wasps, and nickel-plated Chinese puzzles inlaid with ivory. By now it was so commonplace that people had forgotten how it all began, that it was little Aarmens who first infected the Base with this mania when he started confiscating his six-year-old son's toys before going out on patrol.

The honeymoon lasted not quite a year—up until the time the ships stopped reporting back from their missions.

In those halcyon times, patrol duty was still a cause for bitching, just as being assigned to a "space-combing mission" was interpreted as a sign of the CO's personal malice. Pirx, on the other hand, took the news completely in stride. Patrols were like a bout of the measles: sooner or later everyone was bound to get them.

Then Thomas failed to report back—big tubby Tom, who wore size 16 shoes, was always good for a gag, and who kept a bunch of poodles, the world's smartest, of course. The pockets of his space suit were frequently home to hot-dog bits and sugar cubes, and the CO suspected him of occasionally sneaking the poodles aboard ship, though Thomas vehemently proclaimed his innocence. Maybe he was innocent, though the truth will probably never be known. Because one July afternoon Thomas embarked on a patrol mission—his last—loaded down with two Thermoses of coffee (he was also a coffee addict), and leaving behind a third in the pilots' mess, filled to the brim, to make sure his favorite brew was waiting for him on his return: coffee mixed with grounds and boiled with sugar. The coffee was a long time waiting. The third day after takeoff, at 7:00 P.M., after the customary grace period had expired, Thomas's name appeared—all by its lonesome—on the control-room blackboard. Such things were a relic of the past; only the oldest veterans could recall a time when missions were aborted, and they loved to fluster the younger pilots with grim stories of the days when meteorite warnings came fifteen seconds before impact—just enough time for a pilot to say his good-byes. By radio, of course. But such stuff was now ancient history. The blackboard in the control room was always empty, a permanent fixture sustained only through the sheer force of inertia.

At nine o'clock it was still light outside; the pilots on duty, having just emerged from the control tower, stood on the lawn surrounding the concrete landing strip, gazing skyward. The tower was declared off limits. That evening the CO drove back from town, fished the tapes out of the canisters— the ones with the signal recordings of Thomas's automatic transmitter—and went upstairs to where a glass-domed observatory gyrated in a madman's frenzy as it combed the skies with its black radar dishes.

Thomas was flying a small, one-man AMU, though its fuel supply was enough to propel the craft halfway around the Milky Way and back, as the NCO from the tanker squadron, a man unanimously regarded as a jerk, hastened to reassure the pilots. "Up yours, pal," someone muttered the moment the NCO turned his back. Because the truth was the oxygen supply aboard an AMU—a five-day ration, with an eight-hour emergency store—was a mere drop in the bucket, and everybody knew it. For four consecutive days, then, the station's eighty-some-odd pilots scoured the sector where Thomas was supposed to have disappeared, logging a total of nearly five thousand rocket hours. And each time they came back empty-handed, as if the man had simply vanished into space.

The second one to disappear was Wilmer, who, if the truth

be told, was beloved by hardly anyone. Although there was no one major reason to account for his unpopularity, there was also no shortage of minor ones. He was forever butting into the conversation, not content unless allowed to have his say; he had a goofy laugh, a knack for cackling in the least appropriate places, and the more he got under your skin, the louder the cackle. Whenever he didn't feel like landing by the book, he'd think nothing of setting his ship down on the lawn adjoining the landing field, incinerating grass, roots, and topsoil to a depth of one meter. But let anyone encroach on his patrol sector, by as much as a milliparsec, and right away he'd report it, even if it meant ratting on a fellow rocket jockey from the Base. Not to mention a few other annoying habits, almost too petty to be mentioned, such as drying himself with other people's towels, just to keep his own clean longer. The moment he failed to report back from patrol duty, however, Wilmer suddenly turned out to be a prince of a guy, a regular bosom buddy. Again the radar went berserk, the pilots were put on a round-the-clock shift, the flight controllers worked overtime, people took turns catnapping on a bench by the wall and had dinner brought upstairs; the CO, who was on vacation, flew back by special plane and ordered a four-day search mission, the Base morale having sunk so low by now that in retaliation for a single, lousy, imperfectly fitted rivet the men were ready to crack the skull of the mechanic responsible. Two commissions of experts came, an AMU-16—a twin copy of the ship flown by Wilmer—was dismantled screw by screw, clock-fashion, but the results were nil: not a single defective part was found.

Although the sector measured 1,600 billion cubic kilometers, it was also thought to be a relatively tame one, undisturbed by any meteorite showers or the cold remnants of old comet tails, last seen hundreds of years ago—all the more remarkable, considering that comets of that vintage have been known to disintegrate in the vicinity of Jupiter, in its "perturbation mill," and later to discard pieces of their nucleus onto their former course. But the sector was as good as empty, unmarred by any satellites or asteroids, and least of all by the Belt. And just because it was so "clean," no one had a hankering to patrol it.

Even so, Wilmer's made the second disappearance in a row. His tape, which was played and replayed countless times, photocopied, blown up, and forwarded to the Institute, yielded as much information as Thomas's: zilch. Sporadic signals for a while, then nothing. The signals sent by the transmitter had come at infrequent intervals, on the average of one per hour. Thomas had transmitted a total of eleven signals; Wilmer, fourteen. That was all.

After the second disappearance, the CO swung into action. For starters, he had all the ships checked out from bow to stern—atomic pile, flight control systems, every nut and screw; one scratched dial and you were docked a week's vacation. The timers in the transmitters had to be replaced—as if it were all their fault!—and ships on patrol were now required to radio back at eighteen-minute intervals. Not that there was anything wrong with that; what *was* bad was that henceforth two senior officers were stationed by the launch ramp, where they ruthlessly confiscated anything in a pilot's possession—everything from windup birds (of both the feeding and tweeting variety), butterflies, and bees, to various games of skill—in time, transforming the CO's office into a storeroom for every conceivable sort of novelty. The Base cynics maintained that the CO always kept his door locked because he liked to play with his toys in private.

Given such obstacles, one is better able to appreciate the masterful cunning exercised by Pirx in smuggling aboard his AMU the little house with the three pigs. This despite the fact that, apart from a certain moral satisfaction, he derived little actual benefit from it.

The patrol flight was grinding into its ninth consecutive

hour. "Grinding" was precisely the word for it. Pirx reclining in his contour couch, all bound and belted in, mummylike, with only his arms and legs free, and his listless gaze fixed on the screens. For six weeks they had been flying in teams of two, at a distance of 300 kilometers, when Base Command decided to revert to its original tactic, leaving the sector deserted, clean as a whistle, so that even one patrolship was one too many. But just so there wouldn't be any stellar "holes" on the maps, the solo flights were resumed. Pirx's was the eighteenth mission to be flown after the team flights were scrubbed.

For lack of anything better to do, he began turning over in his mind all the possible things that could have happened to Thomas and Wilmer. The names of the missing pilots were seldom mentioned at the Base anymore, but nothing is more conducive to idle speculation than prolonged isolation during a manned space flight. He had logged not quite three years' flight time—two years and four months, to be precise—and already he thought of himself as an old pro. Even so, this time the astro-boredom was beginning to get to him, though he was the last person to advertise it.

Patrol flights have been compared, and aptly so, to waiting one's turn at the dentist's—the difference being that here the dentist never shows. Stars that never move, an Earth that either can't be seen at all or, if you're extremely lucky, looms as big as the tiny crescent of a bruised fingernail—during the first two hours of flight, that is, after which it assumes the same appearance as any star, in this case a moving one. And staring into the Sun, as everyone knows, is not too advisable, either. It's times like these that a Chinese puzzle or a brain-teaser becomes an absolute must.

Still, it was a pilot's duty to hang suspended in a cocoon of belts, to monitor each and every screen—both radar and video—to check the reactor's idling gauge, and to radio back at regular intervals. Once in a great while, it's true, he might pick up a distress call—even an SOS!—coming from some-where inside his sector, and off he'd go, at breakneck speed; but a pilot could count himself lucky if this happened more than once or twice a year.

Under the circumstances, it is hardly astonishing that pilots are subject to myriad fantasies, fantasies which from the point of view of Earth, or of ordinary passengers, might seem wicked, but which in fact are quite normal. When you're out there, surrounded by 1.5 trillion cubic kilometers of empty space, without so much as a flake of cigarette ash for company, the desire for action—be it even some hideous calamity—can grow to a genuine obsession.

In the course of his 172 patrol flights, Pirx had run the gamut of psychic responses, having been subject to attacks of drowsiness, crotchetiness, even fits of feebleminded ec-centricity . . . and once was on the verge of committing some far-from-harmless prank. Lately he had begun concoct-ing plots to various stories, a hangover from his student days, some of which turned out to be so intricate in construction as to defy finding a resolution before the end of the flight. But did it help to relieve the boredom? Not a bit.

As he ventured into the labyrinth of lonely contemplation, Pirx realized he would never solve the mystery of his two missing comrades, not when the most high-powered experts at the Base had been beating their brains out, for months on end, without cracking it. No, he was better off with his piggy game, a no less idle but certainly more harmless pastime—if only he could get it to work! But the engines were quiet, nor was there any reason to fire them up, what with the ship now cruising along the segment of a protracted ellipsis, one of whose foci was the Sun. No, the piggies would have to wait for sunnier days.

Okay, so what could have happened to Thomas and Wilmer?

An ordinary layman would have presumed a collision with

something —with a meteor, for example, with a cloud of cosmic dust, a comet's tail, or the wreckage of some old rocket ship. But the chances of such a collision's occurring were about as remote as finding a mammoth diamond in the middle of a busy street; statistics showed, in fact, that the odds in favor of finding the diamond were much greater.

From sheer boredom, Pirx began feeding figures into his computer and formulating equations to compute the probability of a collision. The result was a figure so large that the computer would have had to drop the last eighteen decimal places just to accommodate the number on its displays.

Besides, the sector was empty. No comet tails, no clouds of cosmic dust—nothing. Theoretically, the wreckage of an earlier ship might just as well have turned up here as anywhere else in the universe—but only after an inconceivable number of years. But if that were the case, surely Thomas and Wilmer would have sighted it—say, from a distance of 250 kilometers. Suppose it had approached from the side of the Sun; in that case, the meteoradar would have sounded the alarm a good thirty seconds before impact. And even if the pilot had slept through the alarm, the automatic control would have triggered the yaw maneuver, whereas a malfunction in the automatic yaw control was practically unheard of: it might happen once, but not twice in a row in the space of a few days.

All this a layman might have deduced, a layman who knew nothing of the hazards present aboard ship during a manned space flight—perils far greater than colliding with a meteorite or a decayed comet. A spacecraft, even one as small as an AMU, is made up of nearly 114,000 major parts—major in the sense that a malfunction in any one of them could have disastrous consequences. The minor parts number more than a million. But even assuming a fatal accident, a spaceship would not simply disintegrate into ether—since, to cite an old spaceman's adage, nothing is ever lost in space: toss out a cigarette lighter, and all you have to do is to plot its trajectory and be in the right place at the right time, and the lighter, following its own orbital path, will with astronomical precision plop into your hand at the designated second. The fact that in space a body will orbit about another to infinity means that sooner or later the wreckage of any spaceship is almost always bound to turn up. The Institute's megacomputers had plotted more than forty million possible orbits in which the missing ships could be traveling, each of which was probed by concentrated pencils of the most powerful radar tracking equipment available on Earth. With the aforementioned results.

This is not to say that the entire solar system was systematically probed. Compared to the vastness of space, a rocket ship is something infinitesimally small, smaller even than an atom in relation to Earth. Still, they searched high and low, anywhere the ships might have been—assuming, of course, the pilots had not simply abandoned their assigned sector. But then, what reason would they have had to leave it? They had received no radio commands or distress calls, nor were they the victims of any collision—that much, at least, had been established.

All indications were that Thomas and Wilmer had evaporated, spaceships and all, like drops of water on a blazing hot grill.

A layman endowed with some imagination, unlike his more pedestrian colleague, would have hastened to attribute the mysterious disappearances to those enigmatic creatures from other planets, creatures possessed of an awesome yet sinister intelligence who are always on the prowl in space.

But who in that advanced age of manned space exploration still believed in the existence of such creatures, not one of which had ever been encountered in the known universe? By this time the number of jokes about "creatures from outer space" far exceeded the number of cubic kilometers contained in the solar system. No one, except for the greenest recruits, whose only flight experience was in a chair suspended from the laboratory ceiling, would have bet a plugged nickel on them. If there *were* any inhabitants on other stars, then only on ones belonging to a distant galaxy.

Add up the handful of primitive mollusks, lichens, bacteria, infusoria—all unknown on Earth—and you have the grand total of many years' expeditions. Even were such creatures to exist, would they really have nothing better to do than to ambush measly little patrolships in one of the most desolate, godforsaken regions of space? And how could they get within striking distance without being noticed?

The effect of such questions—and there seemed to be no end to them—was to reduce the whole hypothesis to a grand, monumental absurdity, to deprive the game of any semblance of reality. But prone as he was to the wildest fantasies during his ninth hour of flight, when faced with such ruthlessly sobering facts, even Pirx would have been strained to entertain something as preposterous as demonic beings from outer space.

From time to time, despite the zero gravity, he would tire of sitting in the same position, adjust the angle of the contour couch in which he was pinioned, and shift his gaze from left to right—without, strange as it may seem, distinguishing any of the 311 gauges, instrument lights, and pulsating dials and displays, as routinely familiar to him as the features of a face whose expression can be read without reference to any parting of the brows, arching of the lips, or pattern of wrinkles on the forehead. Just so, one glance, and dials, control lights—everything—would merge to form a single whole, a message telling him that all systems were go. Looking straight ahead, he commanded a view of both stellar screens—and between them, framed by a yellow, dome-shaped helmet partially obscuring chin and forehead, his own face.

In between the two stellar screens was a mirror, rather modest in size but mounted in such a way that a pilot could not possibly escape his own reflection. What it was actually doing there, what purpose it served, was never explained. That is to say, it was explained, but the rationale given, while ingenious, fooled hardly anyone. The mirrors were the brainchild of psychologists. Man, according to them, when subjected to long periods of unrelieved solitude, is apt to lose control over his own mind and emotions, can be lulled imperceptibly into a dreamless, wakeful sleep from which he is not always able to waken in time. Some have been known to fall victim to hallucinations of obscure origin, to fits of anxiety or severe emotional outbursts, and the ability to control one's own physiognomy is thought to be an excellent corrective, though, to be sure, it was no fun having to stare at one's own face for hours on end and dutifully record its every expression. And no one can appreciate this better than the pilots of patrolships. It may begin innocently enough: you make a face, you frown or grin at your own reflection, and that unleashes a torrent of grimaces, one more contorted than the next. That's what can happen when a situation so contrary to nature goes beyond normal human endurance.

Fortunately, Pirx was not so infatuated with his own image as others were with theirs. Though difficult to verify, stories were told of those who, overcome by a debilitating boredom, were given to such embarrassing acts as spitting at their own reflection, and how, overwhelmed with shame, and in violation of all the rules, they would unfasten their straps, get up, and proceed to walk—or rather to swim—through the cabin's zero-gravity atmosphere to the mirror, to somehow clean it before landing. There were some who stubbornly maintained that Wuertz had drilled his ship thirty-three meters into the concrete landing strip because he had put off cleaning his mirror until the moment of reentry.

Pilot Pirx had never experienced such symptoms, much less

felt the temptation to spit at his own reflection—the struggle to resist often led to severe psychological damage that could have been amusing only to those who have never flown a lonely patrol. In the end, even during his worst spells, Pirx had always found something to distract him, some dependable spool around which to wind his jumbled thoughts and emotions, like a long and tangled thread.

The dial—the normal one, measuring time—showed 11:00 P.M. In thirteen minutes he would reach his orbit's aphelion. He coughed once or twice into the microphone to test it, on a whim made the computer derive the fourth root of 8769983410567396, then showed not the slightest interest when the computer displayed the answer with the utmost speed, grinding out the digits and jiggling them nervously in its CRTs as if it were a matter of life and death; and was thinking that the first thing he'd do after landing would be to toss a glove out through the hatch door—just for kicks—light up a smoke, march down to the mess hall, order himself something hot and spicy, seasoned with paprika, and wash it down with a tall draft of beer (he was a great beer lover)—when he spotted a light.

He had been monitoring the left-front video screen, with one of those seemingly unseeing looks of his, but mentally already back in the mess hall (where he could almost smell the dark-brown camp fries, a whole batch of them, prepared especially for him), when into the center of the screen crept this luminous white dot, the sight of which stiffened his whole body with such a jolt that if not for his straps he would have slammed right into the ceiling.

The screen measured about a meter in diameter, pitch-black except for Rho Ophiuchi in the center, and the Milky Way, dissected by a yawning black void that stretched clear to the other side of the screen, which was bordered on either side by glittering stardust. This perfect still-life spectacle was, slowly but steadily, invaded by a tiny brilliant light, which was not so tiny, however, that it couldn't be distinguished from the stars. But then, it was not the brightness of it that had caught his attention, as much as the fact that it moved.

Luminous moving dots in space usually mean one thing: a ship's navigation lights. As a rule, a ship's lights are not turned on except in response to a radio call, for purposes of identification. Different ships display different kinds of lights: passenger ships are identified by one kind, freighters by another, and the same applies to high-speed ballistic rockets, patrolships, rescue ships, tankers, and so on. The lights are mounted variously, depending on the ship, and they come in every conceivable color except one—white—to make the ships distinguishable at all times from the stars. When two or more vehicles are flying in tandem, a white light on the lead ship can too easily be mistaken for a stationary light, in which case the pilot following behind runs the risk of going off course.

But the little speck floating leisurely across the screen was white as could be, and Pirx could actually feel his eyeballs coming loose from their sockets. Not once did he blink, afraid that he might lose track of it if he did—but the white dot sauntered gingerly along, undisturbed, now only a dozen or so centimeters away from the opposite side of the screen. Another minute and it would vanish from sight.

Instinctively, Pirx's hands went straight for the controls. The reactor, which had been idling, responded with instantaneous thrust, the acceleration shoving Pirx back into the seat's foam-rubber cushion . . . stars scudding across the screen . . . the Milky Way running downhill, very much like a road of milk. . . . This brought the mobile speck to a standstill, with the ship's nose following right on its tail, aiming at it like a hunting dog pointing at a pheasant in the brush. Now was that classy handling, or wasn't it?

The whole maneuver consumed a mere ten seconds.

Now, for the first time, he had the leisure to reflect, and it slowly dawned on him that what he was seeing was a hallucination, because such things were unprecedented. This deduction did him credit. On the whole, people tend to trust too much in the evidence of their senses; if they should happen to see a deceased acquaintance in public, they would sooner believe in a resurrection than admit to their own insanity.

Pilot Pirx groped in one of the seat's side pockets, pulled out a small flask, inserted its two small glass tubes into his nostrils, and inhaled until his eyes began to water. Psychraine was potent enough to disrupt the cataleptic trances of a Yogi or the mystical visions of a saint. But, much to his chagrin, the light continued its peregrinations in the center of the left screen. Having done the prescribed thing, he returned the flask to its proper place, maneuvered the ship's rudders slightly to align himself with the other, and checked the radar to get a fix on the luminous object.

And here he was in for his second shock: the meteoradar screen was blank. Its green tracing beam, incandescent as a strip of phosphorus exposed to a strong dose of solar radiation, swept around in a continuous circle, but without showing the slightest trace of any light—nothing. An absolute blank.

Pirx was not so foolish as to think that he was pursuing a spirit with a shining halo. The fact was, he didn't believe in spirits, although occasionally, especially in the company of women, he might shoot the breeze about them, but even then it was not born of any spiritualistic convictions.

Of one thing he was sure: what he was following was not a dead celestial body, because such an object will always reflect a radar tracking beam, will always show up as a blip. Only objects that are artificially made and externally treated with a substance capable of absorbing, neutralizing, and dispersing centimeter waves will not produce any optical echoes.

Pilot Pirx cleared his throat and spoke deliberately, his

Adam's apple, with each measured phrase, bobbing up and down and pressing lightly against the laryngophone attached to his neck.

"Patrolship AMU-111 calling object flying in sector one-thousand-two-point-two, steering a course approaching sector one-thousand-four-hundred-four, and showing one navigation light. Request your call numbers. Over."

He waited for the response.

Seconds passed, the seconds turned into minutes—still no answer. Instead, Pirx noticed that the light was fading, which meant it was receding. Although the radar telemeter had flunked the test, he still had the more primitive optical range finder in reserve. He stretched one leg, pushed a pedal, and the range finder, similar in appearance to a telescope, dropped down from above.

Pirx brought it up close to his eyes and adjusted the focus.

He located the dot immediately—and discovered something else while he was at it. Magnified now by the lens, the speck assumed the proportions of a pea when see from a distance of 5 meters—which, by standards prevailing in outer space, was nothing short of gargantuan. Not only that, but its somewhat flattened surface was traversed by a number of tiny dark squiggles, much as if several thick black hairs were being pulled across the front lens. The squiggles were just as blurry and indistinct, though constantly in motion—always from right to left.

Pirx tried to increase the sharpness of the image, but the luminous speck adamantly refused to be focused; so, using a second prism, one designed especially for this purpose, he cut the image in two, brought the two halves together—with positive results—checked the scale, and received his third shock.

The shining object was only 4 kilometers away!

This was equivalent to driving a racing car at top speed and suddenly discovering that 5 millimeters away from you is another car—in space, a proximity of 4 kilometers is just as lethal.

Pirx was running out of ammunition. He directed the outer thermocouple in the direction of the light, with the remote-control lever aimed the target finder straight at the milky-white dot, and read off the temperature out of the corner of his eye: 24 degrees Kelvin.

That meant the light had the same temperature as ambient space—25 degrees above absolute zero.

That cinched it. A luminous, self-propelled light in space? Never! But just because it was there, dead ahead of him, he gave chase.

The light was growing visibly—and rapidly—fainter. A minute later he verified that it had gained a full 100 kilometers on him. He increased his velocity.

Then the most uncanny thing of all happened.

First the light deliberately let him gain ground—letting him get within 80, 70, then 30 kilometers—before jumping out in front again. Pirx accelerated to 75 kilometers per second; the light, to 76. Pirx applied more thrust, but this time he didn't pussyfoot around. He opened the jets to half-power, unleashing a powerful forward thrust; the triple gravity shoved him back into the seat's padded cushion. His AMU had a small rest mass, its rate of acceleration being roughly equivalent to that of a racing car. Before long he was hitting 140.

The little light hit 140.5.

Pirx was beginning to feel hot and clammy. He applied maximum thrust. His AMU-11 hummed; his tachometer, whose readings were based on fixed stars, climbed steadily higher: 155 . . . 168 . . . 190 . . . 200.

At 200 he took a peek through the range finder, which, considering the 4g, was a feat worthy of a decathlon athlete.

He was gaining on the light, which swelled in size as the gap between them closed to 20, then 10, and finally 3 kilometers, at which distance it looked larger than a pea when seen from an arm's length away. The dark, blurry shapes continued to shunt across its surface, whose brightness was comparable to stars of the second magnitude—except that it resembled more a disk than a starlike dot.

His AMU-111 was giving everything it had, swelling Pirx with pride. During that sudden burst to maximum thrust, not a thing in the cabin had shaken—not a single vibration! The reaction was in the axis of acceleration; the jets were performing to perfection; the reactor was working like a champ.

The light kept closing in, though at a slower rate of speed. When it was no more than 2 kilometers off board, Pirx's wheels began to turn.

The whole thing looked fishy as hell. A light, not attached to any terrestrial ship. Hm . . . Space pirates, maybe? What a laugh. Even if there were such things as space pirates, what would they be doing in such a godforsaken hole? The light had an extraordinary speed range; it could accelerate as sharply as it braked. And moody, too; first retreating, then letting itself be gradually overtaken. And that, more than anything, made him antsy. It was almost as if the thing were baiting him, stringing him along like a decoy, like a worm dangling on the end of a hook.

And immediately he conjured up the image of a hook.

"Not so fast, fella!" Pirx said to himself, and he braked as abruptly as if he were on a collision course with an asteroid, though the radar was blank and the video screens likewise empty. Instinctively he bent his neck, tucked in his chin, and felt the automatic compressor fill his suit with an extra supply to compensate for the sudden acceleration, which didn't stop him from having a momentary blackout.

The gravimeter plunged to −7, hovered there for a second, then climbed back up to −4. His AMU-111 had lost nearly a third of its velocity, dropping down to 145 kilometers per second.

Where was the light? For a moment he was afraid he'd lost track of it. No, it was there—just farther away, that's all. The optical tracking device gave the distance as 240 kilometers. During those brief two seconds it could have increased its lead by a great deal more than that. That it hadn't meant that it must have braked within seconds of when he did!

Then—later he was amazed that it could have taken him so long—he realized he was on the trail of that mysterious *something* encountered by Thomas and Wilmer while on patrol.

Until now he had not been conscious of any danger. Suddenly he was afraid—a momentary case of the jitters. It was highly unlikely, of course, but supposing the light *did* belong to an extraterrestrial ship . . . ?

The light was moving closer . . . killing speed . . . closing the gap . . . 60 . . . 50 . . . 30 . . . He decided to nudge a little closer, feathering the thrust . . . and watched in amazement as the thing ballooned—now only 2 kilometers off his bow!

On the other side of the couch was a pocket containing a pair of 24-power night glasses—used mainly in emergencies, in case of a radar malfunction, for example, or when approaching a satellite from the night side. But at the moment they were just what the doctor ordered. Their magnifying power was strong enough to bring the light to within the 100-meter range, and what he saw was a small disk, the color of diluted milk, similar in size to the Moon when viewed from Earth, its otherwise smooth surface marred by a continual procession of vertical smudges. When it eclipsed the stars, they faded only gradually, as if the disk's outer rim was somehow thinner and more transparent than at the center.

But *around* the disk there was nothing, no luminosity to block out the starlight. Now, when examined through binoculars from a distance of 100 meters, a spaceship looks pretty much the size of a desk drawer. But there was nothing like that in sight, not a sign of any vehicle. And the little disk was definitely not somebody's navigation light or exhaust flare.

It was just what it appeared to be: a solitary, self-propelled, little white light.

It was enough to drive a man batty!

He felt a tremendous urge to fire a shot at the thing, but without any weapons aboard—the regulations made no provision for them—that would have been no easy task. There were only two things Pirx could fire from the cabin: himself and a balloon probe. The patrolships were designed such that a pilot could eject himself in his encapsulated seat, together with a braking chute. This was done only as a last resort, and obviously there was no going back once a pilot had bailed out. That left the balloon probe—a remarkably simple device, consisting of a thin-walled rubber balloon that when deflated rolled up tightly enough to be a spear. To enhance its visibility, it was treated with an aluminum coating. Sometimes a pilot has a hard time telling by his aerodynamometer readings whether or not he has entered a planet's atmosphere. Most importantly, he will want to know if any rarefied gas is lying in his path. When in doubt, he will fire the balloon, which inflates automatically and travels at a speed somewhat greater than the ship's velocity. Because of its brightness, it is visible to the naked eye from as far away as 5 to 6 kilometers. If it encounters rarefied gas, the friction will cause it to heat up and explode. That's when the pilot knows it's time to start braking.

Pirx did his level best to aim the ship's nose directly at the milky-white disk. Without the radar to guide him, he had to rely on the telescopic range finder. But trying to hit a target that size from a distance of almost 2 kilometers is no mean feat. Whenever he went to fire the balloon, the little disk would slip out of the line of fire. And no sooner would he bring his nose around, gently feathering his yaw jets, than the disk would do a nifty little sidestep and pop up again in the center of the screen. It repeated this maneuver four times in a row, each time with greater speed and facility, as if it were already starting to second-guess him. And judging by the way it flew slightly off course, at an angle, it was clear the disk had no intention of letting the AMU-111 fire point-blank at it.

This was fantastic. To react to such minute changes in his ship's attitude, at a distance of 200 meters, the disk would have had to be using a telescope of gigantic proportions—of which nary a trace. But not only was it capable of carrying out a tricky evasive maneuver, it did so with only a split-second delay at the most.

His anxiety grew. He had done everything in his power to identify this uncanny flying object—and was not the least bit wiser than at the beginning. Then, while he was sitting there, immobilized, his hands gradually turning numb on the controls, it suddenly hit him that Thomas and Wilmer must have experienced the very same thing. They, too, must have sighted the light, tried to pick up the call numbers of what they took to be a UFO, given chase when they got no answer, kept track of it through the telescopic range finder, spotted the lacy little squiggles, maybe even fired a balloon probe, and then—then done something that made it unlikely that they would ever return.

When he realized how close he was to sharing the same fate, he felt not fear but despair. The whole thing was like a bad dream, a nightmare in which he couldn't tell which part he was playing: himself, Thomas, or Wilmer. Because what was happening now was just a repeat performance—that much was clear. He sat paralyzed, profoundly convinced that the game was up. And worst of all, he couldn't even say what the danger was, or from which direction it would come, with all this empty space around . . .

Empty?

Yes, the sector was empty, but then he had been chasing the little light for well over an hour, up to speeds of 230 kilometers per second. By now it was possible, if not altogether certain, that he was approaching the sector's outer perimeter, or had already crossed it. And beyond that? Sector 1009, another 1.5 trillion kilometers of space. So there he was, surrounded by a void, by millions and millions of kilometers of nothing—and what should he have 2 kilometers off his bow but a pirouetting light!

He exerted all his powers of concentration. What would *they* have done—Thomas and Wilmer—right now, at this very second? Because whatever they had done, he would have to do something altogether different. Otherwise he wouldn't come back alive.

Again he braked, again the needle shook, again his speed dropped—from 30, down to 22, to 13, to 5 kilometers per second—until the needle fluttered gently above zero. Technically speaking, he was already stopped; in space, speed is constant, always relative to something else; there's no such thing as absolute zero, as on Earth.

The light began to shrink, retreating farther and farther . . . becoming dimmer and dimmer; then it reversed the process, gradually gaining in size and color, until it came to a stop again, 2 kilometers off his bow.

What would Thomas and Wilmer *not* have done? he wondered. What was the one thing they definitely would have avoided doing? Would they have made a run for it? Never! Not from a measly little speck, from such a dippy little dot!

He had no desire to turn the ship around—too easy to lose track of the thing—nothing harder than to patrol when something is astern—no fun twisting your head around like a corkscrew to monitor the video screen. . . . No, turning around was definitely out—better to keep it in full view at all times. So he started moving in reverse, using his braking rockets to accelerate—one of the many basic navigational skills a pilot was expected to have mastered. His gravimeter showed 1g . . . then −1.6 . . . −2 . . . The ship was harder to handle in reverse; the nose kept listing to one side. . . . Retro-rockets were meant for braking, not accelerating.

The little light seemed to hesitate. It hung back for a while, gradually diminishing, momentarily eclipsed Alpha Eridani, then slid away, gamboled among a few nameless stars, and—took off after him!

It wasn't about to be given the brush-off.

Relax, he thought. Why should I sweat such a shining little pissant? Screw it. My job is to patrol the sector, and to hell with it.

He might have *thought* this way, but not for a moment did he take his eyes off the light. Nearly two hours had gone by since he first sighted it. His eyes were beginning to sting and get a little watery. Wide-eyed and goggle-eyed, he kept the machine in reverse. Flying in reverse is slow going; the braking rockets were not designed for continuous thrust. He reached a top speed of 8 kilometers per second, and sweated it all the way.

As time went on, he began feeling a funny sensation in his neck, as if someone were tweaking the skin under his chin, stretching it down toward his chest, and his mouth was starting to turn dry. But he refused to let it bother him, having more important things on his mind than a dry mouth and a tweaking sensation in the neck. A couple of times he had the eerie sensation of losing all sense of touch in his hands—but not his legs: he could feel the right one exerting pressure on the braking pedal.

He tried moving his hands, but without taking his eyes off the light. It seemed to be gaining on him; it was now only 1.9 or 1.8 kilometers off his bow. Was it trying to catch up with him, or what?!

He tried lifting his hand, but couldn't. The other one was too numb to even attempt it! No sensation whatever; both hands as good as useless. He tried to catch a glimpse of them—his neck was stiff as a board.

He was panic-stricken. Why had he neglected to do the one thing he was duty-bound to do? Why hadn't he radioed the Base and reported the light at once?

He was afraid of the embarrassment, just as surely as Thomas and Wilmer must have been. What a laugh they'd have had back in the radio shack! A light! A little white light that likes to chase and be chased! Come off it, Pirx! Knock off the dreaming and snap out of it!

With a feeling of resigned indifference, he took another look at the video screen and said:

"Patrolship AMU-111 reporting to Base . . ."

Or at least that's what he *would* have said if his voice hadn't got stuck in his throat. But all that came out was a lot of incoherent mumbling. He strained every muscle and let out a howl. Then, for the very first time, his eyes shifted from the stellar screen to the mirror, where he saw, sitting in the pilot's seat, in a round yellow helmet, the face of a freak.

Huge, swollen, bulging eyes, full of ungodly terror; a gaping, froglike mouth with a blotchy, drooping tongue. Where his neck was he saw a bunch of stiffened cords, vibrating so hard they all but obliterated his lower jaw—and this monstrosity with the bloated, ashen face was yelling, yelling, yelling . . .

He made to close his eyes . . . couldn't. He tried to focus on the screen again . . . couldn't. The freak shackled to the seat was twitching more and more violently, as if bent on snapping his straps. Powerless to do anything else, Pirx stared straight ahead at the monster. He himself was oblivious of the convulsions, of everything except a choking sensation in the chest: he couldn't take in air.

Somewhere in the vicinity he heard a hideous grinding of teeth. He was no longer himself, had no more identity, period; he knew nothing, had lost the use of his limbs and body, of everything except the leg on the braking pedal. His eyesight was dimming, getting blurrier by the second; soon it was teeming with lights—tiny, dazzling, multitudinous. He wiggled his leg; it started twitching. He raised it up; he let it back down. The mutant in the mirror was pale as ash, its mouth flecked with foam, its eyes bulging clear out of their sockets, its body convulsed.

Then he did the only thing that still lay within his power. He cocked his leg, brought it up fast, and kneed himself in the face, full force. The blood ran down his chin; the pain in his mutilated lips blinded him; everything went black.

"Ahhhh," he gurgled. "Ahhhh . . ."

The gurgling was his own voice.

The pain abated, and the old numbness returned. Hey! What gives, anyway? Where the hell was he? He was nowhere; there was nothing anywhere . . .

He went on battering, pulverizing his face with one knee, his body contorted in a madman's convulsions. Then it stopped. The howling, that is. What he heard next was the sound of his own garbled, blood-choked, sickening cry.

He had arms again, arms and hands. They were like wood, and ached with the slightest exertion, like torn ligaments, but he could *move* them. Blindly, with half-numb fingers, he groped for the straps and started undoing them, clutched the armrest with both hands, and stood up. His legs shook; his whole body felt beaten to a pulp. Grabbing hold of the line that stretched across the control room, he advanced toward the mirror and braced himself against its frame.

The man in the mirror was Pirx.

His face was no longer ashen, but bloodied; his nose was a swollen bruise. Blood was oozing from his mangled lips; his cheeks were livid, puffy; there were dark circles under his eyes and faint spasms under his chin—and all this was happening to him, Pirx. He wiped the blood from his chin, spit, coughed, took a few deep breaths—a hopeless physical wreck.

He stepped back to check the screen. The machine was still cruising in reverse, unpowered. Through its own momentum. The white disk was still tailing him, 2 kilometers off his bow.

Steadying himself on the cable, he made his way back to the contour couch—unthinking. His hands began to shake— the normal delayed reaction following a shock, no cause for alarm. Something not quite right in front of the seat . . .

The top of the automatic transmitter cassette. Badly dented. He nudged the lid; it collapsed. Components badly damaged. How had *that* happened? He must have done it himself with his foot. When was that?

He sank into the contour couch, fired his roll jets, went into a turn.

The little disk hesitated, then began gliding toward the edge of the screen; but instead of disappearing, it bounced back out into the middle, like a tennis ball. For crying out loud!

"You bastard!" His voice was full of vile loathing.

Thanks to this latest gambit, he had almost gone into stationary orbit! Yet the fact remained: the light had not left the screen when he turned. That could mean only one thing: the light was artificial, generated by the screen itself. A screen, after all, is not a window. A manned spacecraft is equipped not with windows but with video scanners, with cameras mounted externally on the ship's armored hull, together with a transformer for converting the electrical impulses into images on a cathode-ray tube. Was this just some screwy malfunction in the scanner? Had the same thing happened to Thomas's and Wilmer's? And what became of them, anyway?

No time to think about such things now. Better to flip on the emergency transmitter.

"Patrolship AMU-111 to Base," he said. "AMU-111 to Base. Present reading: sector boundary one-zero-zero-nine-dash-one-zero-one-zero, equatorial zone. Have located trouble, am coming home . . ."

Pirx landed some six hours later, at which time a full-scale inquiry was launched, the investigation lasting an entire month. The first thing to be overhauled was the scanner. It was a new, improved model, installed on all the AMU ships the year before and until now having a perfect performance record. Not a single malfunction had been reported.

After laborious testing, the electronics engineers finally discovered the cause of the light. After several thousand hours of testing, the vacuum in the cathode-ray tube developed a leak, causing a loose charge to appear on the screen's inner surface, observable on the outer screen as a milky-white spot. The movements of the charge were governed by a set of complicated laws. During periods of acceleration, the charge would become distended over a broad area, as if flattened against the inside glass, making it appear as if the speck were approaching. When reverse thrust was applied, the charge would withdraw deeper into the tube. Zero and constant acceleration brought the charge slowly back into the center of the screen. It was capable of unlimited movement, but its favorite resting position, during stationary orbit or periods of unpowered flight, was front center. Research on the charge continued, and its dynamics were represented by a sixth-order differential equation. It was also demonstrated that the charge tended to disperse in response to strong light impulses, and to become more concentrated only when the intensity of impulses received by the CRT was extremely low—such as in space, for example, when a ship was farthest from the Sun. If as much as a ray of sunlight brushed the screen, the charge would vanish for several hours.

The findings of the electronics experts filled an entire volume, copiously laced with mathematical formulas. The next to tackle the case was a team of doctors, psychologists, and specialists in astroneurosis and astropsychosis. And again, after many hours of investigation, it was shown that the loose charge pulsated, which to the naked eye manifested itself as tiny dark squiggles creeping across the luminous disk.

The frequency of these pulsations, too brief to be recorded individually by the eye, affected the so-called theta rhythm of the brain's cortex, intensifying the oscillation potential to such a degree that it could induce a seizure identical to an epileptic fit. Other contributing factors were the state of absolute inertia and the absence of any external stimuli, except for prolonged and uninterrupted exposure to a pulsating light.

The experts credited with these discoveries became internationally famous. Today electronics experts the world over are conversant with the Ledieux-Harper effect, caused by the formation of loose charges in high-vacuum cathode-ray tubes, whereas astrobiologists are familiar with Nuggelheimer's atactic-catatonic-clonic syndrome.

Pirx remained an unknown in the world of science. Only the most assiduous readers could infer, from remarks printed in fine type in some of the evening editions, that, thanks to Pirx, pilots of the future would be spared the fate of Thomas and Wilmer, those two unfortunate victims who perished in the outer regions of space after losing consciousness in a high-speed chase after an illusory light.

The denial of fame did not bother Pirx in the slightest. Nor did he mind having a new tooth put in to replace the one demolished by his knee, nor even the fact that he had to pay for it out of his own pocket.

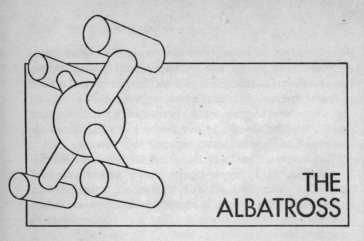

THE ALBATROSS

It was a six-course meal—not counting the trimmings. Wine carts rolled noiselessly up and down the glass aisles. Spotlights illuminated the tables from above: lemon-yellow for the turtle soup, bluish-white for the fish dish, the roast chicken entrée being bathed in a rosy-pink, tinged with a warm, silky gray. Fortunately, there was no dimming of the lights with the espresso—because Pirx's mood was somber enough as it was. The dinner had sapped all his energy. He swore that from now on he'd stick to the snack bar on the lower deck. Too swanky in here for his taste, too much time spent worrying about his elbows. And what a fashion show!

A sunken dining room, with the floor half a flight below level and a circular landing: an enormous, creamish-gold plate, arrayed with the world's most sumptuous appetizers. The rustling of stiff, semitransparent gowns at his back. A gay and festive crowd. Live dance music . . . and live waiters, each decked out like a philharmonic conductor. "The *Transgalactic* offers you nonautomated service, cordial and intimate surroundings, genuinely human hospitality, and a completely live crew, each a master of his trade. . . ."

Over coffee and a cigarette, Pirx tried to find a corner, some quiet place of refuge, to rest his eyes. A woman seated at a nearby table caught his fancy. Her neckline was shaded by a flat but rough stone. Not chrysoprase or chalcedony—most likely a souvenir from Mars. Must have cost a fortune, he thought, even though it looked like little more than a chunk of asphalt. Women shouldn't have so much money.

He wasn't overwhelmed. And he wasn't appalled—just observant. Gradually he felt an urge to stretch his limbs. A stroll on the promenade deck, maybe?

He got up from the table, made a slight bow, and left the dining room. As he passed between some reflecting polygonal columns, he caught a glimpse of himself: a button was showing beneath the knot in his tie. Honestly, nobody wore these kinds of neckties anymore! In the corridor he paused to straighten his collar, stepped into the elevator, and zoomed up to the prom deck. The elevator door slid open without a sound. A sigh of relief: not a living soul in sight. One third of the vaulted ceiling, its glassed roof arching over several rows of deck chairs, resembled a gigantic eye fixed on the stars. The chairs were stacked with blankets, but were otherwise quite empty. Only one was occupied, at the very back—by an elderly eccentric, bundled to the neck, whose habit it was to dine an hour after everyone else, alone, in an empty dining room, veiling his face with a napkin if anyone so much as glanced in his direction.

Pirx settled himself in one of the chairs. Intermittently the deck was fanned by an undulating breeze that seemed to have its origin in the darkest recesses of space but was, in fact, pumped out by the ship's invisible air-conditioning outlets. The engineers on the *Transgalactic* staff knew their stuff, all right. The deck chair was comfortable, more comfortable even than a pilot's electronically designed contour couch. Pirx felt a slight chill, remembered the blankets, and bundled himself up as if making himself snug in a comforter.

Someone was coming. By way of the stairs—not the elevator. His dining-room neighbor. He tried to guess her age—no luck. She had on another dress, and he wondered whether it was the same woman. She stretched herself out, three chairs away from him, and opened a book. The artificial breeze ruffled the pages. Pirx looked straight ahead. The Southern Cross was palpably visible, as was the tail end of the Little Dipper, truncated by the window frame: a luminous speck against a black backdrop. A seven-day flight cruise. Hm. A lot could happen in a week's time. He stirred deliberately, causing the thickish, neatly folded document in his inner pocket to crinkle softly. A surge of contentment: waiting for him on the other end was a second navigator's berth. He knew his itinerary—the plane ride from North Land to Eurasia, then on to India. In his voucher were enough tickets to make a book, each blank a different color and in duplicate, stubs, coupons, gold trim—indeed, everything that belonged to the *Transgalactic*'s package deal fairly oozed with gold and silver. The woman sitting three chairs away from him was good-looking, very good-looking. The same, all right. Should he strike up a conversation? Introduce himself, at least? What a drag having such a short name—a name that was almost over before it began. And then, "Pirx" often came out sounding like something else. Talking on the telephone was the worst. Come on, say something. Fine, but what?!

He felt enervated again. From Mars the cruise had looked altogether different. Luckily for him, the shipowners on Earth were footing the bill—less out of generosity than for purely business reasons. He had logged nearly 3 billion kilometers, but this was his first trip on anything like a Titan. And what a far cry from a freighter! A rest mass of 180,000 tons; four main thrust reactors; a cruising speed of 65 kilometers per second; living accommodations for 1,200 passengers, with a choice of singles, doubles, or suites, all with private bath; guaranteed stable gravitation except during takeoff and landing; maximum safety conditions; all the modern conveniences; a 40-man crew, plus a staff of 260.

Ceramite, steel, gold, palladium, chrome, nickel, iridium, plastic, Carrara marble, oak, mahogany, silver, crystal. Two swimming pools. Four movie theaters. Eighteen direct hookups with Earth—for the passengers alone! A concert hall. Six main decks, four promenade decks, automatic elevators, on-board booking on any ship in the fleet—a year in advance. Bars. Casinos. A department store. An artisans' row—a true facsimile of an old-fashioned city lane, complete with wine cellars, gas lanterns, a moon, and a back-alley wall traversed by genuine back-alley cats. A greenhouse. And God knows what else. It would have taken a good month to make the grand tour, and then only one way!

The woman was still reading. Why do women have to dye their hair like that? That color was enough to turn . . . But on her it worked, somehow. Now, if he just had a cigarette in his hand, he thought, the right words would pop into his mouth automatically. He reached into his pocket.

The moment he whipped out the cigarette case—a present from Boman, which he kept out of friendship, never having owned one before in his life—it felt a little heavier than usual. Just a shade. But heavier it was. Was the ship accelerating, or what?

He strained his ears. Sure enough, the engines were pulling at greater thrust. An ordinary passenger might not have noticed; a series of four-ply insulating bulkheads separated the Titan's engine room from the ship's living quarters.

Singling out a pale star in one corner of the window frame, Pirx kept a watchful eye on it. If they're accelerating, he thought, the star will stay put. But if it so much as jiggles . . .

It jiggled, drifting slowly, but ever so slowly, to one side.

It's turning along its longitudinal axis, he reckoned.

The Titan was flying through a "cosmic tunnel," unobstructed by any dust or meteorites—nothing but empty space. The pilot of the Titan, whose job it was to make sure the giant ship had clear passage, flew on ahead at a distance of 1,900 kilometers. The reason? For safety's sake—even though, under the terms of an agreement negotiated by the United Astronavigation Association, the Transgalactic Line was granted undisputed right-of-way along its segment of the parabola. And ever since unmanned space probes were used to patrol thousands of transuranic sectors, making it possible for meteorite warnings to be issued as much as six hours in advance, the threat of any external hazards had been all but eliminated. The belt—those billion or so meteorites orbiting between Earth and Mars—was kept under special surveillance, whereas the remnants of any vehicles were bound to pass beyond the ecliptic plane. The progress achieved in this area, even since the time Pirx had been flying patrol, was staggering.

With no obstacles to avoid, the Titan had no reason to alter course. But veering off course it was—Pirx no longer had to verify it by the stars, he could feel it in his bones. So confident was he that he could easily have plotted the ship's trajectory, knowing as he did its velocity, mass, and the rate of stellar displacement.

Something's up, he thought.

There were no public announcements. Why all the secrecy? A layman when it came to the customs observed aboard luxury liners, he had enough savvy about engine rooms and cockpits to know there were only two courses of action: in the event of an emergency a ship could either maintain its previous velocity . . . or cut its engines. But the Titan was doing neither. . . .

The whole maneuver lasted a total of four seconds. That meant a forty-five-degree turn. Hm.

The stars once again assumed a stationary position.

They were back on a straight course; yet the cigarette case in Pirx's hand kept getting heavier.

Steering a straight course and gaining speed at the same

time . . . That cinched it. For a moment he sat perfectly still, then rose to his feet, now feeling the effects of the increased gravitation. The gray-eyed beauty was watching his every move.

"Is something wrong?" she asked.

"Nothing to worry about, ma'am."

"Something feels different. Do you notice it, too?"

"It's nothing. Just a little increase in velocity." Now was his chance to strike up a casual conversation. He gave her the once-over, no longer disturbed by the color of her hair. A real doll.

He shuffled off, leisurely at first, but with each step gradually quickening his pace. She must take me for a mental case, he thought. Colorful wall paintings ran the length of the deck. He passed through a door marked OFF LIMITS and headed down a long, deserted corridor, flooded with a bright electric glare. A row of numbered doors. He kept going, relying more on his sense of hearing. Some stairs brought him out on a landing, face-to-face with a metal door.

STELLAR PERSONNEL ONLY read the sign. Wow, nothing like having fancy names!

No doorknob—by special key only. Which key he lacked. He rubbed his nose in a moment of concentration.

Tap . . . tap . . . tatatap . . . tap . . . tap . . .

He waited. The door opened slightly, and a surly, ruddy-complexioned face showed in the crack.

"What can I do for you?"

"I'm from Patrol."

The door opened wide enough to admit him, and he entered what looked to be an auxiliary control room: double row of steering controls, video screens lining the opposite wall, facing which were several vacant chairs. A small, squat-looking unit was monitoring the pulsating dials. Standing on a narrow side table by the wall were some half-empty cups and saucers. The air was redolent of freshly brewed coffee, and of something that smelled vaguely like heated plastic laced with a whiff of ozone. Another door stood slightly ajar, emitting the purring drone of a transformer.

"An SOS?" he inquired of the man who had let him in. Stocky, with a slight swelling on one side of his face: a toothache kind of swelling; headset band creasing the hair; gray, partially unbuttoned *Transgalactic* uniform emblazoned with lightning insignia. Shirttail hanging out.

"Yes." A moment's hesitation. "From Patrol, you say?"

"From the Base. Just back from a two-year tour on the *Transuran*. I'm a navigator. Pirx is the name."

A handshake.

"Mindell's mine. Nucleonics."

Without exchanging another word, the two moved into the adjoining room. It was the communications room. Very big. Ten or more people were huddled around the main transmitter. Two radiotelegraph operators, each equipped with earphones, wrote continuously against a background of clicking instruments, electrical humming, and an incessant, below-decks whine. Swarms of control lights on every wall: the place looked the inside of a trunk exchange. The two radiomen were almost prostrate over their desks; both in shirt sleeves, both with drenched faces—one pale, the other older and more average-looking, with a head scar plainly visible in the place where the headset band made a parting in his hair. Two men were seated a little distance away, one of whom Pirx recognized as the commander.

They were already mildly acquainted. The commander of the Titan was a short, grizzly-haired man with a small poker face. He sat with one leg crossed over the other, seemingly distracted by one of his shoe tips.

Pirx treaded softly up to the radiomen, craned his whole body, and began reading over the shoulder of the man with the head scar.

". . . six-eighteen-point-three proceeding at full thrust time of arrival eight-zero-twelve. Out."

The radioman slid a blank over with his left hand and kept on writing.

"Luna Base to Albatross-4 Aresluna. Check on-board contamination stop answer in Morse stop too far out of range for radio stop how many hours can you maintain emergency thrust stop estimated drift zero-six-point-twenty-one stop. Over."

"Dasher-2 Aresterra to Luna Base. Am proceeding at full thrust destination Albatross sector sixty-four have overheated reactor but proceeding on course anyway stop am now six milliparsecs away from designated point of SOS. Out."

The second operator, the more pallid-looking of the two, let out a muffled groan. Immediately everyone leaned over his shoulder. Mindell, the man who had met Pirx at the door, relayed the recorded messages back to the commander while the operator went on transcribing.

"Albatross-4 to all ships. Am lying in orbit, drift ellipsis T-341 sector sixty-five stop breach in hull widening stop leakage in stern bulkheads stop emergency thrust at 3g stop reactor going out of control stop multiple damages to main bulkhead stop third-degree on-board contamination and rising in response to emergency thrust stop will attempt to seal leaks am transferring crew to bow. Out."

As he wrote, the operator's hands trembled. One of the crew grabbed him by his shirt collar, yanked him to his feet, and rushed him out the door. A short while later he came back—alone—and took the other man's place.

"He has a brother aboard the Albatross," he said by way of explanation, addressing no one in particular.

Pirx peered over the older man's shoulder.

"Luna Base to Albatross-4 Aresluna. The following ships have been dispatched stop Dasher from sector sixty-four Titan from sector sixty-seven Ballistic-8 from sector forty-four Sprite-702 from sector ninety-four stop seal breach in bulkhead stop wear pressure suits behind air locks stop report present course stop."

"The Albatross!" exclaimed the young operator's replacement, and everyone craned to read the message:

"Albatross-4 to all ships. Uncontrolled drifting stop leakage in hull stop losing atmosphere stop crew in pressure suits stop engine room flooded with coolant stop screens punctured stop temperature sixty-three degrees in control room stop initial breach in control room sealed stop coolant boiling stop main transmitter flooded stop switching over to radio stop we'll be waiting for you fellows. Out."

Practically everyone was smoking, the smoke curling upward in blue ribbons before being sucked out through the vents. Pirx was just rummaging through his pockets, likewise feeling the urge to light up, when someone—he couldn't tell who—stuck an open pack into his hand. He lit up.

"Mr. Mindell," said the commander, biting his lip. "Full thrust!"

Mindell registered some momentary astonishment but said nothing.

"Sound the alert?" asked the man seated next to the commander.

"This one's mine."

At that, he swung the mike around on its swivel arm and began speaking:

"Titan Aresterra to Albatross-4. We're proceeding at full thrust. Presently crossing over into your sector. Arrival time one hour. Advise escaping through emergency hatch. We'll be alongside you in one hour. Hang in there. Hang in there. Out."

He pushed the mike away and stood up. Mindell was giving orders into the intercom on the other side of the room.

"Okay, gang—full thrust in five minutes."

"Aye aye," came the reply on the other end of the line.

The commander stepped out for a moment, his voice trailing in from the other room.

"Attention all passengers! Attention all passengers! I have an important announcement. Four minutes from now there will be a significant increase in the ship's velocity. We've received a distress call and are responding with all due—"

Someone shut the door. Mindell gave Pirx a friendly nudge on the arm.

"Better brace yourself. We'll be pushing 2g or better."

Pirx nodded. By his standards 2g was a breeze, but now was not the time to flaunt his physical endurance. Dutifully, therefore, he gripped the armrest of the chair occupied by the older of the two radiomen.

"Albatross-4 to Titan. Won't last another hour on board stop emergency hatch jammed by exploding bulkheads stop temperature eighty-one degrees in control room stop steaming up fast stop will try to escape by cutting through nose shield. Out."

Mindell tore the slip of paper out of the operator's hand and raced out of the room. As he was opening the door, the deck shook slightly and there was an immediate increase in everyone's bodily weight.

The commander labored into the room, each step costing him obvious physical exertion, and plopped down into a chair. Someone handed him a mike on a cable. In his other hand was the last crumpled radiogram received from the Albatross. The skipper spread it out before him and studied it for a good long while.

"Titan Aresterra to Albatross-4," he said at last. "We'll be there in fifty minutes. Approaching on course eighty-four-point-fifteen stop eighty-one-point-two stop abandon ship. Abandon ship. We'll find you. Hang in there. Out."

The man sitting in for the younger operator, his tunic now unbuttoned, suddenly sprang to his feet and shot an urgent glance at the commander, who came over on the double. The operator yanked off his earphones, handed them to the skipper, who slipped them on over his head and listened while the other man adjusted the crackling loudspeaker. A split second later, everyone froze.

In that room were veterans of many years' flight experience, but what they heard now was unprecedented. A voice—barely audible, accompanied by a protracted roar, as if trapped behind a wall of flame—was shouting:

"Albatross . . . every man . . . coolant in cockpit . . . temperature unbearable . . . crew standing by to the end . . . so long . . . all lines . . . out . . ."

The voice faded, being gradually overwhelmed by the roar in the background.

Then—only loudspeaker static. It took no small effort to keep on one's feet—yet all remained standing, hunched over and braced against the metal bulkheads.

"Ballistic-8 to Luna Base," a voice suddenly piped up, loud and clear. "Am proceeding to Albatross-4. Request clearance through sector sixty-seven. Proceeding at full thrust—will be impossible to carry out any passing maneuvers. Over."

There was a pause lasting several seconds.

"Luna Base to all ships in sectors sixty-six, sixty-seven, sixty-eight, forty-six, forty-seven, forty-eight, ninety-six. All sectors closed. All ships not proceeding at full thrust for Albatross-4 are to stop immediately, place reactors on idling, and switch on navigation lights. Attention, Dasher! Attention, Titan Aresterra! Attention, Ballistic-8! Attention, Sprite-702! I'm giving you a clear field to Albatross-4. All traffic within radius vector of SOS has been halted. Commence braking one milliparsec in advance of SOS point. Be careful to extinguish braking rockets once you have Albatross on video—crew may already have abandoned ship. Good luck. Good luck. Out."

Dasher was the first to respond—in Morse. Pirx listened closely to the bleeping signals.

"Dasher Aresterra to all rescue ships. Have entered Albatross's sector. Will be joining her in eighteen minutes stop reactor overheated cooling system damaged stop will need medical assistance following rescue operation stop am commencing braking maneuver at full thrust. Out."

"The guy's nuts," someone muttered, prompting those

standing—until now so stock-still they looked more like statues—to search out the culprit with their eyes. An angry murmur passed through the men, then quickly subsided.

"Dasher will be there first," said Mindell, casting a side glance at the commander, "and forty minutes from now she'll be radioing for help herself—"

He broke off as a voice filtered through the loudspeaker static.

"Dasher Aresterra to all those answering Albatross's distress call. I have her on the monitor. She's drifting on a course approximating ellipsis T-348 and her tail is cherry-red. No trace of any signal lights. SOS ship does not respond. Am shutting down to commence rescue operation. Out."

Buzzers sounded next door. Mindell and another crew member stepped out of the room. Pirx's muscles were cable-tense. Gawd, how he'd like to have been out there! A moment later Mindell came back.

"What's all the ruckus?" inquired the commander.

"The passengers would like to know when they can resume dancing." Mindell's reply went unnoticed by Pirx, whose eyes remained riveted to the loudspeaker.

"It won't be long now," answered the skipper, calmly and without inflection. "Switch on the monitor; we're coming within range. In a couple of minutes we should have a sighting. Mr. Mindell, better sound the alert again—we're about to brake down to overdrive."

"Aye aye, sir," Mindell replied, and he left the room.

A voice came over the loudspeaker.

"Luna Base to Titan Aresterra, Sprite-702! Attention! Attention! Attention! Ballistic-8 reports sighting a flash with a luminosity of minus four in the center of sector sixty-five. No response from Dasher or Albatross. Possibility of a reactor explosion aboard Albatross. For reasons of passenger safety, Titan Aresterra is instructed to stop and report immediately. Ballistic-8 and Sprite-702 are to proceed at their own discretion. I repeat: Titan Aresterra is instructed . . ."

All eyes were on the commander.

"Mr. Mindell, can we stop within a milliparsec?"

Mindell consulted his wristwatch.

"No, sir. We're coming in on video. I'd need at least 6 g's."

"If we changed course?"

"Even then we'd get only 3 g's," Mindell said.

"Well, that settles it."

The commander got up and strode over to the microphone.

"Titan Aresterra to Luna Base. Impossible to stop at present velocity. Am altering course with a roll maneuver at half-thrust. Abandoning sector sixty-five for sector sixty-six, on a course of two-hundred-and-two. Clearance requested. Over."

"Stand by for confirmation," he said, turning and addressing the man who had been seated next to him earlier. Mindell barked into the intercom, buzzers sounded, lights flickered on the wall panels, and the room seemed to grow darker—a case of "dimout," caused by a draining of blood from the eyes. Pirx planted his feet squarely on the floor. They were braking and turning at the same time. There were mild vibrations, the long, shrill whine of laboring engines.

"Sit down, all of you!" the commander suddenly yelled. "I don't need any heroes around here!"

Everyone sat—or rather flopped—down on the floor, which was padded with a thick layer of foam rubber.

"All hell's gonna break loose down below," muttered a man sprawled at Pirx's elbow. The commander overheard him.

"The insurance company will pay for it," he said from his chair. The g-force was now three or better; Pirx could barely touch his face with his hand. By now all the passengers would be safe and sound in their cabins, he thought—but egads, what must it be like in the galleys and dining rooms! A whole shipload of broken china! And he could just see the greenhouse—what was left of it, that is!

"Ballistic-8 to all ships. I have the Albatross within scanner range. Hull completely clouded over, all except for stern, which is cherry-red. Am completing braking maneuver and sending out a search team to look for survivors. No response from Dasher. Out."

The acceleration gradually lessened. Someone poked his head in through the door, permission was given to stand, and there was a quiet stampede to the door. Pirx was the last to enter the main control room. As in some movie theater for giants, the wall was taken up by a huge convex screen, measuring eight meters wide and sixteen meters tall. All lights were off in the control room. Against the black, star-studded background of space, in the left quadrant, lying somewhat below the Titan's main axis, was the Albatross—a smoldering, incandescent sliver, its stern a glowing, fiery-red coal, not unlike the lit end of a cigarette. And this speck, this minute streak, formed the nucleus of a slightly flattened, diaphanous bubble, bristling with myriads of prickly, barb-like extensions—a cloud blister gradually dissolving into starlight. Suddenly there was a slight surge in the direction of the screen. Down at the very bottom, in the lower-right-hand corner, a luminous dot had begun to pulsate. The Dasher!

"Uncontrollable chain reaction aboard the Albatross stop have casualties stop severe burns stop request doctors stop transmitter damaged by explosion stop reactor leaking stop preparing to jettison reactor if unable to control leakage stop"—Pirx deciphered from the steadily blinking light.

The hull of the Albatross was no longer to be seen—only a blistery, yellowish, amber-colored clump suspended among the stars. The farther it drifted into the lower-left-hand corner, the more the Titan towered over it as it steered a new course out of the disaster-ridden sector.

The door to the radio room was ajar, allowing a shaft of light to penetrate the darkness within—along with the sound of a radio transmission.

"Ballistic-8 to Luna Base. Am parked in the central region

of sector sixty-five. Dasher located milliparsec below me. Reports casualties and reactor leakage. Signals that she's preparing to jettison reactor. Am answering her call for medical assistance. Search mission hampered by contamination caused by radioactive cloud with a surface temperature in excess of 1,200. Titan Aresterra in range, passing over me at full thrust and heading for sector sixty-six. Am waiting for arrival of Sprite-702 to launch joint rescue operation. Out."

"To your stations, men!" someone boomed just as the lights at the back of the control room flickered on. There was a sudden flurry of activity, a scattering in several directions at once; Mindell stood by the control desk, giving orders; a number of buzzers went off at the same time . . . Before long the only ones left in the room were the commander, Mindell, and Pirx—and the young radiotelegraph operator, who stood alone in the corner, opposite the screen, and watched as the bubble gradually swelled and faded into the background.

"Oh, I didn't recognize you," said the commander, his hand extended in a handshake, as if just noticing Pirx for the first time. "Any word from the Sprite?" he inquired over Pirx's shoulder of someone standing in the doorway.

"Yes, sir. She's backing up."

"Good."

They lingered for a while longer, their eyes resting on the screen. The last trace of polluted cloud had evaporated, the screen once again filling with a raw and starry blackness.

"What do you think? Any survivors?" asked Pirx, assuming for some reason that the commander was more in the know than he was. A commander, after all, was supposed to know everything.

"Their deadlights must have jammed," the skipper replied. He was at least a head shorter than Pirx, with hair the color of lead. Pirx couldn't remember whether it had always been that gray.

"Mindell!" the commander called out, catching sight of his

engineer passing by. "Lift the passenger alert, will you? They can go back to their dancing now." Addressing the silent Pirx, he said, "Ever aboard the Albatross?"

"No."

"A western company. Twenty-three thousand tons." He was interrupted. "Yes? What is it?"

The radio operator handed him a message. Pirx could make out only the beginning: "Ballistic to . . ."

He stepped back out of the way. When he saw that he was still blocking traffic, he retreated into the corner and stood against the wall. Presently Mindell came barging in.

"Any news of the Dasher?" asked Pirx. Mindell was mopping his brow with a handkerchief, this man whom Pirx was beginning to feel he had known for years.

"A close shave," said Mindell, trying to catch his breath. "Got hit by the blast, sprang a leak in the cooling system— that sonofabitch is always the first to blow. First- and second-degree burns. The medics are already there."

"Ballistic's team?"

"Yep."

"Commander! Luna Base!" Someone called out from the door leading to the radio room, taking the commander away. Pirx stood facing Mindell, who pocketed his handkerchief and instinctively touched his swollen cheek.

Pirx could have gone on grilling him, but thinking better of it, gave him only a slight nod and ducked into the radio room. The loudspeaker was deluged with inquiries about the Albatross and the Dasher—from ships scattered in five different sectors. Finally, Luna Base had to silence everyone so it could go about unscrambling the snarl that had sprung up around sector 65 as a result of the recent ban on traffic.

The Titan's commander could be seen sitting and writing at his desk. Suddenly the telegraph operator took off his earphones and shoved them to one side, as if they were no longer needed—at least that was how Pirx interpreted his

gesture. He was on the verge of asking about the crew of the
Albatross, whether anyone had managed to escape, when the
operator, sensing that someone was standing behind him,
raised his head and looked him straight in the eye. Without
saying another word, Pirx took his leave, through the door
marked STELLAR PERSONNEL ONLY.

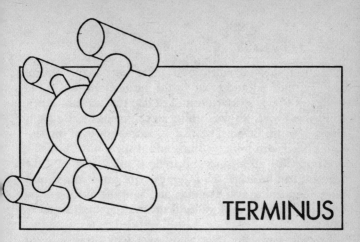

TERMINUS

It was still quite a hike from the stop, all the more so for someone carrying a suitcase. A predawn fog hugged the ground, spectral white in the half-light. Diesel trucks, announced by silvered columns of exhaust, tore along the asphalt highway with their tires humming, their taillights flashing bright red as they rounded the bend. Pirx shifted his suitcase to the other hand and gazed skyward. A low-lying fog, he thought, seeing stars overhead. Routinely he scouted the sky for the Mars reference star. Just then the gray dawn quivered and the fog was shot through with a searing green. Instinctively he lowered his jaw. There was a low rumble, a hot blast. Ground tremors. Seconds later a green sun rose above the land. The snow glared sinisterly all the way to the horizon, the shadows of the road posts skipped on ahead, and those things not already tinted a brilliant green were suffused with ember-red. Pirx set his suitcase down and, rubbing his hands, watched as one of the spiring minarets—eerily luminous, towering above the basin's hilly skyline as though obeying some strange architectural whim—wrenched itself loose from Earth and began its majestic ascent atop a pinnacle of fire. The thunderous roar soon became something palpable, filling the atmosphere; through his fingers he saw in the distance a cluster of towers, buildings, and reservoirs bathed in a brilliant aureole. The windows of the control tower were ablaze, much as if a fire were raging inside; contours buckled and broke in the incandescent air as the instigator of this spectacle vanished into the heavens with a triumphant roar, leaving behind an enormous black ring of smoking earth. Before long a thick, warm shower of condensation descended from the star-studded sky.

Pirx picked up his bag and trudged on. It was as if the blast-off had breached the night; daylight came with a rush now, brightening everything around him: the melting snow lying in the ditches, the valley floor emerging from its misty cover.

Skirting the shiny, wet ships were long, grass-covered bunkers, the place where the ground crews took cover. The dead, water-soaked grass was slippery, hard to get a foothold on; but Pirx was in too much of a hurry to bother hunting for the nearest crossing. He took the grassy slope in one leaping charge—and feasted his eyes on her.

She stood alone, tall as a steeple, surpassing all others in height. An obsolete giant. He picked his way among the puddles on the concrete, the puddles soon tapering off where the water had been instantly evaporated by the thermal blast, until the rectangular slabs rang out hard and crisp under his feet as after a summer dry spell. The closer he got, the farther back went his head. The ship's armored hull looked as if it had been plastered with glue, then buffed with mud-caked rags. An attempt had obviously been made to reinforce the tungsten shield with carbide asbestos fiber. And with good reason. Ships of that mass could have their hulls ripped to shreds—literally skinned—by the heat of air friction during atmospheric reentry. And stripping it did no good, either; the process just repeated itself, so horrendous was its aerodynamic drag. As for its stability, its maneuverability . . . it was downright criminal, a matter for the Cosmic Tribunal.

The suitcase was getting heavier, but Pirx took his sweet time, the itch to inspect the ship carefully from the outside being much too powerful to resist. The gantry stood etched against the sky like Jacob's ladder; everything was coated the same dull gray: the hull, the empty crates strewn about on the concrete, the metal cylinders, the rusty scrap iron, the coils of metal hose . . . The random chaos testified to an expeditious loading. When he was within twenty paces of the gantry, he put down his suitcase and surveyed the launchpad. Hm, cargo already aboard, he thought, seeing the huge mobile loading ramp standing less than two meters from the ship's hull, its grappling hooks dangling in midair. He circled the steel hold-down clamp being used to anchor the ship—now a soaring black tower against the crimson dawn—and stepped under the skirt. The concrete around the base of the clamp sagged under the tremendous weight, with cracklike fissures radiating in all directions.

Ouch! They'll pay a pretty penny for that, he thought, referring to the shipowners, and he stepped into the pool of shadow under the tail section. When he stood directly beneath the main thrust chamber, he tilted back his head. Its gaping flange, too high for him to reach, was caked with soot. He sniffed the air suspiciously. The engines were cold, but the acrid and familiar stench of ionized gas was still in the air.

"Over here!" someone shouted in back of him. He spun around but saw no one. The same voice again, coming from what seemed like no more than three steps away.

"Hey, anyone home?" he yelled, his voice rebounding under the black, domelike tail bristling with nozzles.

Silence.

He cut across to the other side. Three hundred meters away, some men, strung out in a line, were in the process of hauling a fuel hose across the ground. The pad was otherwise deserted. He kept his ears open; then he again heard voices—distorted and unintelligible—this time coming from higher up. The exhaust ducts, he thought—they're acting like dish reflectors . . . He trotted back, picked up his bag, and headed for the gantry.

He climbed the six-story flight unthinkingly, his mind on

matters he would have been hard put to name. The gantry ended in a platform surrounded by an aluminum guardrail, but Pirx did not so much as pause for a glimpse of the scenery. No farewell glances, no fond good-byes. Before flipping open the hatch, he ran his fingers along the armor plating. Rough as a rasp, as a badly corroded rock.

"Just my luck," he muttered. The hatch gave grudgingly, as if blocked by a boulder. A pressure chamber like the inside of a wine barrel. He ran his hand along the pipes and rubbed the dust between his fingers. Rust.

As he was squeezing through the inner hatch, he had a chance to observe that the gasket was a patch job. Passageways lined with flush-mounted lamps ran up and down like vertical tunnels, the light coalescing at the far end into a bluish blur. In the background the steady hum of electric fans, the nasal clucking of an invisible pump. He pulled himself up straight. He was surrounded by such a solid mass of deck and armor plate that it nearly felt a part of him, a prolongation of his own body. Nineteen thousand tons . . . Goddam!

On his way to the cockpit, he met no one, saw no one. A dead, vacuumlike silence reigned in the passageway, as if the ship were already spaceborne. The padded walls were stained, the guide lines slack and decayed. He saw sleeve joints that had been spliced and welded so many times they looked more like charred bulbs left over from a fire. He crossed one ramp, then another, and came out in a hexagonal compartment with rounded metal doors set in each of the walls. Cord-wrapped copper handles instead of pneumatic releases.

The displays stared vacantly, like glass cataracts. He punched the keyboard; the relay clicked and the metal console hummed. The screen remained dark.

"Now what?" he sighed. "Run and complain to the SSA?"

He opened the hatch. It looked more like a throne room than a cockpit. He saw himself mirrored in the blank screens;

in his rain-crumpled hat, light overcoat, and with his suitcase at his side, he made the impression of some errant, law-abiding citizen. The contoured pilot seats, rather imposing in size, their backrests still preserving the deep imprint of a man's body, stood on a dais. Setting his suitcase down on the floor, he went up to the nearest one, its shadowy projection looming like the last navigator's ghost. He slapped the backrest until the dust tickled his nose, broke out in a fit of sneezing, then anger, and wound up laughing. The foam-rubber padding on the armrest was shot, the computers like nothing he'd ever seen before. Their designer must have modeled them on a Wurlitzer, he mused. The consoles were peppered with dials; no man could have monitored them all at the same time, not with a hundred eyes. He made a slow about-face and let his eyes roam from wall to wall surveying the tangle of soldered cables, corroded isolation plates, emergency manual hatches polished smooth from handling, the faded red finish of the fire extinguishers. . . . Everything about this ship was so old and decrepit and dingy. . . .

He kicked the seat's shock absorbers, and immediately the hydraulics sprang a leak.

Oh well, he thought, if others can get her up, so can I; went back out into the passageway, came out through another hatch into the outboard passage, and kept on going. Just past the elevator shaft he noticed that the wall bulged a little and was a shade darker in one spot. One touch of the hand, palm down, bore out his suspicions: a cement patch. He scoured the passageway for signs of other ruptures but couldn't find any; the rest of the walls and the ceiling were like new. His eyes meandered back to the patch. The cement was bumpy in places; Pirx thought he could make out the vague outline of handprints, proof of a job executed in terrific haste. He got into the elevator and rode down to the reactor, the different deck levels indicated by lighted numerals flashing through the window: 7 . . . 6 . . . 5 . . .

It was cold down below. The passageway curved before

joining up with others to become a long and narrow corridor, at the end of which he sighted the door to the reactor chamber. The closer he came, the lower the temperature dropped, turning his breath to silver vapor in the light of the dusty lamps. He shook his head in consternation. The freezers, he thought. They must be somewhere close by. He paused to listen. The metal bulkheads pulsated with a weak but steady vibration. As he passed under the ceiling—a steeply inclined ceiling, echoing his every footstep—he couldn't rid himself of the impression that he was descending underground. The door was hermetically sealed. He exerted all his weight on the handle; it wouldn't budge. He was just about to force it with his foot when he realized that the safety bolt needed pulling out first.

A double door, as sturdy as a bank vault door, followed. At eye level, in places where the enamel finish hadn't completely flaked away, a few letters painted in red were still legible: NG R.

The door opened onto an even narrower passage, this one almost pitch-black. The moment he set foot inside the door, something clicked, his face was struck by a blinding light, and a warning sign flashed a skull and crossbones.

They weren't taking any chances in those days, were they? he thought. The metal stairway reverberated with a loud clanging as he went down into the chamber. Down below, he had the sensation of standing at the bottom of a dry moat; opposite him, rising up like the battlement of some medieval fortress, was the reactor's gray, two-story shielding, its surface pitted with yellowish-green, pockmarklike indentations: scars of old radiation leaks. He started to do a quick count but gave up as soon as he walked out onto the catwalk and examined the reactor from above; in some places the concrete wall was totally obliterated by the sealed leaks.

Supported by metal uprights, the catwalk was insulated from the rest of the chamber by glass panels wrapping all the way around: a huge transparent cube. Lead glass, probably—to cut down the radiation. A relic of atomic architecture. How quaint.

The gamma-ray counters were clustered under a small canopy, fanlike, each one aimed straight at the reactor's belly. He found the gauges housed in a separate compartment, all of them on zero except for one: the reactor's idling gauge.

Pirx worked his way down, knelt, and peered into the observation well. The periscope mirrors were discolored with age. Too much radiation exposure, he thought. So what? This was a trip to Mars, not Jupiter—with a ten-day turnaround. Fuel supply okay, enough for several runs. He activated the cadmium rods. The needle quivered and grudgingly shifted to the other end of the scale. He checked the delay: it was close enough to squeak by the SSA, but just barely.

Something stirred in the corner. A pair of luminous green dots. He kept an eye on them, flinching as they slowly slinked away. He closed in on it. It was a cat. A black and bony cat. Meowing softly, it rubbed its spine against his shin. Pirx smiled, canvassed the room until his eye landed on something high up on a metal shelf: a row of cages. Now and then something white flickered inside, a glittering black bead would show through the netting. Mice. They were still in use on some of the older ships—as live radiation gauges. He stooped down to stroke the cat, but it slipped away from him, stopped dead in its tracks, and turned in the direction of the room's darkest, narrowest corner. Arching its back, meowing softly, it crept on outstretched paws toward a concrete buttress, beyond which the mouth of a passage gaped rectangularly. Wiggling the end of its tail, now stiffly perpendicular, it advanced slowly, so black as to be almost indistinguishable in the dark. Pirx, intrigued, crouched down for a better look. A small door, halfway open, was set in a sloping wall; something glinted inside, which at first he took to be a coil of metal hose. The cat stood transfixed and immobile, its hair on end, its stiffened tail describing little curls in the air.

"Aw hell, there's nothing in there," he grumbled, at the same time squatting down for a closer view inside the dark compartment. Someone was sitting inside, the upper half of its body giving off a dull, metallic sheen. The cat, meowing all the while, started for the chute. Pirx's eyes gradually got accustomed to the dark; soon he could make out a pair of pointed knees raised up high, and shinguards, made of a low-luster metal, around which a pair of segmented arms was wrapped. Its head was lost in the shadows.

"Me-o-w-w," went the cat.

One of the arms creaked, reached out, and laid its metal fingertips down to form a sloping ramp; instantly the cat sprinted up the arm and onto the shoulder of the hunched-over figure.

"Hey, you!" Pirx cried out, not sure himself whether he meant to address the cat or that other creature. The arm had begun to retract slowly, as if having to overcome a powerful resistance, when Pirx's barking cry paralyzed it, causing its fingers to clank against the concrete.

"Who-is-there?" came a voice that sounded as if it were being filtered through a metal tube.

"What are you doing here?" asked Pirx.

"Ter-minus . . . free-freezing in he-here . . . ca-can't see . . ." the robot stuttered in a husky voice.

"Are you in charge of the reactor?" asked Pirx, who was beginning to despair of learning anything from the robot, whose condition seemed as run-down and dilapidated as the ship itself. But something—the green eyes?—urged him on.

"Ter-minus . . . re-reactor . . ." it stammered from its concrete refuge. "Terminus in charge . . . reactor," it repeated with something like moronic self-complacency.

"Get up!" Pirx shouted for lack of anything better to say. He heard a crunching of metal, stepped back a little, and watched as two iron gauntlets with splayed fingers came out of the dark, swiveled around, clamped hold of the rim, and began hoisting the rest of its creaking torso. A metal hulk, half doubled up, soon emerged and, with a lot of grinding and screeching in the joints, drew itself up straight. Oil leaks in the couplings had combined with the dust to form a dark sludge. The robot rocked back and forth, more like a knight in armor than an automaton.

"Is this your station?" asked Pirx.

The robot's glass eyes rotated in opposite directions in 180-degree sweeps, lending the flat metal face a look of even greater vacuity.

"Sealant pre-prepared . . . two, six, eight pounds . . . can't see too well . . . cold . . ."

The voice issued not from the head but from the robot's breastplate.

The cat, curled into a ball, contemplated Pirx from its perch on the robot's shoulder.

"Seal-ant pre-pared . . ." Terminus continued to grunt, accompanying his words now with a scooping and shoveling of the hands—the preliminary gesture of a procedure well known to Pirx: the sealing of radioactive leaks. As the rocking of the oxidized trunk gained momentum, the black cat hissed and clawed the metal plating, then lost its balance and bolted down, brushing Pirx's leg in flight. The robot appeared not to notice. The words had stopped, but not the hands, whose movement became more and more convulsive, residual, a mute echo of his words, until finally grinding to a halt.

Pirx glanced up at the reactor wall, its surface scarred and fossillike, riddled all around with the dark stains of cement patches, then back at Terminus. He must have been as old as the ship itself, maybe older. His right shoulder didn't match his left, there were welding scars on his hips and thighs, and the treated metal around the seams had taken on a gray-blue luster.

"Terminus!" He hollered as loudly as if he were addressing a deaf man. "Report to your station!"

"I hear and obey. Terminus."

The robot retreated, crablike, to his sanctuary and began

squeezing inside to the sound of crushing metal. Pirx's gaze swept the room in search of the cat; it was nowhere to be seen. He climbed back up the stairs, sealed the airtight door behind him, and rode the elevator up to the navigation room on the fourth deck.

A squat and spacious room, with reddish oak paneling, a low beamed ceiling, and brass-ringed portholes that let in the daylight, it had more the feel of a ship's cabin. Forty years ago such nautical decor had been the rage, even the vinyl wall coverings were a deliberate imitation of the old-style wainscoting. He opened one of the portholes and nearly rammed his head into a blank wall: the daylight was fake, artificially simulated by means of camouflaged lighting. He slammed the window shut and turned around. Star maps, colored a pale marine-blue, like the sea illustrations in a world atlas, draped from the chart tables clear down to the floor; the corners were littered with reams of carbon paper decorated with course diagrams; a plotting board, its surface embossed with circular depressions, stood under a small spotlamp; there was a desk in the corner, next to it a swivel oak desk chair, bolted to the floor and flanked by a hefty recessed bookshelf.

A real Noah's Ark.

Is that why the agent had commented, after the signing of the contract, "You're getting a historic ship"?

But "old" was not quite the same as "historic."

He began pulling out the desk drawers, one by one, until he found what he was looking for: the log—a big, glossy, leather-bound book with tarnished clasps. He examined it standing up, not yet having mustered the courage to sit down in the sprawling, worn-out desk chair. He turned back the cover. The first page bore the date of the ship's trial run, along with a photocopy insert of its technical specs. He glanced at the date again and batted his eyes; he wasn't even born then! He turned to the last, and most crucial, entry. It confirmed what the agent had told him: for the past week the ship had been taking on machine equipment and general cargo for Mars. Lift-off, originally scheduled for the twenty-eighth, had been several times postponed, making this the third demurrage day. That explained the rush; the demurrage fees in a terrestrial spaceport were steep enough to bust a millionaire.

He thumbed through the book slowly, his eye occasionally lingering over a bit of navigational lingo, course data, or computer figures—but only in passing, as if on the lookout for something else. Only one page stood out from all the others, the one headed:

Ship consigned to Ampers-Hart Shipyard for class A repairs.

The entry was three years old.

Let's see what repairs were made. Out of idle curiosity he scanned the itemized list of part replacements, his incredulity growing from one item to the next: ablation shield, sixteen deck sections, shielding braces, airtight bulkheads . . .

New bulkheads and shielding braces?!

Okay, the agent *had* said something about an accident in the past. But accident, hell! *Disaster* would be more like it!

He flipped back a page to see what he could dig out of the entries that came before:

Port of destination: Mars. Payload: General cargo. Crew: Pratt—engineer and first officer. Wayne—second officer. Potter and Nolan—pilots. Simon—mechanic . . .

Hm. No mention of the skipper.

He turned back another page and winced.

The date of the ship's first command was—nineteen years ago! The signature of the ship's first commanding officer read *Momssen, first navigator.*

Momssen!

A dry heat engulfed him.

It can't be! Not *the* Momssen! But . . . that was on another ship!

The date squared, though; it was exactly nineteen years ago that . . . Whoa, there! Easy does it . . .

He went back to the log. A strong and legible hand, in faded ink. First day out. Second day, third day . . . Moderate reactor leakage: 0.42 roentgen per hour. All leaks sealed. Course coordinates such-and-such . . . Stellar fix . . .

Come on, come on!

He was no longer reading, just skimming over the hand-written lines.

There it was!

The date he had been forced to memorize as a schoolkid, and underneath it:

1640 hours. Rec'd. Deimos's met. warning re: cloud headed our way from Jupiter perturbation of the Leonids. Cloud approaching on a collision course at vel. 40 km/sec. MW confirmed. PM alert sounded for crew. Despite persistent reactor leakage of 0.42 roentgen per hour, full-thrust escape maneuver on a course approximating Orion delta.

New paragraph:

1651. Im—

The rest of the page was blank.

No marks, no scribbling, no ink stains—nothing except for the final vertical stroke of the letter *m,* dipping down in willful defiance of the rules of good penmanship.

This wobbly, several-millimeters-long extension, breaking off the text to wander aimlessly across the white expanse of paper, told the whole story: the crash on impact, the exploding decompression, the shrieks of men at the moment their throats and eyeballs burst . . .

But Momssen's ship had a different name. What was it called?

It was unreal. A ship almost as famous as Columbus's, and he couldn't remember the name of it!

What was the name of that ship, Momssen's last ship?

He hopped over to the bookshelf. The fat volume of *Lloyd's Shipping Register* seemed to plunk down right into his hands. A word that began with C. *Cosmonaut?* No. *Condor?* Not it, either. A longer name . . . the title of a play . . . a hero, a knight . . .

He flung the book down on the desk and squinted at the walls. Hanging between the chart cabinet and the bookshelf were some instruments: a hygrometer, a radiation counter, a carbon-dioxide gauge . . .

He scrutinized each of them, turning them this way and that. Not one inscription. They looked brand new, in fact.

Over in the corner!

Screwed into the oak paneling was a chronometer, plainly visible because of its shiny dial. A rather quaint-looking model, an antique, with cute little brass doodads around the dial . . . Wasting no time, he undid the screws, carefully slipped the chassis out with his fingertips, and cradled it in his palm. The glossy, brass-plated bottom bore the engraving CORIOLANUS.

That was it—the name of Momssen's ship.

His eyes swept the cabin. So it was in this room and in this very same chair that Momssen had sat during the final moments!

He opened *Lloyd's Shipping Register* to the *C*'s. CONDOR, CORINTHIAN, CORSAIR, CORIOLANUS: *Registered with the company of . . . rest mass 19,000 tons . . . launched in the year . . . uranium-hydrogen reactor, type . . . cooling system . . . maximum thrust . . . introduced on the Terra–Mars line; listed as missing following a collision with the Leonids; located sixteen years later by a patrolship in the aphelion of its orbit . . . underwent class A repairs at Ampers-Hart . . . reintroduced by the Southern Company on the Terra–Mars line . . . licensed as general cargo transport . . . insurance premium . . .* Ho hum . . . Ha, here it is: . . . *under the name* THE BLUE STAR.

He shut his eyes . . . Gosh, it's quiet in here. So that's it—they changed the name. To make it easier to hire a crew, I bet. Maybe that's what the agent had meant when he said . . .

He began thinking back to when he was still a cadet. One of their patrolships from the Base had discovered the wreckage . . . Those were the days when meteorite warnings always came too late . . . Then there was the Commission's report, brief and to the point: "Conditions beyond control. No one at fault." . . . What about the crew? The evidence indicated that not all of them had been killed instantly . . . that among the survivors was the skipper, and that, thanks to him, the crew—though cut off from one another by the collapsing bulkheads and with no hope of being rescued—had held out to the end, down to the last oxygen bottle . . . But there was something else, some morbid detail that the press had played up for weeks, until some new sensation had put it out of the public's mind . . . What in the world was it?

Suddenly he saw the Institute's huge lecture auditorium . . . his pal Smiga, caked with chalk, plodding his way through a blackboard full of math equations . . . and himself, his head bent over an open desk drawer, reading on the sly the newspaper spread out flat on the bottom: *"Only the Dead Survive"* . . . Of course! There was only one who *could* have survived, who was not in need of any oxygen or food . . . The robot! Sixteen years, and all that time it was lying there, buried under the rubble!

Pirx rose to his feet. Terminus! The lone surviver *had* to be Terminus! And to think that he had him right here on board his ship . . . Now was his chance, his golden opportunity . . .

To what? Pump a mechanical moron, a machine programmed for sealing leaks, by now so old it was almost deaf and blind? What a laugh. It was the press's fault, the press in its eternal effort to sensationalize the hell out of everything, whose glaring headlines had made him a "mysterious witness" of the tragedy, even had him being interviewed by the Commission behind closed doors. He thought of Terminus's imbecilic patter. What a put-on!

He slammed the log shut, tossed it back into the drawer, and checked the time.

0800 hours. No time to lose. He started rounding up the shipping papers. Everything was set for lift-off: hatches closed, health and port inspection out of the way, flight clearance, customs declarations. . . . He skimmed through the bill of lading and was surprised not to find any cargo manifest. Machines, okay—but what kind of machines? What about the tare weight? And why no loading chart specifying the ballast? Nothing except for the gross tonnage and a rough plan showing the freight distribution in the holds. Why only 300,000 tons back aft? Was it to lighten the maximum load for takeoff? Say, why wasn't this brought to his attention earlier? While he was rummaging through the files in search of something, he became so distracted that he completely forgot about the ship's past history; the moment he laid eyes on the dismantled chronometer, however, he winced in recollection. A second later he found what he was after: a little slip of paper on which it was noted that the last hold—the one abutting on the reactor chamber—was stocked with forty-eight crates of what was generally described as "food perishables." Why in the hold with the worst ventilation? he wondered. Didn't they care about the spoilage?

There was a knock at the door.

"Come in!" he hollered, hurriedly gathering up the papers scattered on the desktop and stuffing them back into their folders. Two men entered but ventured no farther than the doorway.

"Boman, nuclear engineer."

"Sims, engineer-electrician."

Pirx got up from his desk. Sims was a young, lean man with squirrelish features, a nervous cough, and flickering eyes. One glance at Boman was enough for Pirx to know that he was dealing with a space veteran. His sunburned face had that peculiar orangish tint that comes from prolonged expo-

sure to cosmic radiation. He barely came up to Pirx's shoulder
(ever since he had begun flying, Pirx had been accustomed to
counting every kilo aboard ship). His face, in contrast to his
scrawny build, was puffy, bloated, and there were dark bags
under his eyes—the mark of a man who's been tested many
times over the years. He had a drooping lower lip.

"You'll be looking like that yourself, one day"—it crossed
Pirx's mind as he went to greet them with outstretched hand.

Hell began at 0900 hours. The launch site was the scene of
the usual bedlam: ships lining up for takeoff; loudspeakers
blaring away every six minutes; warning rockets being fired;
the screeching, rumbling, deafening roar of test-firing engines; the dust cascading down out of the sky after every
blast-off, which no sooner would settle than the tower was
already giving the go-ahead to the next ship; the constant
hustling to gain a few extra minutes' time—a familiar enough
scene at any shipping port during the peak hours. Most of the
ships were bound for Mars, now desperate for machines and
fresh produce. People there hadn't seen a piece of fruit or a
vegetable in months, construction on the hydroponic solari-
ums having barely got under way.

Meanwhile, last-minute deliveries continued right up until
countdown: cranes, girders, bales of fiberglass, cement vats,
crude oil, medical supplies . . . At the sound of a warning
buzzer, the ground crews would take cover wherever they
could—in the antiradiation bunkers, in special armored
crawlers—and were back at their jobs before the pads had
had time to cool. By ten o'clock a smoky, crimson, bloated
sun hung over the horizon, the concrete safety barriers
dividing the stands were already cracked, blackened with
soot, and eaten away by exhaust. The deeper fissures were
immediately doused with quick-drying cement, which shot up
out of the hoses in a fountainlike spray, while antiradiation
crews in helmeted suits piled out of transport vehicles and

sandblasted the residue of radioactive fallout. Black-and-red-checkered patrol Jeeps careened in and out, their sirens wailing. Someone in the control tower was yelling himself hoarse over a megaphone. Huge, boomerang-shaped radar dishes combed the skies from the tops of gaunt towers . . . In a word, a routine workday.

Pirx was all over the place—taking aboard a last-minute shipment of meat, tanking up on drinking water, having his cooling system inspected (when the best it could do was −5, the SSA inspector shook his head but mercifully relented in the end), attending to the compressors, which, though just recently overhauled, began sweating around the valves . . . Pirx's voice was beginning to sound more and more like the trumpet of Jericho. At one point it was discovered that the water ballast was off because some idiot had switched off the valve before the lower tanks had been properly filled. There were papers, up to a half-dozen at a time, that had to be signed—more often than not, blindly. It was 1100 hours, with one hour to go before lift-off, when the bombshell came.

The control tower was denying them clearance. The *Star's* jet system was too old, they said, the radioactive fallout too risky; they should have had an auxiliary borohydride propulsion system like the one on the *Giant,* the freighter that took off at six . . . Pirx, now hoarse from shouting, took the news calmly. Did the traffic controller realize what he was saying? Had he just now noticed the *Star?* Another delay was bound to mean trouble—big trouble. Beg your pardon? Additional safeguards? What sorts of safeguards? Sandbags? How many? Three thousand? No sweat. You bet your sweet ass—lift-off as scheduled. Bill the Company? Be my guest.

He was dripping with perspiration. Everything was conspiring to make an already chaotic situation even more hopeless. The electrician was chewing out the mechanic for not checking out the emergency system; the second pilot had taken off on a "five-minute break"—to say farewell to his fiancée—and was still not back on board; the medical orderly was missing; the ship was besieged by an army of forty armored crawlers, and by men in dark overalls who, urged on by frantic semaphore signals from the tower, went about the job of piling sandbags; a radiogram came, was taken not by the pilot but by the electrician, who forgot to record it ("Sorry, not my department") . . . Pirx went about in a daze, only pretending to be in control of things. At T minus twenty minutes he made a dramatic decision: he ordered all the water pumped from the nose tanks to the tail section. What the heck, in the worst case it might boil up a bit . . . but anything to get greater stability!

1140 hours. Time to test-fire the engines. The point of no return. As it turned out, not everybody on board was a bumbler. Take Boman, for instance—now there was a man to his liking. You might not see or hear him, but he had everything running like clockwork: engine purge, low thrust, full thrust . . . At T minus six minutes, by the time they got the signal to prepare for lift-off, they were ready. They were already strapped down when the orderly showed up, followed by the second pilot, who came back from his fiancée looking very down at the mouth. The loudspeaker snarled, bawled, barked until the automatic sequencer hit zero: lift-off.

Pirx knew enough to know that a 19,000-ton vessel wasn't a patrol skiff where a man barely had room to crack a joke. He also knew that a spaceship wasn't a flea: it didn't just *hop* into the air; it had to build up thrust gradually. But he wasn't prepared for anything like *this!* The gauge showed only half-thrust, the hull was on the verge of a breakup—and they hadn't even left the pad yet! He was beginning to wonder if they hadn't snagged on something—freak accidents like that were rare, but they happened—when the needle started fluttering. They went up on the fire column; the *Star* shook; the gravimeter went wild. Pirx sighed, sank back into his couch, and relaxed his muscles; from now on, it was out of his hands. They were no sooner in the ascent stage than they were reprimanded by radio: the Company was being fined for lifting off at full thrust, prohibited on account of the excess radioactivity. The Company? thought Pirx. Go right ahead. The Company be damned! Pirx brushed it off with a sneer; he didn't even bother to dispute the charge by pointing out that he had bootstrapped at half-thrust. What was he supposed to do? Land, request a hearing, and demand that the reprimand be withdrawn from his uranographs? Like hell he would.

Besides, he had plenty of other things to worry about at the moment. Like the way they were breaking through the atmosphere. Never had he been aboard a ship that vibrated so much. He now knew how it must have felt to be at the head of a battering ram when storming a castle wall. The whole ship jumped, the men jumped—in their straps, no less!—even the accelerometer was jumping around: 3.8, then 4.9, at one point pushing its way up to 5, only to plummet pusillanimously back down to 3. What were those rockets firing, anyway? Dumplings? With the ship now on full power, Pirx had to squeeze his helmet with both hands to hear the pilot's voice in his earphones. The noise was tremendous, but it was not a triumphant ballistic roar—more like a life-and-death struggle with Earth's gravity. There were moments when he had the sensation not of a lift-off but of hanging in midair and repelling the planet by force, so physically palpable was the *Star*'s agonizing ordeal. The vibrations blurred the contours of everything—bulkheads, joints . . . At one point, Pirx thought he heard the seams giving way. But it was only an illusion; in that madhouse he would have been lucky to hear the horn of the Last Judgment.

The nose-cone heat sensor was the only instrument whose needle didn't waver, didn't fluctuate wildly, but climbed steadily higher: 2,500, 2,800 . . . There were only a few more scale marks left on the gauge when Pirx happened to check the accelerometer. They weren't even close to orbital velocity!

Fourteen minutes of flight and the best they could do was 6.6 kilometers per second. Pirx was struck by a horrible thought, one of those nightmarish fantasies with which space pilots are continually haunted: What if those weren't clouds drifting by on the scanner but vapors escaping from the cooling ducts? Luckily it wasn't so; they were definitely spaceborne. The orderly lay there pale as a sheet. A lot of help he'll be in an emergency, thought Pirx. The engineers were holding up better. Boman wasn't even perspiring; he lay there, a little peaked in the face, relaxed, scrawny—like a kid with its eyes shut. By now the hydraulic fluid was leaking out onto the floor with a vengeance; the pistons were in almost all the way. What happens when they *really* go? Pirx wondered.

Because he was used to more modern consoles, Pirx's head kept turning in the wrong direction every time he went to check the thrust performance, cooling, velocity, thermal load, and, most important, their position relative to the synergic curve.

The pilot, who had to scream over the intercom to make himself heard, was having trouble keeping on course. True, they were only fractional deviations, but that was all it took, when escaping Earth's atmosphere, to make one side heat up more than the other, setting up powerful thermal stresses in the outer structure, often with fatal consequences. Pirx's only consolation was that the *Star* had survived plenty of other lift-offs in the past; chances were, it would make this one as well.

The thermocouple was now on maximum: 3,500 degrees. Ten more minutes of this and the hull would come apart at the seams, carbide or no carbide. What gauge was the skin? he wondered. No telling—except that it was, for sure, hot. He felt warmer himself, but it was only his imagination: the temperature in the control room was the same as at lift-off: 27 degrees. They were at the 61-kilometer mark, Earth's atmosphere practically behind them, flying at a velocity of 7.4

kilometers per second, with less turbulence but still at $3g$. The *Star* had as much oomph as a block of lead, its rapid acceleration nil. Damned if he could understand why.

A half hour later they were steering a course for the Arbiter; once past the last navigational satellite, they would be veering onto the Earth–Mars ellipsis. The crew was sitting up now; Boman was massaging his face; Pirx, too, felt swollen around the mouth, especially in the region of the lower lip. Everyone had bloodshot, stinging eyes, a dry cough, and a sore throat—all the usual symptoms, normally disappearing within an hour.

The reactor was working, but that was about all; if its performance didn't decrease, neither did it increase, as well it should have in a vacuum. The *Star* appeared to defy even the laws of physics. They were up to 11 kilometers per second, barely above escape velocity. They would have to bring her up to cruising speed if they didn't want to take months getting to Mars.

Pirx, like every other navigator, was expecting nothing but hassles from the Arbiter. Like getting reprimanded for having too big an exhaust flare, or getting bumped to make way for some more important mission, or hearing complaints about how his ionization discharge was causing radio interference. A false alarm. The Arbiter let them through without a boo, just a belated radiogram warning of a "high vacuum" ahead. Pirx acknowledged the warning, and thus ended this exchange of cosmic civilities.

As soon as they were locked onto Mars, Pirx ordered an increase in thrust, people got up, stretched, moved about, and the radio mechanic, who also doubled as crew cook, headed off to the galley. Everyone was famished, most of all Pirx, who had flown on an empty stomach and sweated pounds during takeoff.

The temperature in the cockpit was rising, as the heat generated by the shield began to make itself felt inside. There was also a faint odor in the air—the oil that had escaped from the hydraulics and which now formed neat little puddles around the seats.

The nuclear engineer went down to the reactor chamber to check for neutron leakage. Keeping one eye on the stars, Pirx shot the breeze with the ship's electrician; it turned out they moved in the same crowd. For the first time since coming aboard, Pirx began to unwind, to see the brighter side of things. Whatever else the *Star* might be, 19,000 tons was nothing to sneeze at. Commanding a clunker that size was a lot tougher than piloting your ordinary freighter. Tougher, yeah, but also more prestigious, a good thing to fatten your dossier with.

They were 1.5 million kilometers out beyond the Arbiter when their morale suffered its first blow: the lunch was unfit for human consumption. The radio mechanic, it turned out, was no cook. But the man with the biggest gripe was the orderly, already nursing an upset stomach. Just before lift-off, the orderly had made a bargain on some chickens, one of which he had entrusted to the mechanic's culinary art; the result was a broth full of quills. The rest of the crew was served rump steak, tough enough to consume a lifetime of hard labor.

"A little tough, eh?" commented the second pilot, who pronged his meat with such gusto that it flipped off the plate.

The mechanic, who also had a tough skin, told the orderly there was nothing wrong with the broth that a little straining wouldn't cure. Pirx felt obliged to act as mediator in the dispute, to exercise some authority as the ship's CO, but he was too choked with laughter to even open his mouth.

After a canned lunch, Pirx moseyed on back to the cockpit. He had the pilot take a star fix, entered the accelerometer readings in the log, and whistled when his glance landed on the reactor gauge. That was no reactor, brother—that was a volcano! Eight hundred degrees in the shielding after only four hours of flight was no laughing matter. Coolant circulated at a maximum pressure of 20 atmospheres. Hm. The worst was probably over. Landing on Mars would be a breeze—thinner atmosphere, with a gravity less than half Earth's . . . But the reactor, what to do about the reactor . . . ? He went over to the computer, to calculate how long it would take to reach a cruising velocity at their present rate of thrust. Anything less than 80 kilometers per second would mean a ferocious delay.

"Seventy-eight hours to go," registered the display.

Seventy-eight hours?! By then the reactor would be blown to bits, splattered like an egg. As sure as his name was Pirx. He decided to build up speed gradually. It'll mean screwing up the flight plan a little, thought Pirx, it'll mean going without thrust for a while . . . it won't be no joyride without any gravitation . . . but, well, it's that or nothing. He told the pilot to keep an eye on the astrocompass, then took the elevator down to the reactor chamber. He was working his way down a dim passageway, with cargo holds to the right and left of him, when he heard something on the order of a hollow drumming—the sound an armored squadron riding over metal might make. He quickened his step. A cat—the same black cat—sprang out of nowhere and squirmed between his legs; not far off, a door banged shut. By the time he reached the cavelike mouth of the main passageway, it was quiet again. Before him lay a desolate stretch of bleakly blackened walls, an emptiness relieved only by a solitary lightbulb at the far end, still jittering from the impact of the slamming door.

"Terminus!" he called out blindly, but he got only an echo in reply. He turned and followed the passageway all the way back to the reactor chamber. Boman, who had already come down earlier on the elevator, was gone. The arid, desertlike air irritated his eyes. A hot wind seethed inside the air ducts, blending with all the boiler-room racket. The reactor was performing like any other reactor—in silence. The noise came from the cooling system, now strained to the maximum—a strangely rueful, yammering whine produced by the kilometers of tubing that circulated the ice-cold liquid deep inside the concrete shielding. The needles on the lenslike gauges of the pumps were uniformly tilted to the right. Standing out prominently from all the others, its dial radiant as the Moon, was the most critical gauge of all: the one measuring neutron flux density. Its indicator was verging on the red, a sight guaranteed to give any SSA inspector cardiac arrest.

The rugged, rocklike surface of the shielding gave off a deadly heat; the catwalk's sheet-metal construction vibrated, sending unpleasant ripples through his body; the electric lights cast an oily glare on the vent covers. A white light flickered and went out; in its place a red warning signal came on. He ducked under the catwalk to check the timing switches but saw that Boman had already beat him to it; the automatic timer was programmed to interrupt the chain reaction in four hours. Without tampering with the timer, he checked the gamma-ray counters. They were ticking gingerly away. The radiation monitor indicated a slight leak of 0.3 roentgen per hour. He tossed a glance into the chamber's darkest corner. Empty.

"Hey, Terminus!"

No answer. The mice fidgeted in their cages—back and forth, like white specks—manifestly miserable in the subtropical temperature. Pirx climbed back up the stairs and bolted the door behind him. He felt a chill the moment he hit the cooler air in the passageway: his shirt was soaked through. On a whim he made his way aft, down a series of passageways that kept getting narrower as they approached the tail section, and came to a dead end. He placed one hand on the bulkhead. It was warm. He sighed, retraced his steps, rode the elevator up to the fourth deck, and entered the navigation room. The chronometer showed 2100 hours by the time he had finished plotting the ship's course. Must have lost track of the time, he thought, a bit bewildered. He hit the lights and went out.

The deck seemed to slide out from under his feet the moment he stepped into the elevator. The timer had shut down the reactor as programmed.

At midships the passageway purred with the steady hum of fans in the subdued lighting. The lightbulbs on ahead smoldered in the circulating air currents. Using the elevator door as a springboard, he propelled himself swimmer-style down the passageway, one side of which was almost totally immersed in darkness. In the bluish haze he passed a series of hatches—hitherto unexplored—and black walls set off by ruby-red lights: the emergency escape hatches. With a fluent, somnolent motion, he glided weightlessly beneath the vaulted ceiling, his elusive, untrodden shadow creeping along the deck, wriggled through a partially open door, and entered the former mess hall. Below him, its surface streaked with light, stretched a long table flanked by chairs. He hung suspended above the furniture like a deep-sea diver exploring the interior of a sunken ship. Lights played in the shimmering panes along the wall before dispersing in a shower of blue sparks. The mess hall opened onto another, even darker room. Though his eyes were accustomed by now to the dark, he had to feel his way, blindly fingering everything as he went. His fingertips brushed something pliable—deck or ceiling, he couldn't tell. He pushed himself away, twisted around like a swimmer, and glided on in silence. A row of white, geometrically shaped objects sparkled in the velvety darkness. Their smooth surface felt cold to the touch. Washbasins. The one closest to him was flecked with spots. Blood?

He stuck out his hand—cautiously. Grease spots.

A third hatch door. He opened it and, suspended obliquely in space, was confronted by an eerie procession of paper and books fluttering by in the shadowy penumbra before withdrawing with a faint rustling noise. He propelled himself in the opposite direction, using his feet this time, and wound up back in the passageway, hounded by a cloud of dust, which clung to him instead of dispersing—trailed after him like a long, reddish-brown veil.

The string of night-lights burned with a serene calm, inundating the decks with a watery blue shimmer. He swam up to a rope dangling from the ceiling; the moment he let go of the end, it coiled itself up lazily, snakelike, as if suddenly animated by his touch.

His head snapped back. A clunking noise, similar to a hammering on metal, sounded nearby. He swam in the direction of the echoes, their volume now rising, now falling; along the way spotted a set of rusty tracks embedded in the deck—once used for wheeling dollies to and from the holds, he guessed—and soon was sailing along so fast he could feel the air buffeting his face. The clanging kept getting louder. He sighted a pipe angling around the corner from the next passageway and running along the ceiling. A section of old, one-inch pipeline. He touched it with his hand; it jiggled. The resonances now came in clusters of twos and threes. That's when it hit him. The banging was in Morse.

"A-t-t-e-n-t-i-o-n . . ."

The series came again:

"A-t-t-e-n-t-i-o-n . . ."

And again:

"A-t-t-e-n-t-i-o-n . . ."

Then the pipe chimed, "A-m-b-e-h-i-n-d-b-u-l-k-h-e-a-d." By force of habit, he spliced the letters together, syllable by syllable.

"I-c-e-e-v-e-r-y-w-h-e-r-e . . ."

Ice? he wondered, caught completely off guard. What in . . . ? Ice? What ice?

"R-e-a-c-t-o-r-v-e-s-s-e-l-c-r-a-c-k-e-d," the pipe resonated. He wrapped his hand around it. Who was signaling? And where was it coming from? He tried to figure out which way the pipe ran—from the bow or back aft. If looked like one of those emergency pipelines, obsolete, with branches on every deck. Maybe someone was practicing his Morse . . . ? That's crazy. The pilot up in the control room, maybe?

"C-o-m-e-i-n-p-r-a-t-t-c-o-m-e-i-n . . ."

A pause.

Pirx was breathless. The mention of that name was like a blow to the gut. For a second he stared wide-eyed at the pipe, then suddenly lurched forward. That's it—the name of that second pilot, he thought as he hit the bend, bounced off, and made for the control room, gathering speed as he went, the pipe all the while reverberating overhead.

"W-a-y-n-e-h-e-r-e-s-i-m-o-n . . ."

The echoes receded. Pirx momentarily lost sight of the pipe, picked it up again where it swerved into the next passageway, lunged after it, was bounced off the wall by his own momentum, and saw something through the dust cloud: a gnarled stump of metal, fixed with a rusty cap. A pipe bend. Severed. So it came from the tail section, not the cockpit . . . Huh? There was nobody back aft . . .

"P-r-a-t-t-i-n-s-i-x-t-h-t-o-l-a-s-t-h-o-l-d . . . ," the pipe chimed.

He hung like a bat under the ceiling, clutching the pipe with his fingers, and felt the vibrations throbbing in his head. The banging resumed after a short intermission.

"H-i-s-b-o-t-t-l-e-d-o-w-n-t-o-t-h-i-r-t-y-m-i-n-u-s . . ."

Another series of three.

"C-o-m-e-i-n-m-o-m-s-s-e-n . . ."

A pause.

He looked around. Dead silence except for a faint whirring noise in one of the fan outlets. The incoming fresh air sent particles of dirt swirling up to the ceiling, where under the light they took on the aspect of misshapen moths. Then came a torrent of clanging, rapid and staccatolike:

"P-r-a-t-t-p-r-a-t-t-p-r-a-t-t-m-o-m-s-s-e-n-d-o-e-s-n-t-a-n-s-w-e-r-o-x-y-g-e-n-i-n-n-u-m-b-e-r-s-e-v-e-n-c-a-n-y-o-u-t-r-a-n-s-f-e-r-o-v-e-r . . ."

A pause. The lighting remained constant; the dust and

waste particles continued their pirouette in slow motion. Pirx felt like letting go of the pipe, but something prevented him. He waited. Then it started up again.

"S-i-m-o-n-t-o-m-o-m-s-s-e-n-p-r-a-t-t-i-n-n-u-m-b-e-r-s-i-x-b-e-h-i-n-d-b-u-l-k-h-e-a-d-t-o-l-a-s-t-b-o-t-t-l-e-m-o-m-s-s-e-n-c-o-m-e-i-n-m-o-m-s-s-e-n . . ."

This last sequence, hard and intense; the pipe went on vibrating long after it was over.

A pause. A dozen or so unintelligible taps, followed by a brisk series:

"R-e-c-e-p-t-i-o-n-w-e-a-k-r-e-c-e-p-t-i-o-n-w-e-a-k . . ."
Silence.

"C-o-m-e-i-n-p-r-a-t-t-c-o-m-e-i-n-p-r-a-t-t-o-v-e-r . . ."
Silence.

The pipe barely palpitated. The next series came at faint intervals, as though from far off: three dots, three dashes, three dots. SOS. There was a gradual tapering off. Two more dashes . . . one . . . then a long-drawn-out screeching noise, similar to a scraping or scratching against metal, amplified only by the aura of total silence.

He thrust himself away and swam headfirst along the pipe, veering where it veered, now climbing, now dipping, while the parting air brushed his face. An open shaft. A ramp. Narrowing walls. The cargo holds. Number one, number two, number three . . . He could barely see, it was so dark. He ran his fingertips along the pipe in order not to lose it, the brittle dust coating his hands charcoal-black, and found himself in another part of the ship, one not enclosed by any decks or ceilings, in the space between the armored hull and the holds. The bloated carcasses of the reserve tanks loomed up darkly between the crossframes, with only an occasional dust-speckled light beam knifing through the darkness. At one point he looked up and spotted a double row of lights in a black shaft, the bulbs encrusted with the same reddish-brown dust that kept trailing him like a cloud, like smoke from an undetected fire. The air was stuffy, stale, permeated with the

smell of treated metal. He was sailing among the vaguely
adumbrated shadows of the trusses when the clanking
reverberations started up again:

"C-o-m-e-i-n-p-r-a-t-t-c-o-m-e-i-n . . ."

The pipe suddenly forked. He wrapped one hand around
each of the forking branches, but he failed to tell from which
direction the sound was being transmitted. He gambled on
the left. A hatch tunnel, pitch-dark, constricting to a bright
disk at the other end, brought him out into a well-lighted
room. The entrance to the reactor chamber.

"W-a-y-n-e-h-e-r-e-p-r-a-t-t-d-o-e-s-n-t-a-n-s-w-e-r . . ."
the pipe went on resonating while he unbolted the door. A
blast of hot air hit him flush in the face. He climbed up onto
the catwalk. The compressors were humming away. A warm
wind ruffled his hair. From the catwalk he saw, in foreshort-
ened perspective, the reactor's concrete wall, the luminous
gauges, the warning lights shimmering like red drops.

"S-i-m-o-n-t-o-w-a-y-n-e-i-h-e-a-r-m-o-m-s-s-e-n-b-e-l-o-w-
m-e . . ." the pipe reverberated, hammerlike, only a short
distance away. At the point where it looped down out of the
wall to join up with the main pipe inlet, standing with legs
astride in front of the reactor shielding, was the robot; with
quick jablike movements, as in some imaginary sparring
match, he was applying cement filler by the fistful, slapping it
around, smoothing it, molding it, before moving on to the
next section. Pirx concentrated his ear on the rhythm of his
movements, on the cadence produced by his pistonlike arms:

"M-o-m-s-s-e-n-c-u-t-o-f-f-p-r-a-t-t-l-o-s-i-n̄-g-o-x-y-
g-e-n. . ."

Terminus stopped, with both arms uplifted, and poised
opposite his deceptively human shadow. First to the left and
then to the right he pivoted his box-shaped head in search of
the next seam. He bent down, scooped up the sealant with his
trowellike claws, and again the driving rhythm of his arms
pulsated through the pipe:

"D-o-e-s-n-t-a-n-s-w-e-r-d-o-e-s-n-t-a-n-s-w-e-r . . ."

Pirx side-vaulted over the railing and floated down.

"Terminus!" he yelled before his feet had even touched down.

"I hear and obey," came the robot's instantaneous reply. One eye—the left—remained fixed on the man while the other rotated in its orbit, oblivious of the hands, which went on plastering to a steady beat:

"C-o-m-e-i-n-p-r-a-t-t-c-o-m-e-i-n-o-v-e-r . . ."

"Terminus! What are you doing?" hollered Pirx.

"Reactor leak. Four-tenths of roentgen per hour. Repair leak," the robot replied in a hollow bass while his hands kept drumming away:

"W-a-y-n-e-h-e-r-e-c-o-m-e-i-n-m-o-m-s-s-e-n-c-o-m-e-i-n. . ."

"Terminus!" Pirx yelled a third time, now glancing up at the metal face staring cross-eyed at him, now down at the blinding flurry of metal claws.

"I hear and obey," answered the robot in the same singsong lilt.

"What are you signaling in Morse?"

"Repair leak," the deep voice intoned.

"S-i-m-o-n-w-a-y-n-e-p-o-t-t-e-r-p-r-a-t-t-d-o-w-n-t-o-z-e-r-o-m-o-m-s-s-e-n-d-o-e-s-n-t-a-n-s-w-e-r . . ." the tube reverberated in response to the pelting, swishing jabs of steel. When the viscous paste began to run, the metal claws were immediately there to scrape it back up, pack it, and mold it to the cylindrical surface. For an instant the upraised arms remained poised in midair; then the robot bent down, scooped up another batch of cement, and let loose with a barrage of lightning-quick jabs:

"M-o-m-s-s-e-n-m-o-m-s-s-e-n-m-o-m-s-s-e-n-c-o-m-e-i-n-m-o-m-s-s-e-n-m-o-m-s-s-e-n-m-o-m-s-s-e-n . . ." The cadence reached a frenzied pitch; the piping shook and wailed from the unrelenting shower of blows—at times verging on a prolonged human cry.

"Terminus! Stop it!" He made a stab for the robot's oily wrists, but they slipped out of his grasp. Terminus suddenly went stiff; not a sound was heard except for the whining, whimpering pumps behind the concrete containment wall. Before him loomed a metal hulk, bathed in the oil that oozed down his stiltlike legs. He stepped back.

"Terminus . . ." he said, his voice lowering to a whisper. "What are you . . . ?"

He broke off at the sound of metal grinding against metal; the robot was rubbing his claws together, trying to peel away the leftover scabs of dry cement. Instead of dropping to the floor, the flakes spiraled up and scattered like wisps of smoke.

"What . . . have you been up to?" asked Pirx.

"Repair leak. Four tenths of roentgen per hour. May I proceed?"

"What were you signaling in Morse?"

"In Morse," the robot repeated after him, mimicking his exact tone, and then added, "Not understand. May I proceed?"

"You may," muttered Pirx, watching as the powerful arms straightened. "Yes, you may . . ."

Pirx waited. Terminus, seemingly unmindful of him now, ladled up some cement with his left hand, slung it against the shielding, and in three brisk strokes packed it, flattened it, smoothed it. Then the right hand came up and the pipe responded with a rat-a-tat-tat:

"P-r-a-t-t-t-r-a-p-p-e-d-i-n-s-i-x-t-h . . . m-o-m-s-s-e-n . . . c-o-m-e-i-n-m-o-m-s-s-e-n . . ."

"Where is Pratt?" Pirx burst out in a shrill voice.

Terminus, his arms converted by the light into luminous bolts, replied at once, "Don't know," at the same time thumping away with such speed that Pirx had trouble deciphering the Morse.

"P-r-a-t-t-d-o-e-s-n-t-a-n-s-w-e-r . . ."

Then an amazing thing occurred. The first series, produced

by the right hand, was joined by a second set, much weaker in intensity, this one coming from the fingers of the left hand; the signals overlapped, and for a while the pipe reverberated with the percussions of a double hammering, incomprehensible except for one gradually dissolving sequence: -

"F-r-z-i-g-h-a-n-d-s-i-m-p-o-s-s-i-b-l-e-t-o . . ."

"Terminus," Pirx said with his lips only, slowly retreating in the direction of the metal staircase. The robot was too distracted to pay him any heed; his torso, glistening with oil, went on rocking to the rhythm of his work. Pirx didn't need to listen to the pounding signals anymore; he could read them in the back and forth movement of his arms, in the play of light on the metal plating:

"C-o-m-e-i-n-m-o-m-s-s-e-n . . ."

He lay on his back, wide awake. The darkness teemed with a proliferation of flickering images. Let's see, Pratt must have wandered back aft, then run out of oxygen. Wayne and Simon knew where he was but couldn't get to him. Why didn't Momssen return their signals? Maybe he was already a goner. Impossible—Simon said he heard him. In which case he must have been quite close by—next door, even. Next door? That would mean there was air in Momssen's compartment. Otherwise, Simon wouldn't have heard anything. What did he hear, I wonder? Footsteps? Why were they calling him in the first place? And why no answer?

The voices of a life-and-death struggle, reduced to a lot of dashes and dots . . . Terminus. But how? Hold it. Wasn't he found in the wreckage? Hm. I'll bet I know where, too—in the spot where the piping runs outside. From there he could have picked up all the signaling back and forth. . . . I wonder how long they were able to keep it up. With a good oxygen supply, they could have held out for months. Food supply, ditto. Okay, so he was trapped in the wreckage. . . . Wait a minute. If there was zero gravity, what immobilized

him? The cold temperature, probably. Robots can't function
at extremely low temperatures. The oil congeals in the joints.
The hydraulic fluid freezes up, busts the lines. All that's left
then is the electronic brain. Terminus's computerized brain
must have picked up and recorded the signals, preserved
them in the electronic coils of his memory. And he doesn't
know. . . . He doesn't realize that those signals are regulating
the rhythm of his work. Or was he lying? Nah, robots don't
lie.

Fatigue overran his senses like a black liquid. Maybe it was
wrong of him to eavesdrop. There was something obscene
about it, about being a spectator to someone else's death
throes, witnessing it in all its gruesome detail and later
analyzing every signal, every plea for oxygen, every shriek
. . . It was immoral—if you could do nothing to help. . . .

He was fading fast, now so far gone he could no longer
keep track of his thoughts, though his lips kept repeating,
inaudibly, as if in protest:

"No . . . no . . . no . . ."

Then nothing—a total blank.

He woke up with a start, circumscribed by darkness. He
tried to sit up but was held back by the restraining blanket,
fumbled blindly with the straps, then switched on the light.

The engines were running. Wrapping a coat around his
shoulders, he did a few knee bends to gauge the rate of
acceleration. His body must have weighed a good 100 kilos.
He pegged the acceleration at about $1.5g$. The ship was
turning; he could feel the vibrations. The wall cabinets rattled
ominously, one of the cabinet doors flew open with an angry
bang; everything that wasn't secured—shoes, clothes—
started sliding, imperceptibly and in unison, aft, as if
animated by some conspiratorial plot.

He walked over to the intercom box, flipped open a little
door, and spoke into a gadget reminiscent of the old-style
telephone receiver.

"Control room!" he barked, wincing at the sound of his own voice. He had a headache. "First navigator speaking. What in hell is going on up there?"

"Course correction, sir," came the pilot's distant reply. "We strayed off course a little, that's all."

"How much off course?"

"Six . . . maybe seven seconds."

"Reactor temperature?" he demanded in a slow, deliberate voice.

"Six hundred twenty in the shielding."

"How about the holds?"

"Fifty-two in the port holds, forty-seven in the bow, twenty-nine and fifty in the stern."

"Give me the yaw correction again, Munro."

"Seven."

"Uh-huh, uh-huh," he said, and he slammed the receiver down. The pilot was lying through his teeth. You didn't need that much acceleration to make a seven-second correction. He guessed the deviation to be more in the neighborhood of several degrees.

Those holds were getting too damned hot. What did they have stored back aft, anyway? Food? He sat down at the desk.

Blue Star Terra–Mars to Compo Earth. Skipper to shipping agent. Reactor causing overheating in holds stop cargo in jeopardy stop no manifest available for cargo aft stop guidance requested navigator Pirx out.

He was still writing when the engines shut down, eliminating the last vestige of gravity, with the result that when he pressed down on the pencil he was catapulted up out of his seat. He bounced impatiently off the ceiling, settled back down in his chair, and ran through the radiogram message again.

On second thought, he tore up the radiogram and stuffed the scraps into a drawer. He decided not to get dressed—

always a rather tricky affair during weightlessness, involving a lot of awkward gymnastics and a fair amount of wrestling—and so, dressed as he was, with a coat draped over his pajamas, he left the cabin.

The bluish ambience made the dismal state of the wall padding less conspicuous. The nearby fresh-air vents—recessed, gaping, black—were sucking up the particles of dirt eddying in the corners. The whole ship was blanketed by silence, deep and unbroken. Hanging almost immobile above his own shadow, whose oblique extension could be seen climbing the wall, he shut his eyes in silent concentration. It happened that people sometimes fell asleep in this position, which was a hazardous thing to do, since the slightest burst in acceleration—in preparation, say, for a maneuver—could slam a person smack against the deck or ceiling.

Soon he couldn't hear a sound—not the fans, not even his own heartbeat. The nocturnal silence aboard ship was unlike any he had ever experienced. Earthly silence has limits; one senses its finite, transitory quality. Even when you're out among the lunar dunes, you're always accompanied by your own private little silence; trapped by your space suit, it magnifies every squeak of your shoulder straps, every crack of your bone joints, every beat of your pulse—even the act of breathing itself. Only on a ship at night can you be truly immersed in a black and glacial silence.

He brought his watch up to eye level: it was going on 3:00 A.M.

If this keeps up, I'll collapse, he thought. He caromed off a convex partition wall and, stretching out his arms like a bird braking its speed, landed on the cabin doorstep. It was then he heard it—a faintly audible sound that seemed to resonate from an iron interior:

Bong—bong—bong.

Three times.

He uttered a profanity, slammed the hatch door shut, and

recklessly flung his coat into space, where it swelled and ascended upward like some grotesque phantom. He turned off the light, climbed under the covers, and buried his head in the pillow.

"Idiot! Goddamned metal-plated idiot!" He kept muttering with his eyelids closed, shaking with a rage that even he found hard to justify. But fatigue got the better of him, and he was out before he knew what hit him.

It was going on seven when he opened his eyes. Still half-asleep, he lifted his arm up high; it didn't want to come back down. Zero g, he thought. He got dressed, went out. On his way to the control room, he instinctively kept his ears open. A hush. He paused in front of the hatch. The cabin's twilight interior was suffused with the greenish, almost aqueous luminescence given off by the low-luster radar screens. The pilot was reclining in his contour couch, smoking a cigarette; the flat wreaths of smoke hung in front of the screens, refracting the sea-green light. From somewhere came the subdued tinkling of Earthly music, punctuated by cosmic static. Pirx lowered himself into the contour couch directly behind the pilot; he didn't even feel like checking the gravimeter readings.

"How long till the next burn?" he asked.

The pilot saw through his question. "Not till eight. But I can fire 'em up now, skipper, if you feel like a bath."

"Nah . . . We'd better stick to our timetable," mumbled Pirx.

The ensuing silence was marred only by the persistent buzz of the loudspeaker music, monotonous in its endless repetition of the same mindless melody. Pirx felt himself getting sleepy. Several times he would manage to shake it off, be wide awake, then slowly surrender to a drowsy stupor. Or he would have visions of cats' eyes in the dark—big green cats' eyes—which, the moment he blinked, turned into luminous instrument dials. He went on like this, treading that thin line between sleep and reality, until the loudspeaker began to crackle.

"This is Deimos on the air. The time is exactly 0730. Stay tuned for the daily meteorite report for the inner zone. A frontal disturbance influenced by the gravitational field of Mars has been reported in the Draconids, last seen leaving the Van Allen Belt. In the next twenty-four hours the storm is expected to hit sectors eighty-three, eighty-four, and eighty-seven. The meteorite station on Mars estimates the cloud to be in the four-hundred-thousand-kilometer range. Sectors eighty-three, eighty-four, and eighty-seven are hereby declared closed to all traffic until further notice. Stand by for the cloud's composition, as relayed by Phobos's ballistic probes. According to the latest report, the cloud is made up of micrometeorites of the X, XY, and Z type . . ."

"Whew! Am I glad we're not affected," sighed the pilot. "I just ate breakfast, and I'd sorely hate to have to rev up the engines."

"Present velocity?"

"Over fifty."

"Really? Not bad," mumbled Pirx. Before heading off to the mess hall, he took a course reading, consulted the uranograph readings, and checked the radiation count—it was holding steady. The other two officers were already in the mess. Pirx kept waiting for someone to squawk about all the nocturnal clamor, but, to his surprise, the conversation never once left the subject of the next lottery draw. Sims, visibly the more excited of the two, kept up a steady recital of friends and acquaintances who, at one time or another, had hit the jackpot.

After breakfast Pirx stopped by the navigation room to plot the distances already traveled. Suddenly, in the middle of it, he dug his compass into the plotting board, tore open the desk drawer, pulled out the logbook, and scanned the *Coriolanus*'s last crew list:

Officers: Pratt and Wayne. Pilots: Nolan and Potter. Mechanic: Simon . . .

He pondered long and hard the commander's vigorous handwriting. Finally he tossed the book back into the drawer, finished plotting the ship's course, and rode down to the control room, taking the carbons with him. It took him a half hour to compute their exact time of arrival on Mars. On his way back, he peeked through the window in the mess-hall door. The officers were playing chess; the orderly sat slouched in front of the TV, with a heating pad on his stomach.

Pirx shut himself up in his cabin, browsed through the radiograms handed him by the pilot, and, before he knew it, was lulled into a light snooze. Once or twice he thought he heard the engines running, tried to rouse himself, and dreamed instead of having gone down to an empty cockpit and of having combed the pitch-dark passageways back aft in search of one of the crew . . . When he awoke he was seated at his desk, drenched with sweat—peeved at the prospect of a sleepless night brought on by such a long afternoon nap.

When, toward evening, the pilot reignited the engines, Pirx took advantage of the gravity to indulge in a hot bath. Feeling greatly revived, he then stopped by the mess, poured some coffee into himself, and phoned upstairs for a temperature reading. The reactor was up around the 1,000-degree mark, demurring, for some reason, at crossing the danger point. Around 2100 hours he was summoned to the control room: a passing ship was requesting medical assistance—to help out with an acute appendicitis on board. Pirx was debating whether to dispatch his orderly when a nearby passenger liner radioed that it was willing to stop and offer assistance.

Thus began a fairly routine and uneventful day. At 2300 hours sharp, the white lights on all the decks—except for those in the control room and reactor chamber—were switched off, and the blue night-lights came on. Only one light was left on in the mess hall—the one over the chessboard, where Sims, the electrician, stayed up until around midnight playing chess by himself.

Pirx went below to check the temperature in the cargo holds. On the way down, he ran into Boman, just returning from an inspection of the reactor. The ship's engineer was in good spirits; the leakage was stable and the cooling system checked out okay.

The engineer said good night and retired to his cabin, leaving Pirx alone in the dark and deserted passageway. A draft was blowing in the direction of the bow, gently ruffling the remains of spiderwebs clinging to the air vents.

The passageway between the main holds rose up tall and cavernous, like a church nave. Pirx meandered back and forth for a while, until a few minutes after midnight when the engines shut down.

At once a variety of sounds, muted and high-pitched, assailed him from all sides. Liberated by the drop in acceleration, objects not secured began shifting and colliding with walls, ceilings, decks; the reverberations, diverse and multitudinous, bestowed on the ship a strange animation. They hung in the air for a while before giving way to silence, a silence made even more extreme by the monotonous hum of the fans.

Pirx suddenly remembered that a desk drawer in the navigation room needed fixing, so he set off in search of a wood chisel. A long, narrow passageway that ran between the port holds and a cable duct took him to the toolroom; a dirty place at any time, the room now fairly swarmed with dust that wouldn't settle, so that Pirx was almost asphyxiated by the time he groped his way to the exit.

He was almost amidships when footsteps sounded in the passageway. Footsteps? In zero gravity? It could be only one thing, he knew. The clicking of magnetic suction disks gripping the deck was a confirmation. Pirx waited until a dark silhouette appeared in the passageway, its back to the lights at the far end. Terminus advanced with a rocking motion, paddling his arms for balance.

Pirx stepped out of the shadows.

"Hey, Terminus!"

"I hear and obey."

The ponderous figure halted; the upper half of his body was pitched forward by the force of inertia, then gradually righted itself.

"What are you doing up here?"

"Mice restless." A voice resonated from behind the armored breastplate, a voice strongly suggestive of a husky-voiced midget. "Mice cannot sleep. Fidgety. Thirsty. When thirsty, must have water. Mice drink much when temperature high . . ."

"So what are you doing about it?"

The robot swayed on its stiltlike legs.

"High temperature. Must move. Always move when temperature high. Water for mice. When drink and sleep—good. Often errors when temperature high. On duty. Must report back. Water for mice . . ."

"You bring the mice water?"

"Yes. Terminus."

"Where do you get the water?"

Twice the robot repeated the words "high temperature"; then, fully as if some human were prompting him from within, he lifted up both hands in a gesture of surprise—a gesture as abrupt as it was pathetic—passed each hand before the lenses rotating in their socketlike orbits, and fixed his gaze on his sheer metallic palms.

"No water . . . Terminus."

"Well, where *is* the water?" Pirx pressed, squinting up at the towering robot. After uttering a few unintelligible sounds, Terminus unexpectedly intoned in a deep bass:

"I . . . forgot."

It was pronounced with such helplessness that Pirx almost

lost his composure. He studied him for a while, this figure swaying before him, and said:

"Forgot, did you? Go on back to the reactor, y'hear?"

"I hear and obey."

Terminus made a crunching about-face and walked off in the same stiff, almost senile fashion as before, gradually diminishing in the receding distance. He stumbled on one of the ramps, paddled his arms oarlike, managed to regain his balance, and disappeared around the bend into the adjoining passageway. His marching step rebounded off the walls for a while.

Pirx was already on his way back to his cabin when he suddenly changed his mind; hugging the deck, he glided noiselessly along until he came to the sixth ventilator shaft. Although the shafts were strictly off limits, a rule that applied even during engine shutdown, he shoved off from the guardrail and covered the seven flights separating the midships from the tail section in a matter of seconds. This time, however, instead of entering the reactor chamber, he swam up to a sliding trap set at head level in the wall, slid back the metal plate, and found himself staring through a steel-framed, rectangular window of leaded glass. The back of the mice cages. How convenient—an observation port. The littered cages on the other side of the glass were empty; through the wire netting in front his attention was drawn to the center of the chamber, where, reflecting the light from above, his torso glistening with water, the robot hung almost horizontally in space, twirling his arms in a slow, comatose motion. The panoplied body was crawling with white mice; scurrying over brassards and breastplate, they congregated in the hollows of the robot's segmented abdomen—where the water had generously gathered into drops—drank, somer-saulted, and flew strange patterns in the air, while Terminus tried hard to retrieve them, only to have them slip through his metal pincers each time, their tails describing weird ara-

besques as they squirmed their way to freedom . . . It was a
spectacle so bizarre, so comical, that Pirx could hardly
contain himself. Once, as Terminus went about corraling the
mice, his metal face narrowly missed Pirx's gaze. The last of
the mice finally captured, Terminus shut the cages and
vanished from sight, leaving only his behemothian shadow to
fall crosslike from the main pipe joint, clear across the
reactor's concrete wall.

Pirx quietly slid the door back into place, returned to his
cabin, undressed, and climbed under the covers. Unable to
sleep, he opened a volume of Irving's memoirs—of astronavi-
gator fame—and read until his eyes began to burn. With a
groggy head, yet feeling as alert as ever, he contemplated in
despair the number of hours still separating him from
daylight, then climbed out of bed, threw on his coat, and
went out.

He picked up the plodding footsteps at the point where the
main passageway merged with the outboard passage. He
brought his head up close to the air vent; the noise was
coming from below, resonating in the shaft's iron well. A
push of the hands propelled him forward, feet first, toward
the nearest vertical shaft, and he dropped down to the tail
section. The echoing footsteps grew louder, then fainter. He
strained to listen; they started up again, more booming than
before. He was coming back. Pirx hovered motionlessly, high
up under the ceiling, and waited. The deck reverberated with
the clinking, clanking of metal-plated soles. Then silence.
Just as he was running out of patience, the measured treading
resumed, and a large shadow, with Terminus marching at the
rear of it, flooded the passageway. He came toward him,
passing so close underneath that Pirx could hear his hydraulic
heartbeat. After he had taken a dozen or so steps, he stopped
and emitted a high-pitched, hissing sound, tilted several times
to the right and left, as if bowing to the iron bulkheads, and
moved on. When he came to a side passage, he halted just this
side of its gaping mouth, peeked around the corner, and

hissed a second time. His fingertips grazing the high ceiling, Pirx trailed after the hulking figure.

"Ssss . . . Ssss . . ." The closer Pirx came within range of the robot, the more distinct the hissing became. Terminus interrupted his march again, this time in front of a ventilation shaft, tried—but without success—to squeeze his head through the grate, hissed, then straightened up and wobbled on his way. Pirx had heard and seen enough.

"Terminus!" His yell brought the robot to an abrupt standstill, just as he was in the process of leaning over.

"I hear and obey."

"What are you up to now?" Pirx demanded, staring at the same time into that misshapen metal mask of his, too expressionless to be a real face.

"Cat . . . I look for cat," replied Terminus.

"You what?!"

Terminus drew himself up to his full height, his arms dangling listlessly, almost forgetfully, at his sides. It was a slow, rising movement, accompanied by a faint creaking in the joints, so slow it seemed somehow fraught with menace . . .

"I look for cat."

"The cat? What for?"

Terminus, for just a moment, became a mute metal statue.

At last he said, lowering his voice, "I don't know." Pirx was momentarily disoriented. With its dead silence, grim lighting, and rusty bed of rails skirting the sealed hatches, the passageway could have been an abandoned mine tunnel.

"Well, this has got to stop," he said. "Go on back to the reactor—and don't let me see you up here again."

"I hear and obey."

Terminus turned on his heels and tramped back the same way he had come. Pirx lingered for a while, suspended midway between deck and ceiling, while an air current gently nudged him, centimeter by centimeter, into the direction of a gaping ventilator shaft. Bouncing off the wall with his feet, he veered toward the elevator and made his way topside, passing as he went the yawning chasms of the shafts, still reverberating with the robot's footfalls, as regular as the swinging of a pendulum in a gigantic clock.

In the course of the next few days, Pirx was consumed by problems of a more mathematical nature. After each burn, the reactor would heat up a little more and put out a little less. Boman speculated that the neutron reflectors were wearing out—a hunch corroborated by the slow but persistent increase in the amount of radioactive leakage. Using a complicated equation, the engineer tried to proportion the periods of propulsion and cooling; during shutdown, he would reroute the freezing liquid coolant from the portside holds to back aft, where the temperature was reaching truly tropical proportions. This balancing of extremes demanded much patience on Boman's part, and he spent many hours at the computer, searching by trial and error for the right ratio. Thanks to Boman's mathematical endeavors, they were able to cover 43 million kilometers with only a minimal delay. Finally, on the fifth day of the trip, despite Boman's pessimistic predictions, they managed to achieve the desired speed level. Pirx ordered the reactor shut down, to allow for cooling prior to landing, and breathed a discreet sigh of relief. Commanding an old freighter like the *Star* was a full-time job; it left precious little time for stargazing. But then what did Pirx care about the stars, or even the copper-red disk of Mars, when he had the course charts to content him?

On the last day of the flight, late in the evening, when the darkness, only intermittently relieved by the blue-tinted night-lights, seemed to swell the decks, he suddenly remembered that he had neglected to inspect the cargo holds.

He exited from the mess hall, leaving Sims and Boman to finish their nightly game of chess, and rode the elevator down below. Since their last encounter he had neither seen nor heard Terminus. Only one thing served as a reminder—the cat. It had disappeared without leaving a trace, as if it had never been aboard in the first place.

At midships the barely lighted passageway sighed with the continual flow of air. He opened the hatch to the first hold, and the dust-coated lamps filled the interior with a sullied glow. He covered the area, sailing from one end of the hold to the other. A narrow passage divided the crates, some of which were stacked as high as the ceiling. He checked the tension of the steel straps securing the pyramids of cargo to the deck. A draft created by the open hatch started sucking debris out of the dark corners, the sawdust and oakum rocking gently up and down like duckweed on a water swell.

He was already back out in the passageway when he heard a succession of sounds, slow and cadenced:

"A-t-t-e-n-t-i-o-n . . ."

Three taps.

Pirx drifted on an air current, which lifted him imperceptibly higher. Willing or not, he had to listen. It was a two-way transmission he heard now. The signals were weak, restrained, as if the object was to conserve strength. The rhythm varied: now slow, now fast; one of the parties kept making mistakes, as if rusty with the Morse alphabet. At times there would be a prolonged pause; at other times the signals would overlap. The dark, sparsely lit passageway seemed interminable, as if the fanning breeze had its origin in the cosmic void.

"S-i-m-o-n-d-o-y-o-u-h-e-a-r-h-i-m . . ."

"N-e-g-a-t-i-v-e"—pause—"n-e-g-a-t-i-v-e . . ."

Pirx recoiled off the wall, tucked in his legs, and torpedoed his way back aft, each passageway a little darker than the one before, the gradual accumulation of powdery red dust around the lamps a sign that he was nearing the stern. The door to the reactor chamber was open. He peeked inside.

He was struck by its coolness. The compressors, already shut down for the night, were quiet. The piping immured inside the concrete wall now and then emitted a strange, almost gurgling sound—gas bubbles impeding the flow of congealing liquid.

Terminus, cement-splattered from the top down, was diligently at work. A fan whirred frantically just above his head, which kept shifting back and forth with a pendulum-like regularity. Holding on to the railing with one hand, Pirx glided down the stairs without touching the steps. The robot's iron appendages barely echoed, their impact being cushioned by a freshly applied coat of cement.

"N-e-g-a-t-i-v-e . . . o-v-e-r . . ."

Whether by accident or by command of the same source dictating the transmissions in Morse, the fact was that the resonances were abating. Pirx stood an arm's length away from the robot, close enough to see the overlapping segments of its belly, which, every time it doubled up, evoked the image of an insect's crenulated pouch. The lights, reflected in miniature, swung back and forth in his glass eyes. Their impersonal stare impressed on Pirx the fact that he was alone in that empty chamber with its sheer concrete walls. Terminus was a machine, an insensate machine, capable of transmitting a prerecorded set of sounds—that and nothing more.

"C-o-m-e-i-n-s-i-m-o-n . . ." He barely managed to decipher it, so faint and erratic were the signals that came now. Above the slaving robot's head was a half-meter section of pipe; Pirx reached up and grabbed it. As he was adjusting his grip, his knuckles accidentally brushed the metal tubing. Terminus froze momentarily; the tapping broke off in the middle of a series. Seized by a sudden impulse, before he had time to reflect on the folly of his action, on this insane urge to intrude on a conversation from out of the deep past, Pirx rapped out the following quick message:

"W-h-y-d-o-e-s-n-t-m-o-m-s-s-e-n-a-n-s-w-e-r . . ."

At almost the exact instant his knuckles touched the pipe, Terminus responded with a rapping of his own. The two series ran parallel for a while, when suddenly, as if in recognition of his question, the robot's hand stopped, remained poised until Pirx was finished hammering, and a few seconds later began packing cement into the fissures:

"B-e-c-a-u-s-e-h-i-s-r-i-g-h-t . . ."

A pause; Terminus bent over to scoop up another batch of paste. What did he mean by that? Was it the beginning of an answer? Pirx waited with bated breath. The robot straightened again and began pelting the shielding with cement, but so hard and so fast that the reverberating blows seemed to flow into a single, drawn-out drone:

"I-s-t-h-a-t-y-o-u-s-i-m-o-n . . ."

"T-h-i-s-i-s-s-i-m-o-n . . . w-h-o-i-s-s-i-g-n-a-l-i-n-g . . ."

Pirx ducked his head down: it was a regular barrage.

"W-h-o-w-a-s-s-i-g-n-a-l-i-n-g-i-d-e-n-t-i-f-y-y-o-u-r-s-e-l-f-w-h-o-w-a-s-s-i-g-n-a-l-i-n-g . . . w-h-o-w-a-s-s-i-g-n-a-l-i-n-g . . . w-h-o-w-a-s-s-i-g-n-a-l-i-n-g-w-h-o-w-a-s-s-i-g-n-a-l-i-n-g-t-h-i-s-i-s-s-i-m-o-n-t-h-i-s-i-s-w-a-y-n-e-c-o-m-e-i-n. . ."

"Terminus!" he suddenly cried out. "Stop it! Stop it!"

The pounding ceased. Terminus stood up straight. His whole body was shaking—arms, shoulders, claws . . . The robot was convulsed by a fit of metal hiccups, racked by spasmodic jolts that seemed to arrange themselves into a familiar pattern:

"W-h-o-i-s-s-i-g-n-a-l . . . w-h-o . . . w-h-o . . ."

"Stop it!!!" Pirx screamed a second time. He had a profile view of him now: the quaking shoulder blades, the light bouncing off the armored metal in mimicry of the sounds:

"W-h-o . . ."

The storm spent, the robot suddenly went limp. Hovering above the deck, he scraped loudly against the horizontal piece of pipe and hung there, in the dead calm, like a trapped animal. But even from a distance, Pirx could see that one of the robot's drooping hands was still twitching in millimeter spasms:

"W-h-o . . ."

Somehow he wound up back in the passageway. The fans purred ever so softly. He swam topside into a cool, dry breeze coming from the upper decks. Pools of light slid across his face whenever he passed one of the wall lamps.

The cabin was partially open, the desk lamp still on. Flat, wedge-shaped planes of light stretched to the base of the walls, cleaving the darkness.

Who was calling? Was it Simon? Wayne? No, it couldn't be! They've both been dead for nineteen years!

Okay, who else could it have been? Terminus. But he was just a robot, good for patching leaky reactors. Pick his brain? Sure, and listen to a lot of mumbo jumbo about roentgens, neutron leakage, and cement patches! He knew nothing about anything, much less how his labor was being transformed nightly into a ghostly cadence!

One thing was clear: his recorder was far from dead. Whoever those people were—those voices, those signals—you could talk to them, converse with them. You just had to have the guts, that was all . . .

He pushed off from the ceiling and drifted leisurely over to the other wall. Goddamnit! He wanted to walk, to feel the ground under his feet again, to feel his own weight, to bang his fist down on the table! Oh, it was a cozy feeling, all right, this constant weightlessness that kept turning everything, including his own body, into flimsy shadows—as cozy as a bad dream! Everything he touched slipped away, drifted off—precarious, disembodied, fraudulent, a sham, a dream . . .

A dream?

Hold it. If I dream about someone, ask that person a question, I won't know what that person has said until he has said it. Yet that someone is a product of my brain, a brief and momentary extension of it. It happens almost every day, or rather every night—in dreams, when the self splits up, divides, and begets pseudopersonalities. These dream personalities can be invented, or taken from real life. Don't we sometimes dream of the dead? Carry on conversations with them?

They were dead.

Did that mean Terminus was . . . ?

Immersed in such thoughts, he circled around the cabin, ricocheting off the hard surfaces of the walls until he stood hovering in the hatchway. Holding on to the rim, he contemplated the long, dark passageway, the light trailing off into the darkness. . . .

Should he go back?

Go back—and ask?

It must involve some physical mechanism, he thought—one more complicated than the standard recorder. What the hell, a robot is not a sound-recording device. So it must be equipped with something else, some unique kind of recorder, one endowed with a certain autonomy, a certain mutability . . . one capable of being probed, of throwing light on the fates of those men—Simon, Nolan, Potter—and Momssen's silence, that terrifying, inexplicable silence of the commander . . .

What other explanation was there?

None.

He knew there wasn't, but he still couldn't bring himself to budge, to move from the hatchway, as if waiting, hoping for some other explanation . . .

What was Terminus, anyway? An electronically wired box. Hell, anything alive, any living creature would have perished long ago in the wreckage. So now what? Rap out a few questions before his glass eyes? And even if he did that, what would he get out of him? Would they—those dead men—give him a neat and coherent narrative of what happened? Or wouldn't he just hear a lot of screaming and yelling, cries for oxygen, for help. . . . And what was he to tell him? That they didn't exist? That they were only "pseudopersonalities," isolated figments of his electronic brain—an illusion, a case of the hiccups? That the terror of those men was a fake terror, that their death struggle, repeated every single night, had as much meaning as a worn-out record? He recalled the response provoked by his question—that sudden burst of signals, and that cry, so full of shocked bewilderment and hope, and that frantic, urgent, unremitting pleading: "Come in! Who is signaling? Come in!!!"

He could still hear it ringing in his ears, could feel it pulsating in his fingertips: the terrible despair and fury of those banging supplications.

Didn't exist? But then whose voices were those? Who were those people calling out for help? Oh, the experts would have an explanation, all right. They'd blame it on some electrical discharge, on the resonating effect of the vibrating metal. He sat down at his desk, pulled out a drawer, angrily slapped his hand down to keep the papers from fluttering away, fished out the printed form he was looking for, and carefully spread it out before him, pressing it flat so his breath wouldn't disturb it. One by one he began filling in the blanks.

MODEL: *AST-Pm—15/0044.*

TYPE: *Universal maintenance.*

NAME: *Terminus.*

NATURE OF DAMAGE: *Functional disintegration.*

RECOMMENDATIONS: . . .

He hesitated, holding the pen up close to the paper, then pulling it away. He began thinking about the innocence of machines, about how man had endowed them with intelligence and, in doing so, had made them an accomplice of his mad adventures. About how the myth of the golem—the machine that rebelled against its creator—was a lie, a fiction invented by the guilty for the sake of self-exoneration.

RECOMMENDATIONS: *To be scrapped.*

And with a perfectly rigid face, he signed it:

Pirx, first navigator.

NEW FROM BARD
DISTINGUISHED MODERN FICTION

EMPEROR OF THE AMAZON, Marcio Souza 76240 $2.75
A bawdy epic of a Brazilian adventurer. "Mr. Souza belongs in the same room where a Garcia Marquez, a Jose Donoso, a Vargas Llosa, a Carlos Fuentes and a Julio Cortazar disport themselves....A remarkable debut." *New York Times*

THE NEW LIFE HOTEL, Edward Hower 76372 $2.95
A novel of discovery and entangled love, set in an African country on the brink of upheaval. "Powerful, thoughtful, suspenseful...and compassionate." *John Gardner*

IN EVIL HOUR, Gabriel Garcia Marquez 52167 $2.75
This exotically imaginative prelude to ONE HUNDRED YEARS OF SOLITUDE explores the violent longings festering beneath the surface of a South American town. "A celebration of life." *Newsweek*

PICTURES FROM AN INSTITUTION
Randall Jarrell 49650 $2.95
The distinguished American poet Randall Jarrell lampoons a world of intellectual pride and pomposity. "One of the wittiest books of modern times." *New York Times*

PASSION IN THE DESERT, Curt Leviant 76125 $2.25
In the majestic desert of the Sinai, a man embarks on an emotional odyssey, exploring the depths of his memory and passion.

MCKAY'S BEES, Thomas McMahon 53579 $2.75
Set on the eve of the Civil War, this is the comic story of one man's attempt to gain a fortune as he encounters love, sex, slavery, and ambition. "A delightful piece of writing." *Los Angeles Times*

SECRET ISAAC, Jerome Charyn 47126 $2.75
A triumphant tale of villainy, true love and revenge set on the streets of New York. "SECRET ISAAC is a veritable Fourth of July." *New York Times*

SEVENTH BABE, Jerome Charyn 51540 $2.95
A wildly comic novel that delivers a curveball vision of America's national pastime—baseball. "Strange and wonderful." *New York Times*

THE EDUCATION OF PATRICK SILVER
Jerome Charyn 53603 $2.75
A wild and gutsy novel about big city cops, crooks and freaks. "A lead-in-yer-liver cop story." *Boston Globe*

THEOPHILUS NORTH
Thornton Wilder   53108 $3.95

Thornton Wilder, America's most honored writer, explores through young Theophilus North the lives of the saints and sinners, the rich and the servants, the gigolos and the fortune hunters in Newport, Rhode Island in the 1920's.

A CHARMED LIFE, Mary McCarthy   53884 $2.95

Mary McCarthy's celebrated novel of 20th Century love and decadence is set against the backdrop of a New England artists' colony. "A glittering tragedy."
The New York Times

AMERICAN BAROQUE
Lamar Herrin   77362 $3.50

An unforgettable story of the 1960's, and of the imperfect ideals and inescapable truths which sparked the imaginations and sensibilities of American youth. "Herrins's writing has vitality, humor, intelligence and vividness."
The Washington Post

THE WELL OF LONELINESS
Radclyffe Hall   54247 $3.95

This is the controversial and eloquent classic that movingly portrays a woman's love. It paved the way for the popularity of Virginia Woolf and of works such as Vita Sackville-West's THE DARK ISLAND, and Rita Mae Brown's THE RUBYFRUIT JUNGLE.

MASS APPEAL, Bill C. Davis   77396 $2.50

The stormy but underlying tender conflict between a middle-aged priest and a rebellious, idealistic young seminarian is explored in this "wise, moving and very funny comedy."
The New York Times

Available wherever paperbacks are sold, or directly from the publisher. Include 50¢ per copy for postage and handling: allow 6–8 weeks for delivery. Avon Books, Mail Order Dept., 224 West 57th St., N.Y., N.Y. 10019.

AVON Paperback

DESERT NOTES:
Reflections In The Eye Of A Raven
Barry Holstun Lopez   53819 $2.25

In this collection of narrative contemplation, naturalist Lopez invites the reader to discover the beauty of the desert. "A magic evocation, Casteneda purged of chemistry and trappings." *Publishers Weekly*

PRINCIPLES OF AMERICAN NUCLEAR CHEMISTRY: A NOVEL
Thomas McMahon   54122 $2.95

Set in Los Alamos, New Mexico in 1943, this is the story of the intellectual, emotional and sexual ferment that grips a group of American scientists at work on the atomic bomb. "A brilliant and important novel." Kurt Vonnegut, Jr.

A SHORT WALK, Alice Childress   54239 $3.50

From the rustic life of the rural South to the chaos of a Harlem riot to the revelry of a Depression Christmas, this is the moving story of one woman's passionate life, and a striking portrayal of 50 years of the black experience in America.

THE GROVES OF ACADEME
Mary McCarthy   52522 $2.95

In this wicked and witty bestseller Mary McCarthy deftly satirizes American intellectual life. "Brilliant ...funny...bitterly tongue-in-cheek." *New Yorker*

Available wherever paperbacks are sold, or directly from the publisher. Include 50¢ per copy for postage and handling; allow 6–8 weeks for delivery. Avon Books, Mail Order Dept., 224 West 57th St., N.Y., N.Y. 10019.

AVON Paperback